GW00864792

Taken – The Complete Series

Cover design by Cover Shot Creations (covershotcreations.com)

Parts 1-3

TAKEN

MIRANDA DAWSON

Part One

Chapter One

"You dropped your underwear on the floor." Mr. Townsend stared at me from behind his desk as I walked into his office.

"I... Excuse me?" I muttered.

He looked busy and I knew he would rather be doing anything else right now than meeting with me. I had expected him to be abrupt and short-tempered, but that was still a strange introduction.

"Your panties," he said again. "You appear to have dropped them on the floor." He pointed to the floor just behind me in the doorway of his office.

Sure enough, right there on the floor, in plain sight of anyone who happened to pass by, was a pair of sexy red lace panties. They must have fallen out of my bag. I wouldn't have minded quite so much had they been clean, but these were dirty.

I grimaced and quickly bent down to pick them up, then shoved them deep into my handbag where hopefully this time they would remain.

"I'm so sorry," I said. "My name is Amanda

Gibson." I held out my hand to try to get the introduction back on track.

He looked at my hand but didn't extend his to meet it. His raised eyebrows made it perfectly clear he didn't intend to shake my hand after I had picked up my dirty panties. He motioned to the seat opposite his desk, so I sat down and took out my pen and notebook.

"Don't worry, you're not the first woman to lose her underwear in this office. Would you like a minute to finish getting dressed?" Mr. Townsend asked.

"Oh, no," I replied quickly. "That was a spare pair. I'm not going commando."

Without thinking, I pulled down the waistband of my skirt to show him that I was, in fact, wearing underwear.

"I didn't need to see the evidence," he said. I saw his eyes flick to the computer monitor in front of him. Probably checking the time. "We're going to have to keep this short, Ms. Gibson. I have a lot to get done today."

"Of course, of course," I said, scribbling the time of the interview at the top of my notepad. I had been expressly forbidden from using my phone to record Mr. Townsend's comments. "I'm so grateful to you for granting me this interview, Mr. Townsend."

"I wasn't left with much choice," he replied. "A mutual friend of ours called in a favor and I owed him one. And please, call me William."

William? I was supposed to be meeting *Adrian* Townsend, not *William* Townsend. Shit, this could be a problem. I'd been struggling to get anywhere with this story for months and I had been close to giving up when a friend, Emily

6

Saunders, offered to help.

Emily and her boyfriend, Carter Murphy, felt like they owed me a favor, so Carter had arranged this meeting. However, I had explicitly said I wanted to meet Adrian Townsend. Adrian was my lead. I had evidence connecting him to serious allegations of corruption that went all the way to the U.S. Senate and I desperately wanted to get him on record.

Instead of finally interviewing Adrian, I was here in front of someone who was presumably his brother. They looked similar enough that I hadn't immediately noticed the difference, although if I hadn't been busy shoving my panties back into my bag I would have picked up on the subtle distinctions.

William had darker hair than his brother and he didn't have the same youthful expression in his eyes. Adrian was a media darling and loved to be photographed, but William looked troubled, like he didn't get enough sleep and had too much on his plate.

I was a sucker for men with troubled backgrounds and my mind immediately started down a path that was not conducive to work. I couldn't help it; William was sitting there glaring at me with a look that told me there was a secret behind his eyes.

I liked to blame my journalistic instincts for desiring men like him, but the part of my body that was alive right now had nothing to do with work.

William looked tired, and in that respect we had something in common. I'd made an effort to start sleeping more, but this story consumed my every waking hour these days and I found it hard to switch off at night. The events of the last week in Washington, D.C. had left me absolutely exhausted.

"Let's get right to the point, shall we?" William said. "You wanted an interview with one of the big players in the fashion arena. I guess I fit that bill, although I'm not exactly a fashion designer myself. I just run the company. Anyway, ask away. And make it quick."

I had no questions related to running a fashion empire. My interest in fashion, or lack thereof, was probably quite apparent from what I was wearing. I didn't own many formal clothes, so I'd chucked on an old, comfortable skirt with a sweater that I'd purchased in my first year of college—about five years ago. It hadn't even been fashionable then and knowing how little money I'd had in college, it was likely cheap as well. The fact that the sweater was still in one piece was a testament to how little I'd worn it.

Adrian's company was a large producer of organic food and I had prepared questions based on that. There were some nice, easy introductory questions, and then I planned to transition to questions about corruption and bribery. I had been looking forward to asking those questions, but I could hardly use the same ones with William.

"Ms. Gibson?" William said. "I don't have all day."

"Sorry," I muttered, looking down at my notepad to pretend I had prepared some questions. "How does a non-fashion designer like yourself become the majority owner of one of the biggest fashion labels in the world?"

In his tailored suit, he looked like he could model for a fashion label, but he didn't look like the type to run one. He was far too young, for one thing. William was thirty at most, which made him a few years older than his brother, but still far too young to have achieved so much. Fashion was notoriously difficult to get into and he didn't even design clothes. The business seemed an odd fit for him.

"That's your question?" he asked, looking at me sternly.

I met his gaze for a few long seconds before I had to look away. His eyes were intense and I felt sure he would start reading my mind if I lingered on them any longer. I didn't want him to know that I was here by mistake today or that I was having rather inappropriate thoughts about him right now.

I glanced down again at my pad and then looked up. "Yes, that's my first question, but we can move on to another if you'd prefer."

"Ms. Gibson—"

"Please, call me Amanda," I interrupted. If he insisted on being called William, then it seemed silly for him to call me 'Ms. Gibson.'

"Ms. Gibson," he repeated, "the history of how I built up this company and made it into what it is today is a story that has been told many times before. My answer to that exact question has been given in plenty of detail and you could find it in seconds with a quick online search. Please don't tell me you are so unprepared that you didn't do the slightest bit of research on me before this interview?"

William kept staring at me while I desperately racked my brain for other questions. If William weren't Carter's friend, I would have just gotten up and left. William was rude and clearly didn't want me in his office. I suppose Carter had meant well, but he must have misheard me and set me up with the wrong brother.

"I just asked that question to break the ice a little bit," I lied. "Easy questions are supposed to make things more relaxed between the interviewer and the interviewee. At least that's what they taught me in my journalism classes. Sorry, I'm still rather new at this."

"I think you broke the ice by showing me last night's underwear as you walked in, Ms. Gibson. What's your second question?"

Think, Amanda, think. He was more of a business guy than a fashion guy. That meant he was probably more comfortable with the numbers than he was with the clothes.

"How did your biggest investors respond to the announcement in your last quarterly earnings statement?" I asked.

William sat forward, a slight frown appearing on his face as he considered the question. *I did it!* I'd found a sensible question to ask. It had been so vague and ambiguous that I didn't even need to have any idea what the 'announcement' might have been about.

"The announcement?" William said, still thinking.

"Yes," I said, confidently, to fill the silence.

"Swiped, Inc. is a privately owned company, Ms. Gibson. We don't issue quarterly earnings statements. And there are no investors. I own a hundred percent of the company."

Shit. Maybe that hadn't been such a good question. I fumbled around in my head for an excuse, but couldn't find one.

"I don't believe you're a journalist, Ms. Gibson. You had better tell me why you're really here, and I suggest you do it quickly. Carter's friend or not, I will have you forcibly removed from the building if I have to. What is this all about?"

Chapter Two

What is this all about? I wish I knew. I'd spent the last week in Washington, D.C. doing research for my story and had only arrived back in San Francisco a few hours ago. My brain was still groggy with jet lag and I couldn't think on my feet as quickly as usual.

All that might not have been such a problem if I hadn't been thrown into the middle of an interview with someone I didn't know and hadn't done the slightest bit of research on. I still didn't understand how Carter had managed to set me up with the wrong brother, but it was too late to worry about that now. I didn't want to embarrass him, so I had to think of a way out of this.

"I'm sorry," I said, letting my voice shake a little to make William think I was upset. "I definitely am a journalist—a freelancer—but I've had a bad few weeks and my usual level of professionalism has slipped."

"What happened?" William asked. He didn't sound entirely interested; he was probably just asking to be polite.

"I broke up with a boyfriend," I lied. "I'm fine now, but I needed a few weeks to move on. I totally forgot about this meeting, so last night I went out with a friend and ended up having to crash on her sofa."

William raised his eyebrows and looked at me suspiciously. He didn't believe me. "Do you always take a spare pair of panties on a night out, Ms. Gibson? Sounds to me like you weren't expecting to go back to your own place last night."

I felt like I was being grilled by a detective. If I looked behind me right now, I half expected to see a one-way mirror and a locked door.

"I... er..."

"It's okay, Ms. Gibson. I don't need all the details. It's clear you have now moved on from the issues with your ex-boyfriend. Congratulations."

William didn't seem too bothered by what he thought I'd done the night before, so I didn't make any attempt to correct him. I would probably end up tripping myself up with some lie or inconsistency and even an amateur detective would certainly spot it.

"Can we start again?" I asked. "I do want to interview you. If you give me a few moments, I'm sure I can think of some questions to ask."

William let out a noise that was somewhere between a groan and a sigh of frustration. He glanced at his computer again; he was keeping a close eye on the time.

"Listen, Ms. Gibson—Amanda. As I said, I'm really pressed for time. Carter spoke very highly of you, so I'm going to assume that your behavior today is a one-off."

"It is."

"Very well. I apologize if I came across rather harsh. I'm under a significant amount of pressure right now."

"I completely understand," I said, slightly shocked to hear him apologize. "I can't even imagine how much pressure you must be under trying to run a company of this size." I still had to think of some questions to ask him, but at least now he was softening up a bit.

"The company stuff I can handle," William said. "This problem is... tricky. But never mind that. Look, you're not going to come up with any good questions in the next five minutes, so here's what we'll do. I'm going to give you a story—just a short anecdote—and then you can weave that into a longer piece about me. Get the rest of the information from other interviews I've given. You have my permission to pretend I repeated the details to you personally. You can meet your word count and you'll have a unique spin on the facts that no one else knows. Best of all, you can be out of here in five minutes. How does that sound?"

"That sounds great," I replied immediately, as a mixture of relief and disappointment washed over me. I was going to get a story out of this mess, but I couldn't help but feel a little hurt that he wanted me out of his office so quickly. A lifetime of failures with the opposite sex should have me used to that by now, but apparently not.

Not long ago, I had asked Emily and my friend Amy to match me up with eligible bachelors, and right now I was sitting across from an unmarried millionaire. Maybe even a billionaire. My window for impressing him had been short and I suspected I'd blown my chance before I even realized I had one.

"The story of how I made my money is well-known," William began. "*Most* people already know it. I went to college and after graduation I started selling t-shirts from my parents' garage. Those took off and I kept reinvesting the money until I got where I am today. Simple, really."

"If it were simple, everyone would do it."

William nodded. "I suppose. Anyway, what most people don't know is that I was doing something similar at the age of twelve. My mom worked two jobs. During the day she would go to her regular gig and at night she would work on sewing clothes for the local community. She charged for it, but never enough and we were always poor. I fancied myself as a bit of a salesman and I had the cocky swagger to go with it."

William caught the look of confusion on my face as I tried to picture him as a door-to-door salesman. He didn't look like he had the energy for something like that anymore.

"It's true," he insisted. "And I was good at it. I offered deals and discounts to get new customers and kept track of my mom's expenses. Soon she was making triple what she'd been making before."

"Wow, that is a great anecdote. So you've wanted to do this ever since you were a child?"

William shrugged with indifference. "Not really, but you can write that if you want. I just wanted to help my mom make more money from her efforts. I think my later foray into fashion was a coincidence, but if you tie them together it makes for a nice story."

"Definitely," I agreed. "Thank you so much."

"Make sure you send my assistant a copy of

the final article," William said.

"You want to approve it?" I asked. "I know some journalists do that, but I'm not really comfortable having my work approved by—"

William held up a hand and I stopped speaking immediately. For someone who looked stressed and tired, he still managed to command a remarkable amount of authority over me. I stared at his hand and imagined him touching my cheeks and moving it down to my chest. *God, I really need to have sex soon. He's not even trying and I'm already obsessed with him.*

"I'm not asking to review it," William said. "I probably won't even read it. My PR people just like to have all this stuff in one place. You can send me a link to the final version when it's up online. Any idea which publication you're going to sell this to?"

"I'm hoping one of the business websites will take it," I replied.

"They probably will," he said. "If you need some contacts let me know and I'll make some calls."

"Thank you again, William," I said, then stood up and got ready to leave.

William seemed to have forgotten he was in a rush, but then snapped out of his thoughts and showed me out of his office. I left the building feeling like the real story was locked away much deeper in William's head, but I knew he had no intention of letting me in there. Still, what I had what I thought would make a good story and pay the rent for next month.

I knew a few business websites that might be interested, although I'd never worked with any of the big ones before. All my work to date could politely be described as 'local interest' pieces, but this one had some potential.

I couldn't let it take up too much of my time, though. The real story was the one I had been researching in D.C. The story involving William's brother was a much bigger deal. That story could get me into a national publication and put me on the map. More importantly, I could expose a level of corruption that the American public was entirely unaware of.

The events I had witnessed in D.C. last week had sickened me, but I would see those involved punished eventually. This level of corruption was destroying lives and I was going to put an end to it.

Chapter Three

The only thing I wanted to do after that excruciating interview was go home and sleep. The jet lag had affected me more than I'd thought it would and I had barely slept a wink on the red-eye back.

Combined with the busy week I'd had in D.C., it made me less than enthusiastic about meeting my friend. At least we were meeting over coffee; I really needed coffee.

"You look exhausted, Amanda," Natalie said as soon as we'd sat down with our drinks. "Does that mean you had plenty to do in D.C.?"

I nodded and took a sip of my coffee. It burned my tongue, but I had to get a few drops in me before I could hold another conversation.

"I found something, Natalie. Something big, I think."

"Involving Adrian Townsend?" Natalie asked. She sounded uncertain, which wasn't entirely surprising. She had been the voice of caution in my ear ever since I'd shared my suspicions about

Adrian with her.

Natalie was a little naive and she chose to believe that big companies and politicians were not nearly as tied-together as the media would have us believe. I found it tiring to talk to her about it sometimes, but it was good to get the opposing viewpoint.

"He's up to something. I know it."

"How do you know it?" Natalie asked. "Do you have any evidence yet?"

"Nothing that isn't circumstantial at this point. But it's more than enough to confirm I'm on the right track," I added when I saw Natalie roll her eyes.

"Just promise me you'll be careful. I don't see a good outcome for this. If you're right, then you're going to need bulletproof evidence to take down such powerful people. If you're wrong, well, I don't need to tell you the consequences there."

"I know," I said. "And don't worry, I'm taking precautions. This story has been in the works for months, so I'm not about to do something stupid in the rush to get it published."

"Good. Don't you have that interview with Adrian soon? That should prove interesting."

"No," I said with a shake of my head. "That was supposed to be this morning."

"*Supposed* to be? Did he cancel?"

I explained to Natalie how my meeting with Adrian Townsend had been scheduled with his brother by mistake and how I'd only just managed to get out of there without making Carter look like he had misplaced his faith in me.

I even told Natalie how I had dropped my panties on the floor of William's office. That was nowhere near as tawdry as it sounded. I had been on an overnight flight back from D.C. and didn't have time to go home and shower. I wanted to put on fresh underwear, so I got changed in the bathroom at the airport and shoved the old pair into my purse. How I then managed to drop them on the floor of his office was a mystery, but at least William would remember me.

"Sounds like Adrian is the charismatic brother," Natalie said when I had finished telling her my story. "I didn't even know he had an older brother, but then I don't pay much attention to these fashion companies."

"Me neither," I said, gesturing to the clothes I had thrown on to wear for the flight home. "He is nice, though. William, I mean. He had a lot on his plate and was a little short-tempered at first, but he relaxed by the end of it. And from the story he told me, it sounds like he used to be less… dark."

In my head I had already forgiven William for acting like a jerk. Everyone had bad moments, and he'd looked like he was going through one hell of day. He had apologized, which was more than a lot of men did. Perhaps I was being biased because I wanted to excuse the rather inappropriate thoughts I was having about him, but I didn't think that was it. Not entirely, anyway.

"Maybe you could use this whole fiasco to your advantage," Natalie said, putting down her coffee.

"How?"

"You should drop the idea of talking to Adrian and just work on William instead. Try to get him to talk about his brother."

I frowned. The thought of seeing William again did hold some appeal, and it would give me a chance to show him I wasn't a complete idiot.

"I'm willing to bet that William knows nothing about what his brother is doing," I said. "He certainly isn't going to know as much as Adrian himself."

"Think about it," Natalie pleaded. She was getting surprisingly enthusiastic, considering how nervous she was about my story. "What information would you have gotten out of Adrian, anyway? He was hardly likely to spill the beans to you in an interview just because you asked nicely."

"I didn't plan to get a confession out of him," I said. "I was just hoping he would confirm a few facts to let me know I was on the right track."

"*If*, and that's a big *if*, he is guilty of what you allege, don't you think he's clever enough to keep important information from you?"

"I know, but what else can I do?"

"Speak to William. Try to get the facts you need from him. If you're right and he has nothing to do with it, then he might give you details without realizing that he's incriminating his brother."

If only I had thought of that while I was interviewing William that morning. "I'm never going to see him again," I explained. "The interview was a one-off and after my performance today he isn't going to take kindly to a follow-up request."

"Could you call and say you want to follow up on some facts?" Natalie asked. She looked disappointed that her grand plan had hit an early obstacle.

I shook my head. "He told me to get the facts I need from the information that's online. I'm supposed to get in touch with his personal assistant and let her have a copy of the final article, but that's it. I don't see any obvious way to speak to him again."

21

"Damn," Natalie said. That was the closest I had known her to get to swearing. Natalie was always nice and polite to everyone. I had no idea how she had the energy to keep it up all the time. "Maybe you could wait for him after work and 'accidentally' bump into him?"

"I'm not doing that, Natalie. This isn't a romantic comedy."

"I don't know. You did introduce yourself by dropping your dirty underwear on his floor. Sounds like a romantic comedy to me."

"Fair point," I admitted.

Natalie was right. William was my best potential source of information. I just needed to get his attention.

An idea came to me before I finished my coffee. I wouldn't have to track William down; he would find me.

Chapter Four

I took a week to write the article about William, which was about six days longer than I had planned to spend on it. Instead of just bashing out a quick story and selling it to the highest bidder, I crafted every word of it with precision and detail before selling it to a well-known business website that had paid top dollar for it.

If William was going to end up reading it—and that was the plan—I wanted him to think I was a good writer even if I was awful at interviews.

The article did a good job of setting the bait. I was confident my plan would work, although I didn't know how long it would take for him to notice. In the meantime, I needed some new stories to keep me busy while I waited. I tried asking my new roommate, but we tended to be on different wavelengths when it came to important stories.

"Why don't you write about a story about dating in San Francisco?" Sophie asked. "It's a different world now with all these dating apps out there. I don't even have to leave the house to get laid anymore."

"Yes, I've noticed," I replied. I'd seen Sophie invite strange men into her bedroom on countless occasions already and we'd only been living together for a few months. "Those aren't the kind of stories I write," I explained. "I wouldn't even know where to start with something like that."

"Your stories are great," Sophie said, "but they take a long time to produce. You could try writing something lighter in between."

"I just wrote a story on William Townsend," I said, pulling up the article on my laptop. "That ended up paying quite well, actually."

"You wrote about William Townsend?" Sophie asked. "Wow, now I'm impressed. I didn't realize you were into fashion."

"Thanks. And no, I'm not. I wrote the story from a business angle. You want to read it?"

"Are there pictures of William in the article?" Sophie asked.

"Nope, just words," I replied.

"I'll give it a miss, then. Did you meet him in person?"

I nodded. "Yes, in his office. I can't say he was all that charming, though." He didn't have to be—I wanted him anyway.

"I prefer his brother, myself," Sophie said, "but I wouldn't say no to William."

"You don't say no to anyone," I joked. "Do you know Adrian?" I hadn't been entirely surprised that Sophie had known who William was, because half her wardrobe came from his store, but I didn't think she'd know Adrian.

"I make a point to try to know all the multi-millionaires in this city," Sophie said. "I don't know him, but I know *of* him. I've thought about him a lot, if you get my meaning."

I grimaced, not wanting to picture Adrian enjoying pride of place in Sophie's fantasies. He should be locked up in prison, not the object of women's affections.

"He should stay in your fantasies," I said. "Don't go near him. I can't say too much at this point, but he's a nasty piece of work."

"Now you're just making me want him more," Sophie said. "There's nothing more tempting than forbidden fruit."

"Well, please don't bring him back here."

"Okay, okay," Sophie said, holding up her hands. "I'd rather go back to his place, anyway. So, what's this big story you're working on? Anything I can help with?"

"No, I doubt it," I replied. "I did a lot of the work in D.C. last week, but now I need to follow up with some sources."

"D.C.? Is the story about politics?"

I thought for a few seconds and then shook my head. "It involves politicians, but it's a story about corruption."

"Sounds intense. Is that what you like to write about? Far too deep for me."

"I wouldn't say I *like* to write about it, but it's important. I have... personal reasons for my interest in corruption and bribery."

"You can tell me if you like," Sophie offered. "I know I'm a bit of a loudmouth, but I can keep a secret."

"I know you can. It's nothing exciting. Let's just say my family has suffered as the direct result of political corruption. Everyone acts like it doesn't happen anymore—not in America, at least—but it

25

does, and I want to see those involved get punished."

"Fair enough. Well, if you're ever having trouble making rent, just let me know and I'll feed you some gossip on which billionaire is sleeping with which other billionaire's wife. It may be trashy, but it sells."

I laughed. "Thanks, Sophie. I may take you up on that one day. I'm not proud. Not when rent needs to be paid. What are you up to today, anyway?"

"I'm going to meet a friend for a bite in the afternoon and then I start the evening shift waiting tables."

I tagged along with Sophie to get some fresh air and then detoured to a coffee shop when she went to work. I needed some fresh air and a change of scenery. It had been five days since the article was published, and I hadn't heard a thing from William or any of his staff.

With every day that passed, I became less and less certain that he would respond to the bait. My email address was displayed prominently at the top and bottom of the article, so if he wanted to get in touch he could do so quite easily. But there was nothing in my inbox other than a few emails from my mom that I hadn't responded to yet and some emails from food blogs that I subscribed to.

My cooking was atrocious, but I liked to think I could improve if I put my mind to it. The food blogs served as inspiration, but by the time I made it to the grocery store I would forget all my good intentions and buy the usual combination of ready-made meals and token pieces of fruit.

The coffee shop was starting to fill up and I considered leaving. There was a fine line between cafés that had enough background noise to help me zone out and being so busy that I couldn't get any work done.

I closed my laptop and started packing my things away. It took all of three seconds for someone to notice I was leaving and sit down at my table. I hadn't even stood up yet, but manners were fast disappearing in this city.

"Don't mind me," I muttered under my breath as I packed my laptop into my bag.

"Sit down, Amanda," a voice said.

I looked up at the man who had sat across from me; it was William. He'd found me.

"We need to talk."

Chapter Five

My idea had worked. The article I'd written had done its job, although judging by how angry William looked, perhaps I had gone a little over the top.

"What do you want to talk about?" I asked innocently.

"You know full well what I want to talk about," he said before motioning to one of the baristas to bring him a coffee. "I've read your article about me."

"I thought you weren't going to read it."

"I was curious," he said. "I assumed you must have more talent with writing than you do with interviewing or Carter would never have recommended you."

Carter had never seen any of my writing; he'd only done me this favor because he credited me with helping get him and Emily together. I'd never felt like Carter owed me anything, and I had initially resisted his attempts to help. When he told me he knew "Townsend" I'd assumed he meant Adrian and took him up on the offer to set up an interview. Natalie was right, though—Adrian wouldn't have told me anything useful, but William might be very helpful.

"I take it you didn't like the article," I said. My words came out weak and unsure, as if I were intimidated by having him sitting opposite me, staring into my eyes. I wasn't scared of him, but I was worried. Maybe my article *was* a little harsh. William didn't look like he needed criticism right now.

"I'm the owner and CEO of the company," William said, slowly and calmly. "To many people I *am* the company. When you write articles describing me as weak and 'worn down,' you destroy people's confidence in me."

"I just wrote about what I saw," I replied. I had to take a sip of my coffee so that I had an excuse to break eye contact with him. His smoldering glare was sadness mixed with passion. I wanted to rip up the article to make him feel better and then rip off his shirt to make me feel better. It was obvious that he had passion under that cool exterior, but he seemed reluctant to put any of it on display.

"I gave you everything you could have wanted to write a story and you went and wrote some bullshit about me being unable to handle the stress of running a big company."

"From what I saw that day in your office, I believe that's true."

"What the hell do you know about running a company?" he growled. Clearly, I had made him mad. "I wouldn't have minded so much if you'd just published it in some trashy rag, but you managed to get the story into a widely read business journal. I have emails coming in every minute asking if I'm considering selling the company."

"Are you? Considering selling the company?"

"No, of course not," he said, the anger fading from his voice. "Why did you do it? Was the whole thing a big trick? You pretend to be a clueless journalist and I break down in front of you?"

"No," I said quickly. "No, that wasn't it at all. I'm sorry. I didn't mean to cause you so much trouble. I just wanted to be taken seriously for once. I've never had anything published before."

William sank back in his chair and took a long sip of his coffee. He stared at me, sizing me up with those dark eyes, and I tried to match his gaze. Minutes passed in silence with William only taking his eyes off me when he sipped his drink.

I had to say something before he stood up and left, but I had no idea what to say next. His cup was nearly empty—if he walked out, then all my work would have been for nothing. I hadn't enjoyed writing that article about him. My words had been cruel and largely untrue or exaggerated to make the article more publishable. I'd written it to get a reaction from him, but now that the bait had worked I found myself uncertain what to do next.

"I wanted to interview your brother," I said, blurting the words out in one breath. "Carter made a mistake setting up the interview. I'd planned to interview Adrian the entire time."

William frowned. "Why?"

"Because he works in an industry that's hot right now. I know more about organic food than I do fashion."

"So you just wanted to write a business story?"

I nodded. My voice felt too uncertain for me

to lie convincingly right now.

William sat there in silence. I wanted him to say something, but he was carefully thinking over his next words.

"Do I really look like I can't cope?" William asked at last. "Do I look 'like I've been awake for five days,' as you put it?"

"I was too harsh," I said. "I shouldn't have said those things."

"But you meant them?"

"Some of them. You do look like something is troubling you and you aren't sleeping, but I shouldn't have said you were incapable of running the business. That was unfair."

"You're probably right," William admitted. "I'm struggling."

I leaned forward onto my elbows to shrink the gap between us, unconsciously squeezing my breasts up and out in the process. I had been genuinely surprised to hear him be so honest, but I probably looked like I was flirting with him.

"I don't know what I'm talking about," I said. "I didn't even take a business class in college. Trust me, you don't want to take my comments too seriously."

"I didn't say I was struggling with work," William said. "That's not the problem."

"What is the problem?" I asked. "Whatever it is, it must be important to you."

"I can't talk about it," William said quickly. "I shouldn't have come here to see you. I normally just ignore criticism, but this time it struck a nerve."

"I'm glad you came," I said. "It gave me a chance to apologize. I just wanted to make a name for myself, but I made a mess of it. Again.

I'm sorry."

"It wasn't all bad," he said, then stood up to leave. He left some money on the table to leave the waitress a very generous tip and then headed towards the door.

I should have shouted after him, but there was nothing I could say to bring him back. My plan had failed, but that wasn't what was really bugging me right now. There was something big happening in William's life and I had used it to write a story. That made me almost as bad as his brother.

My eyes didn't leave William as he walked towards the door. Then he stopped and walked back in my direction.

"I want you to write another story," William said as he sat back down at my table. "I wasn't at my best the other day—I'm still not—but that was a particularly bad day. They aren't all like that."

"Okay, I'm up for that. Shall we schedule another interview?"

William shook his head. "No interviews. I hate them at the best of times. My company is putting on a fashion show later this week. Come along as my guest. You'll get a behind-the-scenes view of a huge event. That's a good story by itself and no doubt you'll get more material on me as well."

"That sounds perfect," I said.

"My assistant will call you," he said, then stood up and headed for the door once again.

My eyes followed his perfect rear as he left the café. I would find it hard to concentrate on work while being around him, and I had no idea how I would slip his brother into the conversation. Still, my plan had gone about as well as I could ever have expected. I would have plenty of access to William. I just had to keep my mind on the story and not his ass.

Chapter Six

"Sophie, I need you to help dress me," I yelled as soon as I walked in the door.

Sophie was lying on the sofa playing with her phone with the television providing background noise. Nine times out of ten when I came home she was in the exact same position.

"You want me to dress you?" she asked. "You mean you need help getting into a dress?"

"No, no," I said, kicking off my shoes by the door. "I need you to come shopping with me and help me pick up some fashionable clothes."

Sophie dropped her phone and sat up. "Are you serious?"

I nodded. "I'm going someplace where I'll be surrounded by beautiful and fashionably dressed women. I can't go like this." I waved my hand up and down my body to point out the untidy clothing I had thrown on that morning. Even with my limited knowledge of these things, I knew the colors I was wearing didn't match and no doubt Sophie had noticed.

"I've been waiting for this moment since the

day we first met," Sophie said as she stood up and walked over to me. "Get out of these clothes first. I have some shops in mind, but the sales staff won't take us seriously if you walk in there dressed like that." She threw her arms around me and hugged me tight. "This day is going to be so much fun."

Against all my instincts, I did have a good time shopping with Sophie. I'd never taken an interest in fashion because I didn't understand it and found the whole shopping experience to be a large exercise in frustration.

It wasn't that I didn't want to look nice; it was just that I had no idea how. The few times I had made a conscious effort to buy nice outfits I had ended up never finding the confidence to wear the clothes. Comfortable clothes don't tend to get you noticed one way or the other, and I was usually happy to blend into the background.

I had a bit of cash left over from payment for the article I had written on William, so I let Sophie lead me astray with some wild outfits. At least they looked wild to me. I could always return the ones I didn't wear. According to the experts, we were no longer in season for dresses—not in Northern California, at least—so we focused on getting a pair of tight-fitting pants with a light, floaty top.

I glanced at myself briefly in the mirror but was far too self-conscious to linger for long. If I thought about it too much, then I would just put my old clothes on and go back home.

"I like this top," Sophie said as I came out of the fitting room wearing the least comfortable of all the tops so far. "But not with those pants. Let's get this top and the last one, but we need to keep looking for more pants."

"This top shows my bra strap," I complained.

"I'm going to have to tape it to my shoulder to keep it up."

"It's supposed to show your bra strap, dear."

"Oh."

"That reminds me, we need to buy you some new bras."

"I only need one outfit," I said. "Don't you think we have enough clothes for one decent outfit by now?"

"You only need one outfit for now," Sophie agreed. "But let's face it, your whole wardrobe could use some work. I'm not missing this opportunity to help you impress a man like William Townsend, because I don't know when you'll let me help you shop again."

"I'm not doing this to impress William," I insisted. "I'm only doing this so that I don't look like a complete fool in front of all those models. I could do without those women sneering at me all day for dressing in last year's fashions."

"Darling, those rags you wear are not last year's fashions," Sophie said. "I'm not sure what they are, but they're nothing that was ever fashionable in this decade."

"Whatever. I'm just saying that I don't want or need to impress William. Not in that way. As far as he's concerned, I'm just a regular journalist who wants to write a story on him."

"And do you think he offers every young journalist he meets the chance to spend a day with him at a fashion show? Or just the pretty blonde ones with big boobs?"

"That's not what this is," I replied. At no point had it occurred to me that William might be attracted to me. It had taken me a while to realize I was attracted to him. William had obvious good looks and his well-toned physique was obvious even through a suit, but the first time I met him he had been preoccupied. The last thing I expected was for him to take an interest in me.

Either way, I hadn't agreed to spend time with William to satisfy any urges I might have. I needed to find out what his brother was up to, and I wasn't about to let my pent-up sexual desire mess up a huge story.

It didn't help that I slept in the room next to someone who had more sex in a week than I had had in my lifetime.

"You can't honestly tell me there's no attraction there," Sophie said as we walked home with bags full of clothes. "Between you and William. He's dreamy. And rich. Very rich. Let's not forget that."

"That's exactly why nothing will happen," I said, sidestepping around admitting that I found him attractive. "He has women throw themselves at him all the time. He's not going to look twice at me. Besides, he doesn't look like he's in the mood for a relationship right now. He's going through something and I would wager it's causing him the wrong kind of sleepless nights."

"That whole 'wounded animal' thing he has just makes him even more appealing. Just think, you could be the one to help him through his problems. Maybe he's getting past a breakup and needs a rebound fling. That could be you."

"A girl can dream," I said sarcastically. "Let's not forget that he could be like his brother, and trust me, his brother is a nasty piece of work."

"Don't say that," Sophie said. "I'm hoping that

you'll set me up with Adrian once you and William get together."

"No chance. He's involved in some sketchy stuff."

"Sketchy?"

"Illegal," I said.

"Well, nobody's perfect," Sophie said.

We arrived home and I unpacked all my new purchases and started matching the items purchased from different stores into the best possible outfits. Sophie and I eventually agreed on the best choice. On top I wore a yellow short sleeve cut-out top with a chunky necklace that drew attention to my breasts. On the bottom I wore a relatively plain pair of pants. Apparently it was too much for both the top and the bottom to catch the eye.

This time I let myself admire the outfit in the mirror. It looked good. I looked good. I smiled as I thought of William seeing me for the first time in this outfit. He would barely recognize me. I wasn't sure I recognized myself.

Chapter Seven

The fashion show was a far bigger event than I had realized. A crowd had gathered outside the building with everyone keen to get a look at their favorite models and designers in the flesh. The screaming and adoration wasn't quite on par with that at the Oscars or a movie premiere, but I still found it intimidating.

I had no desire to squeeze through the crowd so I looked around for a side exit for use by guests and staff. I found a door guarded by a large, bulky man who was checking IDs before letting people in.

"Excuse me," I said nervously as I approached the door. "Is this the entry for guests?"

"It is if you have a guest pass," the man replied. He sounded bored and I knew he was unlikely to prove very helpful.

"I don't have a pass, but I'm a guest of Mr. Townsend's. Do you have a guest list or anything? I should be on there."

"There's no guest list, ma'am," he snarled. "I

know everyone who is allowed into this building and you're not one of them."

This guy was on an ego trip. There was nothing worse than someone given a position of power and authority when they were already full of their own self-worth.

"Would you please check with Mr. Townsend?" I asked. "He personally invited me here today and I wouldn't want him to think he had been stood up just because his bulldog didn't take the time to engage his brain."

The man's arms flinched, but remained crossed over his chest. He was fighting an instinct to strike out, and only just about managing it.

"Do you have any idea how many women say that? I'm not leaving my post. If you want to contact Mr. Townsend yourself, then I'm sure you can do that by calling his cell. You do have his number, don't you?" The man grinned. He knew I didn't have William's phone number, otherwise I would have called it already.

"It's okay, Joe." I heard William's voice from behind the man, but couldn't see him. "She's telling the truth. You can let her through."

Joe stepped aside and revealed William standing there with a smile. A genuine smile this time, not forced like all the other ones I had seen so far. I had expected the pressure of putting on such a large show to be overwhelming, but if anything William seemed to be reveling in it. Joe smiled at me as I walked past as if he hadn't wanted to hit me just a few moments before.

William leaned forward as if to kiss me on the cheek, but he changed his mind at the last moment and just placed his hand on my back to lead the way. For someone with such good looks, he was remarkably shy around me. Not that I was complaining. It was far preferable to the approach most men took in bars. They would take a kind word as an excuse to move in for the kill.

"Sorry about Joe," William said as he led me down a corridor past lots of dressing rooms. "He's overly aggressive at the best of times, but this show is even more intense than usual. We need to be careful about who we let in today."

"Judging by the crowd outside, the show is going to be popular," I said. "Are they fans of the models or the clothes?"

"The crowd outside is gathered for the models," William said. "Or at least, they're gathered for the models that are usually at events like this."

"But not today?" I asked.

William shook his head. I caught a glimpse of a smile, but it quickly disappeared. "No, not today. This show is going to be… different."

"Okay, now you have my attention."

"I didn't before? That's disappointing."

"You did," I added quickly, feeling a touch embarrassed but uncertain as to why. "But now this whole show has my attention. I don't typically follow fashion that closely, so you'll have to excuse my ignorance."

"I gathered that when you showed up at my office without knowing who I was. Although," William added, pausing to look me up and down, "I must say, you look… ravishing today. Not that you didn't before."

"Thank you." I could feel a touch of red on my cheeks. I felt good in my new outfit and had noticed some stares on the way here. I hated that expensive clothes made me feel better about myself, but there was no denying they did. "I suppose you can tell me exactly who designed it and where I bought it from."

"Good lord, no," William said with a laugh. "I told you, I'm no fashion designer, just a businessman. But I'm not blind, and I'm still perfectly capable of pointing out when a woman looks beautiful. And you look gorgeous."

I smiled, but looked down at the floor to take my eyes from his. I was supposed to be here as a journalist on a story, not some naive young girl listening to compliments. "It's amazing what a good outfit can do."

"It's not the outfit," William said seriously. He looked at me for a few more moments, but didn't say anything else. He led me down a few more corridors and then out to the main stage.

The room was already packed full of people who were talking amongst themselves. I had seen some weird-looking people walking around San Francisco in my time, but the people in the audience were still remarkable in their strange outfits with bits sticking out everywhere and every color of the rainbow fully represented.

"These are our seats," William said as he showed me to the only two empty seats left in the house. We were in the front row, in what were probably considered the best seats in the house, although I could immediately tell that I was going to be straining my neck to look up at the catwalk. I hoped the models were wearing underwear.

The lights dimmed and the audience went silent. Spotlights then lit up the catwalk and doors at the far end opened for the models to strut their stuff on the stage. I had only ever seen short clips of fashion shows on the news, but I had a fair idea what to expect. Lots of stick-thin women would walk up and down the stage in items that barely resembled clothes and that no one would ever wear out in public.

The audience would whisper about which ones looked fabulous and which ones were hideous, as if there were some science to it. That was what I expected, but that was not what transpired.

I had been right about the clothing. The collection was all just a crazy combination of things that looked uncomfortable and sometimes impossible. I made a note on my pad of paper to describe one article as "gravity-defying."

The clothing was typical, but the models were not, and it wasn't long before the audience noticed. Instead of a parade of unhealthy looking women, there was a mixture of all body shapes and sizes on display. Some women were thin, but others were curvy or even overweight.

Some walked out on stage as if they had never done it before, but their confidence grew with each step. Despite the stunned reaction of the audience, the models did not lose their smiles or rush off the stage.

I could see some members of the audience walking out of the room and those who stayed looked shell-shocked. Some were laughing and pointing at the models for having the audacity to be on stage when they weren't a size zero.

I looked over at William, expecting to see a look of horror on his face at how badly the show was going. He was smiling. He made eye contact with every model that walked on the stage and nodded at them or gave them a sign of encouragement.

He must have noticed how badly the show was being received, but he didn't seem to care. In fact, he looked happier than I had ever seen him. There was something William wasn't telling me. It wasn't just his brother who was keeping secrets.

Chapter Eight

William's fashion show had at least got people talking. Unfortunately the conversations among the audience sounded either angry or amused. Some people thought the whole thing had been a joke or an attempt at satire on the industry. I didn't think it was anything so subtle.

After the show William took me backstage where we mixed with the models. They were all delighted to see William and each one approached us to thank him for the opportunity to do the show. It sounded like none of these models had ever done a catwalk show before.

William kissed each of the girls on the cheek, which caused a slight discomfort in my stomach, but I didn't know why. He was in his element here and whatever cloud had been over him when we first met was nowhere to be seen today. Had he been worried about the show and now he was just happy it was over? That could be it, but I didn't think so. He'd seemed relaxed before the show and if he had been nervous about it being a failure, he wouldn't likely be much happier now that it been roundly criticized by everyone in the audience.

"Thank you so much, Mr. Townsend," said a pretty young woman with wide hips and a chest bigger than mine. She had been one of the models laughed at on the catwalk, but she either hadn't noticed or didn't care.

"You're very welcome, Michelle," William replied. "But I just gave you the stage. You're the one who made it a success."

Michelle couldn't hide her delight at being flattered by William. She looked like she was meeting her idol and he'd given her an autograph.

"Isn't he wonderful?" Michelle said to me as William was distracted by two other models approaching him. "You're so lucky to have him."

"Oh, we're not dating," I replied. "We're just friends. No, not friends. I mean, I do like him. Not in that way." Why was I blabbering on like this? *Calm down, Amanda.* "And we're not really friends, but only because I hardly know him. I'm sure he's terrific, though. I'm just here for a story I'm doing."

"Okay," Michelle replied slowly. Her eyes made it clear she hadn't believed a word I'd said. "I'm so grateful for what he's done for me. For all of us, really. He didn't have to do any of it, but he's changed my life completely."

"By giving you this job?" I asked. I didn't want to burst her bubble, but after today I wasn't sure she would be doing many more modeling jobs.

"It's a little more than that," Michelle replied. "He's the reason... never mind. I probably shouldn't talk about it."

"I'm here to write a story on William," I said.

46

"It would help to know more about him. So far all I know is what he tells me, and he's painfully modest. I'd love to hear from the people he's helped. Is he the reason you got this job?"

"Oh, he did a lot more than get me this job," Michelle began. "He's the reason I'm—"

"Amanda," William said, leaving his adoring fans behind, "can you come with me please."

Michelle had been so close to giving me something interesting I could almost taste it, but I still didn't hesitate when William asked me to go with him. His voice carried a conviction I found hard to reject. He led me back to the dressing rooms and motioned for me to go inside one of the empty ones. Maybe this was where we would do a more in-depth interview. Unlike the last time, I now had plenty of questions to ask him.

The dressing room had a bunch of outfits hung up on a rail, but other than that it looked unused. All the make-up on the dressing table was unused and there was no spare set of clothes on the floor.

"One of the models couldn't make it," William said with a strong note of sadness in his voice. "She would have looked wonderful in these clothes."

Anyone would look wonderful in these clothes. They were more minimalistic than most of the outfits that had been on display today and I could imagine wearing them out in public. The dress in particular was beautiful, with a slit up one leg and a plunging neckline that would not leave a lot to the imagination. It was a dress made for an awards show and it was a shame it had to stay hidden in this dressing room.

"You would look phenomenal in that dress,"

William said when he caught me admiring it. "Try it on."

"No, I can't. This dress is too special. I don't even want to touch it in case some of the grease from my fingers spoils it."

"I insist," William said. He walked up behind me and reached his arm over my shoulder to grab the dress off the rack. "I want to see you in this dress," he whispered in my ear.

I felt goosebumps on the back of my neck and shivered as they sped down my spine. I took the dress from William and placed my bag on the floor.

"I won't look," William said as he turned his back to me.

You're supposed to be interviewing him, Amanda, not dressing up for him. I shouldn't be doing this. I had a story to write, but it didn't seem to matter right now. Nothing else mattered except showing William how I looked in a dress that must easily cost a thousand dollars.

My heart raced as I undressed just feet from William. He couldn't see anything, but it still felt weird to be undressing so close to him. I left my panties on, but removed my bra because the dress had plenty of support.

The room was warm, but my nipples were already hard as if they anticipated something more than just a change of clothing. I quickly slipped on the dress to cover them up in case William turned around.

The fabric felt smooth and comforting against my skin. It was a tight fit, but the cut of the dress flattered me, emphasizing curves in the right places and hiding the bits of my body I was less comfortable with.

"Can you zip me up?" I said aloud. William approached and stopped just inches from me. I could feel the heat coming off his body and his breath on the back of my neck.

His right hand pressed against my lower back as he held the dress in place. His other hand slowly pulled the zipper up to the top. I didn't breathe the entire time his hands were on me. When he took his hands away, my lungs finally released and I took a few deep breaths.

William was still standing behind me. If I moved back slightly my behind would be able to rub against him. I wanted him to press up against me, but he didn't move.

"Your skin is glowing," William said. I flinched as the backs of his fingers lightly brushed against my shoulder. "It's as smooth as this dress. You two were made for each other. You should keep it."

"I can't—"

"I insist. I want to see you in this again one day."

He stepped forward and pressed his body against me at last. I stood firm and took in the feel of his member between the cheeks of my ass.

William lifted my hair from my ear and leaned forward. "Perhaps you and I could—"

There was a loud and aggressive knock at the door. I heard William sigh.

"What is it?" he yelled.

"I have a call for you, Mr. Townsend," came a female voice from the other side of the door.

"I'll call them back."

"You'll want to take this call, sir. It's your brother. He says it's urgent."

Chapter Nine

William spoke to his brother on the phone while I got changed back into the clothes I had worn here. Hearing Adrian's name reminded me instantly why I was here and killed any romantic mood that might have been developing. His name acted like a cold bucket of water poured over me. I simultaneously wanted to get out of here as soon as possible to avoid any awkwardness with William, but I also wanted to hear some of the conversation.

I left just as the call was winding down; I'd heard enough. Adrian was meeting someone for lunch at an Italian restaurant in the Financial District. I knew it well and could get there within thirty minutes.

The last thing I heard was William trying to convince Adrian to blow it off. That worried me. Did William know what Adrian was doing? I wanted to think he had nothing to do with it, but the two of them were brothers. They were bound to know each other's secrets. At least William didn't sound entirely supportive of his brother. That was some comfort, at least.

Adrian was almost as rich as his brother, but the restaurant they were meeting at was a relatively affordable place which would likely be busy around lunchtime. That would work out well for me because they would be less likely to notice me in a crowd. While I was in D.C., I spent a lot of time tailing Adrian and following him into restaurants. I doubted he had seen me there, but I wasn't about to take the risk that I might be recognized.

The restaurants in D.C. had been so expensive I stuck to ordering a salad each time. Impressing the politicians and lobbyists no doubt required a more elegant touch than a cheap meal. Whomever he was meeting with today did not need to be wined and dined in that way.

I got there before Adrian and chose a table by the wall within listening distance of a man who was sitting by himself looking at his phone a lot. He was waiting for someone and every other table at the restaurant had two or more people at it already. This was the man Adrian was coming here to meet.

I slipped my phone out of my purse and pretended to check emails while secretly taking pictures of the mystery man Adrian was here to meet. Thank God we lived in a day and age where a young woman could sit in a restaurant taking high-quality photos without anyone being in the least bit suspicious. I could never have been a journalist in the nineties.

The man looked nervous and was fidgeting a lot. He was in a different position in every photo on my phone. My pictures had captured something I somehow hadn't seen with my own eyes. The man had a briefcase which he had placed on the floor at the side of the table.

The man also wasn't dressed like the sort of person who needed to carry around a briefcase for work, especially not one that looked like it cost more than the cheap suit he was sweating in. Was this an old school bag drop? I felt like I was in a spy movie. The stakes felt higher and I started to sweat.

Finally Adrian arrived. He rushed into the restaurant, pushing past the waitress who offered to seat him, and sat down next to the man. He couldn't see me unless he looked over his right shoulder and the other man was far too distracted to notice me eavesdropping on the conversation.

The two men sat at the table in silence until the waitress had taken their order and brought them drinks. Then Adrian started speaking in hushed tones and I had a hard job hearing him. I brought out my phone again and used an app to start recording everything around me.

The quality of the recording would likely be awful. There were far too many conversations going on around me and the speakers were playing a Taylor Swift song loud enough that I was involuntarily moving my foot to the beat. I blamed my old roommate Amy for getting me into that particular type of music. Eventually I managed to block out the surrounding noise and listen to most of the conversation.

"I hope your trip to D.C. was a success," the strange man said. "Did you accomplish your goals?"

"Some of them," Adrian replied. "Things were set in motion, but we're still a long way from the kind of influence I need over there."

"D.C. is a tough place," the other man said between sips of water. He was already on his second glass and still looked like he was far too hot for comfort.

"The way you see it reported on the news, you'd think it would be easy to get one of them to help you out," Adrian said.

He was talking about bribing politicians. He had to be.

"You need more than just money, Adrian. You need power. The two are often the same thing, but not always."

"I know what I need," Adrian snapped back. "Speaking of which, do you have it? I hope that briefcase doesn't just contain your latest law journal article."

"It's in there," the man said. He used his foot to push the briefcase slightly closer to Adrian. "Promise me you won't let any of this lead back to me. I have a family to think of."

"Don't mention family to me," Adrian snapped again.

"You're right," the man said quickly. "I'm sorry. I shouldn't have said that." He paused for a few moments before speaking again. "Please pass on my regards to Olivia when you see her."

"This won't lead back to you," Adrian said, ignoring the comment about Olivia. "You're done. I don't need to see you again after today."

The two men didn't say another word as they sat and ate their meals. Who the hell was Olivia? Was that a mutual friend of theirs? If I could get a surname, I might have another lead.

The strange man got up to leave as soon as he had finished his meal, leaving Adrian to pick up the check. The man went to walk away and then stopped and turned back. For a second, I thought he was about to bend down and pick up the briefcase, but instead he just held out his hand in front of Adrian.

Adrian looked at the hand for five long seconds and then finally reached out and shook it.

"Good luck, Adrian," the man said. "You're going to need it."

Sure enough, Adrian took the briefcase with him when he left. I didn't have much to go on. The conversation would make for some great quotes for my story, but they were useless at the moment without more context.

I was more sure than ever that Adrian was guilty of something—presumably bribery—but I had no proof. The only leads I had gained today were the name Olivia and a tired old man who wrote law journal articles. It wasn't a lot to go on, but I had helped out a friend in the past with less information than that.

I pressed my phone to stop the recording just as a message came through from William.

Meet me tonight for dinner. I want to finish what we started today.

Chapter Ten

William and I agreed to meet for dinner at his apartment. That sounded a lot like a date to me, but he mentioned the article and told me he would answer my questions. We were at least going to pretend this was part of the interview.

In what was fast becoming a bad habit, I spent hours thinking about what I was going to wear before leaving the house. I couldn't go too formal, because the evening was supposed to be about work.

My usual clothes wouldn't do, though. I had set a standard this morning and now I was going to have to keep it up. I dug some clothes out of the pile that were going to be returned to the store and managed to put together an outfit that was professional, but a touch sexy as well.

Here goes nothing.

"Good evening, Amanda," William said as he opened the door to his apartment. His lips pressed against my cheek for a firm kiss. "I'm just finishing up with dinner, but why don't you take a tour of the place? You can wander around at your leisure and get some information for your story."

The apartment was large—huge, even—but mainly open-plan so there weren't many different rooms. The kitchen and living room were part of one large space. There was a massive bedroom and a second bedroom that had been converted into an office. I headed straight for the bookcase to check out his reading material. That would make a great anecdote and I loved looking at what other people read.

William's collection was an eclectic mix of serious literature with genre fiction, mainly fantasy and science fiction. I spotted a number of books I had read myself and even more that I knew I should read but had never quite found the motivation to get through. William apparently had no such difficulty. Even his copy of *War and Peace* looked well worn, as if it had been read more than once.

"I actually prefer *Anna Karenina*," he said from behind me as I placed *War and Peace* back on the shelf. "*War and Peace* is better known, probably because of its length, but I've always found the mixture of war and society to be a little jarring, like it's two separate books mixed into one."

"Isn't that kind of the point?" I asked. "War *and* peace? The clue is in the title."

William looked at me seriously for a few seconds and then laughed. "Yes, true, the title is honest. That doesn't mean I have to like it, though."

I nodded as if I had actually read it. My comment had made it sound like I had; anything else I said would risk making me look stupid.

"Dinner smells splendid," I said, taking a deep breath in through my nose. The aromas had spread through the apartment and I could pick out the flavor of cooked sausage and something spicy.

"It's ready to eat," he said, leading me back into the dining area where the food was laid out on the table. "I'm not much of a cook, so it's just pasta with spicy Italian sausage in a tomato sauce."

The table was immaculately set, but I smiled as I caught a glimpse of the mess in the kitchen. Like me, William had used every imaginable item in the kitchen when just a few would have sufficed. The end result was much better than the frozen pizza dinners I usually ended up with, though.

William poured some red wine while I placed my pen and notebook on the table. It looked completely out of place, but I hoped it would serve to remind me that I was here for a work-related reason.

I had to pretend to be interviewing William, while finding out information about his brother and remembering that this was not a date. I was bound to get confused at some point if I wasn't careful.

The meal might not have been overly complicated, but it was cooked to perfection. The sausage and tomato sauce combined beautifully and I had to force myself not to just pick out all the sausage pieces right away.

"Sorry about how things ended this morning," William said. "Bit of an emergency with my brother, that's all."

"Is he okay?" I asked.

"Yes, he's fine. Everything's always an emergency with him."

"You know," I said, as if a thought had just come to me, "that could make a good angle for the story."

"The emergency with my brother?"

"Your brother in general. How many families have two siblings who both, separately, built billion-dollar companies in completely different industries? I could look at the conflict and the atmosphere over family dinners, that kind of thing."

"Sure, I guess," William replied. "But I doubt you'll find it that exciting. We get along pretty well for the most part. We do things differently, but we grew up together, so we agree more than we disagree. He works in food and I work in fashion, but we're both CEOs, so our day jobs are often similar."

"I did some research on Adrian back when I was going to interview him. His company has a lot of... how do I say this... regulatory issues. Government compliance and that kind of thing. His company spends more on lobbying than it does growing food."

William glared at me for just a second and then smiled. "I can't say I'm jealous of that part of his work. I hate politicians."

That last bit didn't sound like a joke. "I've never understood how companies can spend so much on lobbying. I mean, it's not like they can give money to the politicians—not legally, anyway—so where is all that money going?"

"It goes to law firms and consultants, mainly," William said calmly. "Adrian's company pays people to produce studies and reports that they can then show to the politicians."

"Ah, that makes sense." It was true. The money Adrian's company was spending on lobbying had to be disclosed in the accounts, and that spending would all be above-board and legal. It wasn't the money being reported that I took issue with. It was the spending that went unreported that caused the problems.

"It's not a pleasant process, when you think about it," William admitted. "But my brother has some big ambitions and I think he'll achieve great things one day."

William seemed to have a genuine feeling of pride in his little brother. He wasn't just defending him or covering up his actions. He looked like he really believed in him. *William doesn't know*, I realized. *He has no idea what his brother is doing.* I was at once relieved, but also worried. When I published my story, William would see all the gory details about his brother; he'd be devastated.

"Tell me about your family," William said. "You know about mine, but I know nothing about yours."

"Do you always interview the people who are supposed to be interviewing you?" I asked. I didn't want to answer questions about my family right now.

"No, but I don't invite them to my apartment for dinner, either. Let's end this interview pretense for good. You don't want to interview me and I don't want this to be about work. Deal?"

I swallowed. My mouth felt dry, so I took a quick sip of water to try to calm my nerves.

"Deal," I replied. My work evening had officially turned into a date. I was terrified.

Chapter Eleven

"What do you want to know?" I asked. "I'm not a very interesting person."

"Oh, I don't believe that for a second," William said. "I know that you majored in journalism at college, but instead of going to work for a big publication with decent pay, benefits, and job security, you opted to freelance. That's interesting to me and I want to know why."

"How do you know I didn't try to get a job at one of those places and got rejected?"

"You went to a good school and finished in the top five percent of your class. It's on your professional profile," he added when I was about to question how he knew that information. "You could have gotten a job if you'd wanted one. Besides, you have Carter Murphy in your corner. If you wanted a job, he could have handed you one on a silver platter. No, you *chose* to freelance and I want to know why."

"I'm not as brave and adventurous as you probably think I am. I worry about money all the time and I've had my phone in my hand ready to call Carter for a job on at least half a dozen occasions."

"But you never did?"

"No." I knew why I didn't work for a paper, but I couldn't tell William that reason. "I like having independence. After the freedom of college, the last thing I wanted was to tie myself down to a Monday-to-Friday, nine-to-five thing."

"There's more to it than that," William said. "Journalists can largely set their own schedules and you could have worked remotely, for the most part. I think you're right about the independence thing, but it's not about your work hours. You want to write stories that the big papers would be too scared to publish."

William was getting dangerously close to the correct answer. "That's kind of it, I suppose. It's more that I didn't want to be told what to write. If you work for a big publication you'll be placed in a specific department and you'll only write about that field. I might want to write about politics one day and, say, fashion the next."

William nodded slowly, but he seemed to be waiting for me to expand on my thoughts. I couldn't say any more or I would give something away.

"I have one sister," I said, interrupting William as he was about to speak. "She's a few years younger than me. I'm also really close to my mom. I'm not going to say anything cheesy like 'she's more like a sister to me' but it's not far from that."

"You're not close to your father?" William asked.

I took a deep breath and considered my words carefully. I couldn't tell the truth, but I had to

61

say something. Hopefully William wouldn't ask too many questions.

"My father passed away four years ago," I said softly.

"Oh my God, I'm so sorry, Amanda. I had no idea." He reached out and placed his hand on mine. Suddenly my heart was racing, but not because I was close to giving away my secrets. "What happened?"

"Car accident," I lied. It was the first thing that came to mind, probably because of my friendship with Emily. I hated lying about my father's death, but I had no choice.

"You probably don't want to talk about it," William said. "I shouldn't have asked."

"No, it's okay. There's just not much to talk about. Obviously it's still difficult, but we're all getting on with our lives. My mother has even started dating a new guy."

"That must be tough for you."

"Not as much as I expected it to be," I said. "He's different from my dad and has a family of his own. We all really like him and I want my mom to be happy."

I looked down at my plate and picked at the last few bits of pasta. A silence descended, but at least William didn't want to talk about my family any more. Mentioning my dead father did tend to put a stop to those conversations rather quickly.

"Did you see the press reaction to the show?" William asked.

"No, I didn't." After the show I had spent my time spying on his brother and getting dressed for tonight. I wouldn't have known where to look for that sort of information anyway. "The reaction of the crowd seemed... mixed."

"I don't know if I would say that," William said. "I'd say there was a general consensus. I believe everyone hated it," he added with a grin.

"You don't seem too concerned about that. Aren't you worried about the effect it will have on the company?"

"Not really. We have plenty of money, so I can take some risks. I'm pleased with the show we put on."

"It wasn't what I was expecting."

"You mean the models weren't size zero and looked like normal people?"

I nodded. "Yes. And I think the audience was surprised as well. Why did you use those women?"

"I have my reasons," William said. "They're important to me and deserved a chance in the limelight. Besides, I don't like looking at women that skinny. What did you think?"

"I much preferred the women you chose. They were all beautiful in their own way. Are you close to all of them?"

William nodded. "I know them all personally. And yes, they're all beautiful, but..." William trailed off. My breath caught in my throat. I felt sure he was about to say something to me, but he seemed to change his mind.

"But..." I said, urging William to finish his sentence.

He hesitated before continuing. "I like to think I look for more in a woman than just the beauty on the outside. I hate to think of myself as shallow, but sometimes a woman's beauty captures me from the moment I lay eyes on her. Does that make me a bad person?"

"We can't help who we're attracted to," I

replied. *I'm attracted to someone whose brother I'm investigating for bribery and corruption. If I could change that, I would.* "Hopefully there's more to it than just a physical attraction."

"Definitely," William replied. "She's beautiful, but intelligent and modest as well."

If it turned out he was talking about one of the models from this morning I was going to feel very stupid.

"A man with your power and success could have any woman he wants. Why don't you do something about it?"

William leaned back in his chair and took a sip of wine. "I want to. I want to more than you can imagine. But I don't think she's ready yet. Soon, hopefully, but not yet."

I nearly yelled at him. I wanted to scream "I'm ready!" at the top of my voice. I wanted him to drag me over to the sofa and take me right there. Physically, I was more than ready. I was already wet between my legs and he had barely touched me.

But William was right. I needed a little longer before taking things any further. Just twenty minutes ago I had been interviewing him. I didn't want to put out *before* the first date. Soon, though. It was inevitable now. William would fuck me soon and that day could not come quickly enough.

Chapter Twelve

William told me he would be busy at work for the next few days dealing with the fallout of the fashion show, so we had to delay our first official date until he had some free time.

I would be busy as well. I needed to use this time to focus on my story about Adrian. It was hard enough to get William off my mind, but having to investigate his brother made it nigh on impossible.

"What are you going to do now?" Natalie asked. "Sounds like you're starting from scratch."

I had told Natalie what happened with William. Whereas Sophie would have asked why I didn't fuck him, Natalie just wanted to know how it was going to affect my story.

"I have some leads now. I spied on Adrian the other day and have a name to follow up on. Plus, there was a mysterious guy I want to track down."

"Amanda, this sounds far too serious for one young journalist. You should pass this story off to a bigger team or even bring the police in."

"No way am I doing either of those things. This could be my chance to actually change things. If I can bring this out into the open, then I can expose everyone. If this gets passed off to a big newspaper then there's more chance of Adrian getting a heads-up about the investigation. You can bet he has connections at all the papers."

"This is dangerous. Why don't you just keep doing what you were doing before and get information from his brother? That sounds safer."

"Because we're going to be dating. It's bad enough that I'm writing a story about his brother. I can't get information from him as well. That's not a great way to begin a relationship."

Natalie shook her head, but she smiled and gave a little laugh. "Only you could investigate serious allegations of corruption and end up dating one of the suspects."

"He's not a suspect," I said tersely. Natalie thought of me as her carefree and somewhat loose friend, which was how I thought of Sophie. Maybe Sophie had a friend whom she thought of as the easy one. "I ruled him out. He's not involved at all and knows nothing about what his brother is doing."

"Are you sure about that? You said he was keeping something secret from you."

"He's just stressed about work, I think. Besides, he looks sad and worried about something. It's not the look of a man capable of committing these crimes."

"You can't know that, Amanda. Just be careful, okay?"

"I promise. Now, can you help me brainstorm? I still have no idea what's going on here and it helps to talk these things through with someone."

"Okay, okay. So, what do you know about him so far?" Natalie asked. "What do you *know* he's done wrong?"

"He's bribing politicians in D.C.," I said. "I saw him do it, clear as day."

"You saw him give money to a politician? Who?"

"I don't know. He didn't give it directly to the politician. It went to one of his aides."

"Maybe he's just bribing the aides, then," Natalie suggested. "It's possible, although the story will be far less newsworthy."

"It's not that," I replied. "I heard parts of conversations and one of the aides promised to pass the money on to his boss."

"Any idea which politician he's bribing? Maybe it's more than one."

"I saw him give money to three different aides, but that's just the ones I saw. Who knows how many there were. I couldn't keep tabs on him the entire time he was in D.C. I followed one of the aides after she met with Adrian, and she went into the Hart Senate Office Building."

"He's bribing senators? Okay, Amanda, one last time. You need to seriously consider walking away from this. You cannot go investigating members of the U.S. Senate. Don't you watch *House of Cards*? Those people are dangerous."

"I'll stay clear of any Texans who look like Kevin Spacey, I promise." Natalie was half joking, but only half, and she had a point. I wasn't scared of the senators, but by following people around D.C. I had taken a real risk of attracting attention from the wrong people. I'd been careless, but had gotten away with it. I hoped.

Natalie sighed. "Okay, if you're going ahead with this crazy story, I may as well help you. I'm just going on record as saying it's a bad idea."

"Noted. Now, can you help?"

Natalie nodded. "I don't have a particularly high opinion of our esteemed members of Congress, as you know, but even so, I believe most of them are honest people. If Adrian is bribing some of them, it will just be a select few. He can't risk casting the net too wide or he's more likely to find that rare politician who actually plays by the book. It's an even bigger risk if the members of staff are involved because they're more idealistic and haven't had the integrity kicked out of them yet."

"Plus, we know that it's one of the senators in the Hart building. That narrows it down a bit, because there are another two buildings with senators' offices."

"Yes, but the Hart building is the biggest. I think it has about half the senators, so that's about fifty, give or take a few. But yes, it helps a bit. What you need to focus on is, who would he need to bribe and why?"

"His company is in the organic food business," I said. "Republicans generally vote in favor of farming and food production already. That means he's probably bribing a Democrat."

"Maybe," Natalie said. "But I'm not sure that's it. A Democrat would love a chance to bring down one of the big companies with proof of bribery. The fallout from an investigation would be worth more to that individual than the bribe itself, I bet."

"My biggest issue is figuring out what Adrian would need to bribe someone for. What could be worth taking such a risk?"

"Whatever it is, it must be out of the ordinary," Natalie said. "If he wanted to lobby in favor of his company then he could do that in the normal way. I don't think he's bribing a politician at all. I think he's bribing the staff."

She might be right. Bribing politicians at the U.S. Senate level would be almost impossible. Unless there was one specific issue Adrian wanted to get passed and just one or two votes were needed, it wouldn't work. There was no way to bribe enough people to pass a radical bill. Bribing members of staff, especially interns, would be far easier.

"He's collecting information," I guessed. "He's collecting information on politicians and when the time is right he'll use that to blackmail them."

Natalie nodded. "That could be it. Adrian's playing the long game here. You need to find out what he wants. What is it that's important to his company that's currently off the table? Something so radical he needs to bribe or blackmail politicians to get it passed?"

I had no idea what that was, but I knew where I would start looking. He had met with someone yesterday who had given him important information. Presumably something that couldn't be sent electronically. I pulled out my phone to look at his picture. I had to find out who this man was and what he had given to Adrian.

I opened my laptop and flexed my fingers. I had a few days with nothing to do. That was plenty of time to bring down a criminal.

Chapter Thirteen

I didn't have the time or energy to learn everything there was to know about the organic food industry where Adrian's company made its money. There were far too many nuances about the business and most of them went over my head. I tried reading about all the tax breaks, but without an accounting background I had no way to understand how they worked.

Instead I decided to focus on the mystery man whom Adrian had met for lunch. The man had mentioned writing legal journal articles and there were only three types of people with the mentality to devote months of their lives to writing tens of thousands of words of inane drivel, complete with detailed footnotes on topics that no one would ever read.

Law students were one group, but this guy was far too old to be a law student. Besides, law students might write articles, but they rarely got published unless a more senior attorney put their name to it. The other two types of people were law professors and lawyers who wanted to be law professors. Judging by the way the man was dressed, I was willing to bet he was a law professor and presumably one who worked in the city.

There was a law school close to the restaurant where he had met Adrian, so that was as sensible a place to start as any. The law school was huge, but there was a list of professors on the website so it was just a case of being patient and working my way through all of them. Finally, I found him.

Professor Timothy Winston. Head of the law school's regulatory practice with a specialty in international law. That was not what I had expected, but food businesses probably had some international law issues if they did cross-border trade.

I studied the professor's online biography for clues, but there was such a long laundry list of publications including articles, books, and blog posts that I had no idea where to start.

Adrian and Professor Winston hadn't looked like close friends when they were eating lunch. The whole thing had resembled a business transaction from beginning to end except for the reference to a woman named Olivia. She might have been a mutual friend or acquaintance, but other than that they hadn't spoken about personal affairs.

They looked like two people who hadn't known each other for long and the whole thing with the briefcase had been out of place. My suspicion was that Adrian and Professor Winston had only recently been introduced and therefore Adrian's interest in the professor was likely based on one of his recent publications.

I pulled up all the articles Professor Winston had written over the three years and started scanning them for anything that would be important to someone like Adrian. I couldn't see anything close. Professor Winston didn't work in the field of international transactions or business. All his articles were about issues such as the United Nations and diplomatic relations. Either I was way off track or I was missing something.

I went back to some of the less dense articles—usually blog posts—and read them in more detail to see if that would help. It didn't. One article did mention other large players in the world of farming, but that was in the context of their being fined for overseas corruption and bribery of foreign politicians. I knew Adrian was doing something similar, but he was buying American. If Adrian's company was up to illegal activities overseas, then Adrian wasn't doing the dirty work himself.

I couldn't think of a single reason why any of the articles would have interested Adrian, and Professor Winston's skill set did not appear helpful. I flicked through a few more articles, delving deeper and deeper into the past, but the topics were equally irrelevant.

Something caught my eye as I started closing the tabs on my browser. I reopened the last one I had closed and looked at it again. The article was about international law issues surrounding diplomatic and trade relations between the U.S. and China. That could be a topic of interest to Adrian if his company had Chinese suppliers, but that wasn't what had caught my eye. At the bottom of the article was a short note by the professor where he thanked his research assistant—Olivia Young.

Olivia. That couldn't be a coincidence. She had been a second-year law student at the time the article was published five years ago. That had to be the connection between Adrian and Professor Winston. Adrian knew Olivia and she used to be a research assistant for the professor.

I felt elated to have made the connection, but on reflection none of it helped me figure out what Adrian had been doing in D.C. I quickly came crashing down to the reality that I still didn't have a strong case against Adrian.

I didn't want to speak to William about it. He was likely in the dark and it just felt wrong to use my burgeoning relationship with him to get the dirt on his brother. We had better things to talk about. At least I hoped we did.

Once I'd started thinking about William there was no way I could concentrate on investigating his brother. One of them made me feel angry and the other made me feel horny. This whole situation was getting complicated and messy fast, but I wasn't ready to give up on my story and there was no way I was giving up on William.

I shut my laptop and went into the kitchen. My average meal took about twenty minutes to cook, but today I wanted to do something more complicated. I pulled out a cookbook that my mother had given me for Christmas a few years ago and blew off the dust. Time to put together something a little special.

I intended to use the next few meals to practice my cooking and then have William over for dinner. If I just focused on one meal I should be able to perfect a recipe in time for our date. I put

Adrian to one side and focused on cooking the best meal I had ever prepared.

Chapter Fourteen

"I hope you like Chinese takeout," I said to William as soon as he walked in the door.

"That doesn't smell like Chinese takeout," William said, frowning as he sniffed the aroma from the kitchen.

"That's the meal I tried to prepare for you," I said sheepishly. "It didn't work out too well, so I've ordered Chinese. It'll be here soon."

"Luckily for you, I happen to love Chinese food. I lived in China for a few years, actually."

"I doubt the food from my local takeout will be quite up to par with the real thing," I remarked. The restaurant was highly regarded and really expensive as far as takeout was concerned, so the food should be edible at least.

"Well, I'm not here for the food, anyway," he said as he placed his hand on my hip and pulled me towards him for a kiss.

I thought I was too old to go weak at the knees from just a kiss, but apparently not. William had seemed shy and distant with me before today, but there was a hunger in his eyes that made it clear he had come here tonight with something very specific in mind.

"Can you give me the grand tour?" he asked.

"It's a two-bedroom apartment; you can see most of it already. Or is this your way of getting into my bedroom?" I joked.

"No need, I'll see that later on. Who lives in the other bedroom?"

"My roommate Sophie," I said. "I don't think she's here at the moment." I walked over to her room and opened the door when there was no response to my knocking. "As you can see, the two of us are very different."

"Is Sophie a little uptight, by any chance?" William asked.

"No, far from it," I replied with a frown. "Why do you say that?"

"She's very tidy."

Sophie's room was tidy, but I had always associated that with her obsession with style and presentation, not a need to be clean all the time. She certainly wasn't uptight when it came to tidying up after herself in the kitchen.

"I guess she just likes a neat room," I replied. "She entertains a lot in there," I added. "I guess she doesn't want to look like a slob."

"Entertains? Is that your polite way of saying she sleeps around a little?"

I nodded. "I don't judge her for it, but it's true. I wish I could do the same thing sometimes, but it just never quite feels right."

"The first time I met you was after a one-night stand, wasn't it?"

Shit, I had forgotten about that. I had never told William that I had just come back from D.C., where I had been spying on this brother, so he'd just assumed it was after a night of drunken passion. He hadn't believed my story about sleeping on a friend's sofa, but I could hardly blame him for that.

"That was a one-off," I said quickly.

I heard someone at the door and assumed it was the food being delivered, but a key turned in the lock and Sophie walked in. She was supposed to be out tonight and I had hoped to have the place to myself.

"Hey, Amanda, have you—" Sophie stopped in her tracks when she saw William and she hung up on whoever she had on the phone. "Oh. Hello. I didn't realize you had company tonight."

"Sophie, this is William Townsend. William, this is my roommate Sophie."

The two of them shook hands and for the first time I thought I saw Sophie slightly lost for words in front of a man. She soon came to her senses, but I kept the mental image in my head. It wasn't something I was likely to see repeated any time soon.

"I only came back to change my top. I managed to spill ketchup on this one. I'll just be a minute."

Sophie dashed into the bedroom and changed into a new top. William looked away just in time, because she made no effort to cover up as she did so.

"You have a brother, right?" Sophie asked William. "A couple of years younger than you? Owns a huge company? Looks so good I want to lick him all over?"

"Yes," William replied with a laugh. "His name's Adrian, and at least two out of those three are correct."

"Well, you know where I live now," Sophie continued, still tucking her shirt into her short skirt. "And I have no qualms about you telling your brother where I live, if you get my meaning."

"You might need to be a little less subtle," I said sarcastically. "I'm having difficulty understanding your point."

"I mean that if Adrian was to come over here one night, I would greet him by dragging him into my room, pulling him down onto my—"

"I'll be sure to pass on the message," William said.

"Thanks. Okay, got to dash."

Sophie disappeared and hopefully wouldn't return until the next morning. She'd only been here a few minutes, but she'd left her mark as usual.

"She's... interesting," William said slowly.

"You don't have to mention her to your brother. She's just joking. I think."

"Believe it or not, she's probably my brother's type. They would be well suited."

We sat down in front of the television to eat dinner. There was a baseball game on and we were both Giants fans, which made it the perfect program to have on in the background to fill any awkward silences that might come up.

William looked relaxed and comfortable around me now, but I didn't feel ready to ask him what had been on his mind this whole time. He didn't want to tell me and I didn't want to force him into a lie.

"I hope you're not offended when I say this," William said when the game went to a commercial break, "but did Sophie help you choose the outfits you've been wearing recently?"

"Is it that obvious?" I asked. The clothes I

was wearing tonight were the third combination from my day of shopping with Sophie. I had now worn all but two pieces of clothing and was beginning to accept that I wouldn't be taking any of them back. The money I'd received for my article had only covered about half the total. The rest had gone on credit cards which I'd be paying off for months.

"She's dressed you in her style," William said. "You don't need to make an effort, you know."

"Oh, I do. You wouldn't want to see me in what I usually wear around the house. It isn't a pretty sight."

"I beg to differ," William said. "I think you should take those clothes off now."

"You want me to go change into my sweatpants?"

"No," he said. "I just want you to take those clothes off."

Chapter Fifteen

William leaned in towards me, but stopped just before his lips reached mine. I stopped breathing. I wanted him to keep going, for those lips to touch mine. The intoxicating freshness of his breath drew me in towards him as his hand squeezed my thigh. On instinct, my legs began to part for him as his thumb teased the inside of my thigh, moving temptingly close to my sex.

"I've waited so long for this," William said. "These last few weeks have felt like an eternity. Ever since you walked into my office I've wanted to put my lips on yours."

"Then you should take what you want," I whispered, my breath mixing with his in the air between us.

William's lips pressed against mine as he pushed me back into the sofa. His hand quickly moved between my legs and pressed against my damp panties.

"You're so wet," William whispered in my ear. "I've barely even touched you."

"Just thinking of you inside me is enough." I

grabbed his wrist and pushed his hand harder against my pussy. My panties were soaked through already and I was desperate for him to peel them off.

William's fingers maneuvered underneath the wet cotton and moved between my slick folds. I squirmed under his firm and skillful touch as he worked his fingers inside my opening. I tried to pull open his shirt, but his thumb rubbing lightly against my clit made it impossible for me to concentrate on undoing the buttons.

"I want to feel your cock," I moaned. "Please, I have to have it inside me."

"No," William said, his eyes looking directly into mine as his hand moved faster and faster between my wet thighs. "I want to taste you as you come in my mouth."

He applied more pressure against the upper wall of my tunnel and I felt my insides contract around his fingers.

"You're so fucking tight, Amanda. I can't wait to get inside you."

"Then do it," I moaned. "Please."

"I told you," he said as he pulled his fingers out of my sex. "I want you to come while I'm licking your beautiful pussy. I've dreamt about how you taste ever since I saw your panties on the floor of my office."

William dragged me into the bedroom and threw me down on the bed. My legs fell open as I landed and he immediately moved between them, pulling my panties off in one swift motion. I still had my top and skirt on, but there was no time to remove them before William dived between my

81

legs and started licking at me greedily.

"You taste so sweet," he said. His tongue moved slowly from the base of my opening all the way up, stopping just short of my clit. "Even better than I imagined." He pressed his tongue against my swollen clit.

I moaned and made a noise that would be unrecognizable to any human. "Again," I whimpered. "Please."

"You like me licking your clit?"

I moaned an affirmative reply, unable to form any words. His tongue darted quickly in and out of my tunnel, moving deftly between the folds as he brought me closer and closer to climax.

"Come for me, Amanda." He gripped my thighs hard and buried his face between them, his tongue pushing hard against me.

"I'm close," I moaned. I reached down and grabbed the back of his head as I thrust my sex harder into his face. I squirmed under the movements of his tongue until finally I came hard, waves of pleasure crashing against his face.

William licked up every hint of my essence and then stood up, leaving me writhing on the bed trying to wrestle back control of my body. I heard a condom wrapper being ripped open and soon after William was on top of me, the head of his thick shaft pressing against my engorged, wet lips.

"I need to be inside you, Amanda. I want to hear you scream my name when you come."

I rocked my hips against him, trying to work his cock inside me. My body ached for him and the exhaustion of the last orgasm had already passed. My body was ready and willing for more.

"Stop teasing and fuck me," I ordered.

I looked down and watched my folds part as

he pushed his cock inside me inch by inch. He went deep and entered territory where no man—or even my toys—had ever been. I felt full and complete with him inside me.

"God you're so tight and wet," he whispered as he ground his hips against mine. "I don't know how long I'm going to last inside you."

My hands gripped the soft sheets under my body as he pushed the final inch inside. I lifted my head back and surrendered to William. I moaned his name over and over until his body stiffened and he released his passion inside me.

It wasn't until after we had both come that I finally got undressed and lay naked in William's arms. Almost immediately William's phone started beeping and vibrating with a steady chain of incoming emails and messages. Eventually he gave in and picked up his phone from the floor. I didn't complain because I got a great look at his perfect ass as he bent down to pick it up.

"Work?" I asked.

"No, I turned those notifications off. Family stuff."

"Your brother?"

He shook his head. "Sister."

"I didn't know you had a sister."

William nodded. "Unfortunately she has... issues. It's a difficult relationship." He put his phone down without replying to the message and wrapped his arm around me.

Our sweaty bodies rubbed against each other and I could feel his cock begin to stiffen again under my thigh.

"Already?" I asked. "You only came ten

minutes ago."

"Are you complaining?" William asked.

"Not at all," I said as I took his sticky cock in my hand and brought it to attention once again.

Chapter Sixteen

I was exhausted. Too tired to work and too tired to have fun. I could have used a nap, but the curtains in my room didn't keep out enough of the light. Besides, lying in bed with the sheets still ruffled from last night made me think about William and what we'd done there not so long ago.

No sooner had I shut my eyes than there was a knock on the bedroom door. "Is it safe to come in?" Sophie said.

I looked around for any signs of condom wrappers or similar clues to last night's activities, but there were none. Not that Sophie would have cared.

"Come in," I called back, the last word turning into a loud yawn.

Sophie opened the door and walked in grinning. "Bed's a mess and you look tired. I'm going to guess that last night went well."

"Last night was perfect, thank you. How was yours?"

Sophie shrugged and sat down on my bed. "He was okay. Nothing earth-shattering, if you get my drift. But don't try to change the subject. What was he like? I'm pretty good at guessing a man's ability between the sheets—last night notwithstanding—and I figure William knows what he's doing."

"He does," I said. I could feel my cheeks warming and could tell they were turning red. "He definitely does."

"I'm glad you had a good time. I'm pretty sure you needed that and I know he did."

"What do you mean?" I asked, frowning at Sophie. "I admit it's been a while for me, but I don't think he ever goes long without sex. You should see how women throw themselves at him."

"Oh I don't doubt it," Sophie said. "But he's going to have a stressful day at work today if the news I've seen is anything to go by."

"What news?" I asked. I opened my laptop and searched for William's name and the name of his company.

"You know that fashion show you went to with him recently?"

I nodded. "What about it?"

"Were the models... unusual?"

"No, they were normal women. Well, I guess by the standards of models they weren't normal, but they were beautiful nonetheless."

"There were rumors about the show a week or so ago, but no one was allowed to take pictures so it was just rumor. Now William's company has released an entire line of clothing with, shall we say, unconventional models showing off the clothes."

"Is that bad?" I asked. "Sounds sensible to me. I know I never buy clothes when they're modeled by stick-thin women because I assume they won't fit me properly."

"I agree, actually, but there are a lot of people who don't. Like I said, today could be a stressful day for him."

I decided that trying to sleep was a bad idea, so I just jumped in the shower and headed out to my usual coffee shop. The coffee kept me awake, but not much more than that. I had no energy to do anything overly constructive, so I started reading the articles that were appearing about William's company.

Sophie had been right; most of them were negative. They recognized the choice of models as "admirable" but ultimately reckless. William was the owner of the company, but he wasn't outspoken enough to be considered famous. The blame for the poor choice of models was either directed generally towards the company or at other individuals who were better known in the fashion industry.

I knew those models had been William's decision and no one else's. There had been so much pride on this face when he saw them and they'd all thanked him personally. The press might not know it was him, but the other directors of the company would, and they would make their feelings known to William.

None of the articles I read bothered to name the models, so they were obviously not famous. They were named on the photos, but a quick online search didn't bring up any information on them. Given that models were usually credited in some way, it seemed safe to assume they had never done that sort of work before. In fact, going by the compete lack of an online presence, it was almost like they didn't exist.

Bashing away at my keyboard reinvigorated me more than the coffee had done, so I decided to turn my attention back to Adrian's illicit activities. I knew a lot more now than I had just a week ago, but it still wasn't a lot to go on. He was getting help from a professor at a local law school who practiced in some esoteric area of international law. Adrian's company probably did international trade, but that was the only area which would involve international law in any way.

Olivia Young was easy enough to track down. The name wasn't that common and I knew which law school she had attended. After graduating and passing the California bar exam, she had gone to work for a large law firm and had stayed there for two years.

After that she moved to a smaller firm which probably paid a lot less, but proudly touted offering a "work-life balance" on its website. She had stayed there for three years and that was the last record of her working anywhere.

For the last two years she had seemingly been unemployed and her social profiles were largely untouched. Other than living in the same city, Olivia had nothing in common with Adrian that I could see and I was beginning to think the name could be a red herring. At the very least it didn't seem to be getting me anywhere.

I put the profiles of Adrian and Olivia side-by-side on my screen to see if I could spot any overlap. Maybe she had interned at his company once, or the law firm she'd worked for had assisted Adrian with a big case? But no, there was nothing.

A hand pressed against my upper back, so I tucked my chair in closer under the table, assuming someone behind me was trying to squeeze through the gap between chairs. The hand didn't move. That felt a little creepy, but it wasn't unheard of for guys to be overly hands-on in San Francisco. I turned around to glare up at the man whose hand was still on my back.

"Oh, it's you," I said with a smile when I saw William standing behind me.

He didn't smile back. He looked confused and then angry. "Amanda, what the hell are you doing?"

"I'm just—" I looked back down at my screen and realized the picture of Adrian was still there.

"What the hell is going on?" William asked through gritted teeth. "Why are you investigating my family?"

Chapter Seventeen

I closed my laptop, but it was far too late. He had seen the page of information I had prepared on his brother and there was little I could do to deny it.

"Let's go somewhere to talk about this," I said. People around me were already staring at us and not being too subtle about it.

"My place," he said tersely.

The walk from the coffee shop to his apartment wasn't a long one, but it sure felt like it today. I racked my brain to think of an excuse for why I would be looking for information on his brother.

William knew I had wanted to interview Adrian, but I had promised to stay clear of him. I could just say that I'd changed my mind, or a good opportunity had come up, but that would sound weak. Besides, I would still be admitting I had lied.

I decided to tell William the truth. Well, part of it, anyway. I wouldn't tell him about how I had gone to D.C. to spy on his brother, but I would say he was involved in something illegal. William had a right to know.

We reached his apartment and William went to the kitchen to pour some glasses of water. It was warm outside and the walk had given me quite the thirst so I knocked the drink back in one gulp. My mouth felt refreshed, which was a good thing because I had a lot of explaining to do.

"What's going on, Amanda?" William asked. Those were the first words he had spoken to me since we left the coffee shop. "Why were you snooping on my family? What's going on?"

"Remember how I was originally supposed to interview your brother instead of you?"

William nodded. "And I asked you to drop it. He's working through some personal issues and doesn't need this stress right now. Seems like you ignored my request. Did you do it just to get a good story?"

"Don't be ridiculous," I replied. "Do you really think I would do that? I thought you had a higher opinion of me than that. I *hoped* you did, anyway."

"You can't blame me. What am I supposed to think?"

"It's not me you should be accusing. William, how much do you really know about your brother?"

William frowned. "I grew up with him. I know him better than I know anyone else. Why do you say that?"

"He's been hiding something from you. He's been hiding a lot from you, in fact."

"I don't need to know every little detail about his personal life," William said. "If you have some story about who he's slept with, then I'm not interested. And you shouldn't be, either. You're above writing stories like that."

I sighed. "You're not listening, William. He's

involved in something big. Something illegal. I don't know exactly what he's doing, but—"

"You don't know? So you're digging for information, but you don't have any proof?"

I took a deep breath and looked up at the ceiling before bringing my eyes back down and looking at William. "He's bribing politicians." I paused to allow it to sink in. William blinked, but otherwise didn't react. "I know you think highly of your brother, but you need to accept that he might be doing things you don't approve of."

"It's just lobbying," William said at last. "It looks ugly to outsiders, but it's all completely legal. I can't say I'm a huge fan of the practice myself, but his company has to do it just to keep going."

"This isn't lobbying," I said, shaking my head. "He's flat-out bribing people. I know he is."

"But you don't have any evidence?"

"I'm going to get some," I said defiantly. "You can't stop me from looking into this, and you may not like what I find."

William shook his head and let out a long sigh. Finally he held his hands up in defeat and smiled. "I can see I'm not going to win this one. I guess that's what I get for dating a reporter."

"You're okay with me investigating your brother?"

"I wouldn't say I'm okay with it, but I'm not going to stop you. Just don't go publishing anything without making sure you have all the facts. I'm confident that my brother isn't doing anything wrong, so you can go ahead and look into him as much as you like."

"Thank you," I said, reaching my hand out to lightly touch his. "I appreciate that you trust me in this. I just hope you won't blame me for what I find out."

"You're not going to... never mind. Let's change the subject and do something else."

William was underestimating my ability to dig up dirt online. If he ever talked to my old roommate Amy, he would probably realize what a big mistake he was making. That suited me just fine, though. I figured I had some breathing space now and I had to make the most of it.

"Why were you in the coffee shop, anyway?" I asked. "Did you come to find me for something?"

"No, I was supposed to be meeting someone there, but they rescheduled for later this afternoon. I decided to go in and get a coffee anyway because it's better than the stuff they have at the office."

"You know, you could just make them buy better coffee. You do own the place."

William shrugged. "It's part of company culture to have bad coffee, I think. Who am I to change that?"

William had a few hours to spare and didn't seem to be in a rush to get back to the office, so we chilled out on the sofa and watched some television. Now that everything—well, almost everything—was out in the open, I felt more able to relax around him. I still felt guilty, though; not so much for having lied to him, but for the disappointment he was sure to feel when he found out what his brother was up to.

I should just forget about the story and write something else. I could make a nice living writing about celebrities and if William and I got serious, it wasn't like I would have to worry about money any more.

But I couldn't do that. I owed it to my father's

memory to put a stop to what Adrian was doing. There were real human consequences to bribing politicians and government officials and people sometimes died as a result. I couldn't live with myself if I let that happen again.

I was going to bring Adrian down, and if that affected my relationship with William, then so be it. I liked to think we could work past it together, but who knows. Families could be funny things, so I couldn't take it for granted.

My relationship with William was so new I could barely refer to it as a relationship, but I didn't think it was fragile. We'd already had one small argument and worked through it quite sensibly. I almost felt like a real grown-up.

Fragile or not, the next few weeks would be the ultimate test. Adrian might end up in prison because of me—I hoped he would—and that would be tough for any new couple to handle. But that was for another day. For now, I tried to just enjoy the moment with William as I rested my head on his chest, listening to the steady beating of his heart.

Chapter Eighteen

"Wake up, darling. Amanda?"

I woke up with William lightly shaking me. The same episode of the TV show was on, so I hadn't been asleep long. I felt remarkably refreshed instead of groggy, so I couldn't have slept for more than fifteen minutes.

"I really need to leave," William said as I lay on his chest on the sofa.

"Do we have to leave?" I pleaded, forcing out a final yawn and shaking myself awake. "I just want to spend the rest of the day here with you. I'll make it worth your while," I added as I rubbed my hand up his leg.

"I have to go to that meeting now. You can feel free to stay here, though. I know you love snooping around the place."

"That may be true," I admitted, "but I'd much rather do something a little more exciting."

William looked at me with raised eyebrows. "I thought I'd left you exhausted after last night."

I shrugged. "It's been awhile for me, so I

have a lot of catching up to do."

"I need to go get some more condoms," William said. "We're going to have to wait until tonight."

"Where's your imagination?" I asked as my hands started undoing his pants. "You were very… generous last night. Now it's my turn to repay the favor."

I reached my hand under the waistband of his boxers and pulled out his thick shaft. It stiffened in my hand and was hard by the time my tongue licked the salty tip.

"Oh, shit," William moaned as my mouth closed over the top. He ran his fingers through my hair and massaged my scalp.

I could usually manage to keep a man happy with my mouth, but William was larger down there than anyone I had attempted this with before. I closed my eyes as I lowered my head as far as it could go.

There was still over an inch left, but I couldn't manage any more. I lifted my head up and sucked hard as I did so. There was a loud 'pop' sound as his shaft left my mouth.

"Oh, God, Amanda. That feels so good. Keep going. Take it all into your mouth."

I licked my lips and took a deep breath before going back down on his cock. This time I pushed all the way down and made it all the way to the base. My eyes were watering as much as my mouth, but I kept going up and down his cock.

"You really know how to suck cock, Amanda. Shit, I'm not going to last long."

I couldn't help myself now. I was out of control, desperate to suck him harder and faster than he had ever been sucked before. I knew I had a lot of competition, but I was up for the challenge.

"Open your blouse," William commanded. "I want to come all over those big breasts of yours."

I kept sucking him while my fingers fumbled at the buttons on my blouse. I pulled it open to reveal my breasts, which looked firm in my push-up bra.

"I'm close, baby," William moaned as his fingers pressed firmly against my head.

He pulled his cock out of my mouth and grabbed the shaft just before a thick spray shot forth and spattered against my chest. I felt the sticky substance drip down the crevice between my breasts as he released two more bursts all over me.

I needed to taste his essence, so I quickly took his cock in my hand and sucked the last bits of release from the tip of his shaft.

William collapsed back down on the sofa. "That was amazing."

I looked up at him and licked my lips. "You can go to your meeting now. Hurry back, though."

William left me alone in his apartment and went to his meeting. The first thing I did was jump in the shower to clean my sticky chest and wake myself up a bit. I resisted the urge to snoop and pulled out my laptop to get some work done.

Usually, the first thing I would do was get connected to the Wi-Fi, but I didn't know the password and decided not to ask. For once, I wanted to be offline. I had plenty of information on Adrian, but hadn't spent enough time actually reading and digesting it.

I pulled up my notes and tried to start from scratch. I needed to sort the speculation from the facts and stop letting my imagination run the show.

Adrian had spent time in D.C. recently and he had given something to people who worked for the U.S. Senate. The meetings had been in public, but the people involved had kept their voices down the entire time and had looked over their shoulders a lot.

There had been an exchange between Adrian and a law school professor who specialized in issues surrounding international law. The two things had to be connected.

Then there was Olivia. I was beginning to think she was a red herring, but I kept her in my notes just in case.

Natalie had suggested trying to figure out what Adrian would want, but that was a long list. Adrian's company was having issues with the European Commission, which was investigating the company for breaches of competition law and privacy issues.

The company did a lot of work with China and some other Asian countries that were known to be hotspots for payments in brown envelopes. That didn't explain why Adrian was bribing a senator, though.

The vibration of my phone on the table snapped me out of my daze. A text from Sophie flashed on the screen.

OMG, I just bumped into Adrian as he was going into the toy store on 20th Street. So delicious. Any closer to getting me a date with him? Don't make me beg!

I replied to Sophie to tell her William was

working on it. He wasn't—I hoped—but that should keep her quiet until a new man came along.

Why was Adrian going to a toy store? He didn't have any children, and he wasn't an uncle. Besides, he probably had assistants to go and buy presents for him. I didn't have much journalism experience yet, but I still had a vague idea when something wasn't quite right. That was how I'd gotten started on this case in the first place.

I quickly packed up my things and headed down to the toy store. It was only a ten-minute walk and I ran the entire way. Nine minutes later, I arrived at the toy store and walked inside.

A few of the employees looked at me suspiciously, because I was walking around the store looking at people instead of the toys on the shelves. I probably looked like I was casing the joint.

At the back of the store, down the last aisle I looked in, I finally saw Adrian. He was standing there holding a toy, but clearly had no interest in it. He was talking to someone else who had their back to me.

I walked down the next aisle and stopped at the back near where Adrian was standing. His voice was just about audible from my position. The aisle was full of action figures based on video game characters. Most of them I didn't recognize, but I grabbed one and pretended to examine it while I listened in on the conversation.

Adrian's voice drifted through the aisle. "I've done all I can. What's next?"

There was a reply; a man's voice, but I couldn't quite make out what he said.

"I *have* been careful," Adrian said. "I couldn't have been much more careful. There's nothing tying this back to me or you."

I stepped closer to the shelves. The store was busy and most people were just going about their business, so hopefully no one would pay any attention to the weird woman looking very closely at the rows of toys.

"She's on to you," the other man said. His voice was deep, but he spoke under his breath to avoid being overheard.

"Then get her off me," Adrian said.

"I can't," the other voice said. "Just leave this to me from now on. You can back off."

"You sure?" Adrian asked.

"Positive. It's my turn to handle this."

Adrian was the majority owner and CEO of his company, but this man spoke to Adrian as if Adrian were the subordinate.

The conversation was over and I saw Adrian walk out of the aisle and head straight out of the store. I didn't follow him. I needed to know whom he had been speaking to. I waited in the aisle until the next man walked out.

It was William.

When I saw him, the conversation I had just overheard made some sense. Adrian did not have a boss, but there was one other person who might speak to him like that. An older brother. Everything Adrian had been doing was at the behest of William. He'd been lying to me this entire time.

Suddenly the store felt a lot smaller and the crowds seemed to be closing in around me. I dropped the toy I'd been holding and ran out of the store, ignoring the looks of those around me.

William disappeared around a corner in the distance and I ran in the opposite direction, not stopping until I was out of breath.

I felt dizzy as I took in deep breaths and tried to calm my heart, which felt like it was racing at a dangerous rate. How could I have been so stupid? It seemed so obvious now I thought about it.

I made my way back home in a daze of confusion and anger. By the time I reached my apartment, the confusion had disappeared, but the anger had not. William had treated me like an idiot, but worst of all he had let me fall for him. I was sleeping with the man I was supposed to be investigating. Just minutes ago I had been scrubbing his come off my chest.

Why had he let me get so close? Was he that arrogant that he thought he was invincible? William was confident, but he had never seemed that cocky.

I collapsed onto my bed and cried. There would be time for work later. Time to uncover what the hell William was playing at. For now, I could only let the tears fall and moisten my pillow.

Tomorrow would be a new day. Tomorrow things were going to change.

Part Two

Chapter One

"William came over to see you again," Sophie said, standing in the doorway of my bedroom. "I told him you were out."

"Thanks," I replied. I kept typing on my keyboard to pretend I didn't care, but the words appearing on the screen were gibberish.

"He knew I was lying," Sophie added. "Your shoes were by the door and he could see the light was on in your room."

"That's fine. I've been ignoring him for weeks. He knows that by now."

"And yet he still keeps trying."

Her tone made it clear she thought I was an idiot for abandoning my fledgling relationship with William. I couldn't blame her—she didn't know what I'd overheard William say to his brother.

"He'll give up eventually," I said. I kept my eyes fixed on the screen, hoping Sophie would leave me alone.

"And is that what you want?"

I nodded. I knew my voice would betray me if I tried to speak. I didn't turn around, but I knew Sophie was still standing in the doorway.

"What—" Sophie began, before being interrupted by someone knocking on the door.

William was persistent, I had to give him that. At first there had just been messages asking me why I was ignoring him. Then he kept calling me, and finally he started showing up at my apartment.

I never bothered to tell him why I was ignoring him. I didn't want to hear all the lies and excuses that he would no doubt come up with.

"Tell him to leave me alone," I yelled out as Sophie went to answer the door again.

"It's not William," Sophie said before she had even opened the door.

I grimaced, assuming that Sophie had invited another man around for an afternoon of sex. I could do without hearing her moaning with pleasure through the thin walls. The next voice I heard was a familiar one.

"Natalie?" I asked, stepping out of my bedroom.

Sophie and Natalie had met briefly in passing, but it looked like they had arranged to spend time together this afternoon.

"Hi, Amanda," Natalie said as she took off her shoes and moved over to the sofa.

"What are you doing here?" I asked. It wasn't a great way to greet a close friend, but I was exhausted and stressed out. I just wanted to be alone and couldn't handle social situations right now.

"I invited her," Sophie said. "We both want to

speak to you."

"We're worried about you," Natalie explained. "You've barely left the apartment in weeks."

"She's barely left her room," Sophie added.

"I'm working," I explained. "I've come to a point in my story were I really need to buckle down and get things done. There's no need to be so dramatic about it. Plenty of journalists burn the midnight oil once in a while."

"I'm not so concerned about you working hard," Natalie said. I'd seen her work through the night while we were in college, so she could understand that easily enough. "I'm more concerned about you suddenly abandoning William as well."

"I'm too busy for him right now," I said.

"He says you're ignoring him," Sophie said. "You haven't returned any of his calls in weeks."

Natalie took my hand and gently pulled me down next to her on the sofa. "If he did something to you, you need to tell us, okay?"

"No, no, it's nothing like that." However much I hated William right now, I couldn't have my friends thinking he had abused me. That wasn't fair.

"Did he cheat on you?" Sophie asked. "Because if so, maybe he just didn't realize you two were exclusive. Dating is pretty complicated these days."

I couldn't handle an afternoon of Sophie and Natalie trying to guess all the things that William might or might not have done wrong, so I decided to tell them what I had overheard a few weeks ago at the toy shop.

"Is there any chance you could have misunderstood?" Natalie asked. "You didn't hear the whole thing. Maybe there was some context you missed?"

I shook my head firmly. "For one thing, the whole meeting looked sketchy. They were in a crowded toy store and they weren't there to pick up the latest *Star Wars* action figures. Plus, William said something like 'she's on to you.' That was a clear reference to me."

"That certainly doesn't sound good," Natalie admitted.

"It all makes sense, really," I said. "I'm just annoyed I didn't spot the signs earlier."

"What signs?" Sophie asked.

"William went to a lot of effort to deter me from digging into Adrian's activities. When I told him I wanted to interview his brother, he immediately insisted I interview him instead. I hoped he just wanted to spend more time with me. I was wrong."

"You don't know that," Sophie insisted. "I still think you may be reading too much into all of these suspicious activities. To outsiders like us, it probably looks like bribery, but I bet big companies do it all the time. I suspect it's entirely legal, albeit a touch unethical."

"It's definitely illegal," I said. "I don't like lobbying, but if that's all it was, I wouldn't be so concerned. There's much more to it than that. I have all the evidence on my computer. Sure, most of it's circumstantial, but when you add it all together you can't argue that William is guilty."

"It's just such a shame to blow a potentially awesome relationship when you're not sure," Sophie said.

"You're just annoyed you won't get an introduction to Adrian," I joked.

106

Sophie smiled. "Okay, yes, that is annoying, but I'll meet another rich man one day."

"How close are you to having a story ready?" Natalie asked.

"I have some paragraphs written describing what happened in Washington, D.C., but without all the context it's almost impossible to write a story. And I need some evidence. I suppose you're going to tell me to drop the story again?"

Natalie had been surprisingly quiet so far, Ever since I'd told her about my investigation she had been the voice of caution in my ear. I needed her pragmatism, even if I didn't always agree with what she said.

"No," Natalie replied. "I think you should keep going."

"You do?" Sophie and I asked at the same time.

"I've been thinking of Adrian as some criminal mastermind, but he was just doing as his brother told him. I don't think William is dangerous either. In fact, I think those two are out of their depth. Meetings in toy shops and exchanging briefcases in restaurants sounds like something from a spy movie. Someone's going to catch them—it might as well be you."

"You'd be giving up your relationship with William," Sophie added. "You can't do this and expect to have him trust you ever again."

"And she can't trust him," Natalie said. "I don't want to sound blunt, but it's too late for them."

I knew Natalie was trying to be supportive, but her words were like a punch to the gut. I'd been ignoring William for weeks, but it had never occurred to me that we might not speak again. It should have—Natalie was right to say I couldn't trust him—but a part of me had assumed everything might work out somehow. It wouldn't.

"What are you going to do?" Sophie asked.

"I'm going to stick with the story. I need to find out what's going on. If that means William and I have no future, then so be it."

My friends both nodded agreement, but Natalie looked more pleased by my decision than Sophie. My head was ruling my heart and Natalie would always agree with that type of thing.

"We're here if you need us," Sophie said. "You need to get out of the house once in a while, and we're going for drinks on Friday night. No arguments," she added as I was about to argue.

My phone vibrated with another message from William, but I ignored it. I would speak to him again one day soon, but that would only be to ask him questions about what he was doing. Other than that, we didn't need to talk and I would keep ignoring him.

I didn't trust myself to read his messages without wanting to respond, so I immediately deleted it. I allowed myself to hang out with Natalie and Sophie for a few hours, but after that it was back to work. Natalie was right—if I didn't write this story, someone else would.

Chapter Two

Sophie and Natalie both made a conscious effort to distract me from my story over the next few days. They worked together to practically drag me out of the apartment at least twice a day for some much needed fresh air and exercise.

They both supported me, but I could tell they didn't entirely understand. Sophie always lived for the moment, so she worked as much as she needed to and no more. She didn't take herself at all seriously and I admired that in her, even if I never said so.

Natalie knew what it was like to work hard when you had a passion for something, but she didn't understand where my passion came from. She had slaved over her degree and had striven to get top grades, even in classes she didn't care about. She'd cared about her education and that was enough to motivate her.

I considered telling Sophie and Natalie a number of times, but I didn't know where to start. I ran through the conversation in my head, but I always fumbled over the opening few lines. How should I start to tell that story?

Natalie and Sophie thought my obsession was with lobbying, but that wasn't quite the case. Many businesses in America engaged in somewhat dubious lobbying activities, but my father hadn't been killed because of lobbying. He'd been killed because of companies bribing politicians and those in power. If Sophie and Natalie knew that, they would understand why I had to continue with this story.

But I couldn't tell them. I could mention my dead father in passing, but any extended conversation about him brought me to tears. Even mentioning his name was too much. I could talk about him with my mom and sister, but that was different. When we talked about him, we remembered the fun times we had shared together. Conversations with strangers always had to start with the details of how he had died. I couldn't talk about that.

I stopped dwelling on my father and went back to work. Researching William's brother had been hard enough, but looking for information on William and his company was almost impossible without feeling sick to my stomach.

Every click of my mouse brought up either an image of William or something closely associated with him. He didn't look like a bad person. When I stared at the pictures, he still looked like the man who had been worried and vulnerable the first time we met. He had gradually opened up around me and when he did, the passion was phenomenal. How could that be the same man who would go to jail if I wrote my story?

I had never figured out why Adrian would be

trying to bribe or blackmail a politician, so even though I was starting from square one now, it didn't feel like a huge setback.

All the research I had on the law professor was still valid, but I decided to give up investigating Olivia for the time being. I suspected she belonged in Adrian's past, but she probably had nothing to do with William.

Adrian's company grew and sold food, so there were a lot of applicable government regulations the company had to deal with. It made sense that he might want to speak to a politician. The fashion industry, on the other hand, did not seem a prime candidate for government interference. What problem could William have that he would need to resort to bribery or blackmail?

The press had a lot of stories about William's company, but they were largely about the supposed fashion disaster that had started at the fashion show I had attended. I found it incredible that something as seemingly insignificant as using regularly shaped models could cause such a fuss, but it had done exactly that.

The company had recently added a new section to its website with clothes modeled by these women. The website still contained plenty of more traditional models, but the way the media talked about it, you would think the company had changed the face—and shape—of fashion.

I wished William hadn't done something so morally decent. He was making it hard for me to hate him as much as I should. I loved looking at the pictures of women who looked like people I might pass on the street. I had never been an impulse shopper when it came to clothes, but I wanted to order three different things from William's company after just a quick perusal of the new section.

The women even looked happy. They weren't pouting or looking glum—they were smiling in a way that looked completely genuine. The photos didn't look Photoshopped, either.

Most media articles I read said that the company was taking a huge risk and would likely see its efforts backfire in drastic fashion. Employees were described for the most part as disgruntled and some had already quit.

A few prominent publications had written articles praising the company for its efforts to change "how we perceive beauty," but again the suspicion was that its efforts were misguided.

The company had problems, but none of that had any political link at all. The company was not a big exporter of clothing and most of it was American-made. Some of the raw materials would have come from other parts of the world, but import problems like that were better handled through lobbying. Not to mention, many companies would face similar problems and it would be a big story already.

William's company was as much of a mystery as his brother's and my ego was taking a huge hit with every failed attempt to dig up information that would help answer my questions.

My phone vibrated on the table—another message from William. I ignored it and continued working. I must have turned on the Bluetooth functionality on my laptop because the message from my phone appeared on my screen.

I quickly tried to delete it, but it was impossible to close the box in the top right corner without reading the message.

I'm going to tell you everything. The whole story. Come over tonight.

Chapter Three

"I'm surprised you came," William said when I walked into his apartment.

"So am I," I replied. I hadn't replied to William's message and had had no intention of going to his apartment in the evening. I'd gone on working, but couldn't get the message out of my mind.

I'm going to tell you everything. He was admitting his guilt. I had hoped to find out all the information myself, but by the end of the afternoon it had become clear that I wasn't going to find anything, so I gave in and decided to get the information from the source.

"This isn't another date," I said, as I gave him my jacket. "Let's just be clear on that."

"Crystal."

"You said you were going to tell me everything."

"I did. Shall we sit down on the sofa?"

I followed William over to the sofa and sat down, making sure to keep at least three feet between us. I didn't trust myself to keep my emotions and desires out of this. If I felt his skin on mine, it would be even harder.

I pulled out my pen and notebook in case there were any particular dates or names to write down. "Okay, start talking."

William nodded. "Before I start, why don't you tell me what you think I've done?"

I sighed. "William, please don't drag this on any longer than you have to. I don't know all the details, which is why I'm here. You said you were going to tell me, so get on with it."

"Well, it's not how it looked. We're just friends and always have been. I swear, you're the only woman for me, Amanda."

"What?" I struggled to understand what he'd just said. That was pretty much the last thing I'd expected to hear.

"I haven't cheated on you. Ever since we met, I haven't looked at another woman in that way."

"Is that what you think this is about?" I asked. I felt relieved to hear him say those words, but that wasn't supposed to be important right now.

"Okay, confession time," William said, holding up his hands in surrender. "Don't hate me, but I might have lied to get you over here."

I threw my pen down on the floor. It was a stupid thing to do—I looked like a petulant child—but my brain didn't stop me in time.

"You're not going to tell me?" I asked.

"I don't know *what* to tell you," William said in frustration. "I knew I must have done something wrong for you to stop talking to me so suddenly, but I had no idea what. You kept ignoring me, so eventually I sent you that message saying I wanted to confess. I'll tell you whatever you want to know, Amanda. Just tell me what to say."

It had been a dirty trick, but I blamed myself for falling for it. I'd wanted to see William and my brain had latched on to the first decent excuse that came my way. Still, William had promised me answers and I was going to get them.

"I overheard the conversation you had with your brother." William looked confused and just shrugged his shoulders. "The one in the toy store," I added.

William's face was blank for a few moments, then he looked down in defeat. "What did you hear?" he asked.

"No, that's not how this is going to work. You need to tell me everything. What I did or did not hear is irrelevant."

William rubbed the bridge of his nose with his thumb and forefinger. He was reverting back to the man I had first seen in his office right in front of my eyes. When he looked back at me I could see the worry and stress on his face again.

"I can't tell you about that," William said at last. "I'm sorry, I just can't."

When I first met William, I had almost felt sorry for him. He'd looked like a man consumed with problems that he was keeping hidden deep inside. Now I knew what he was so worried about—getting caught. That had to be it. He was stressed because he was doing something illegal and was worried about the threat of prison.

"In that case, I'm leaving." I stood up and picked up my pen from the floor. "I came here because I thought you were going to confess. I guess I'll just have to figure it all out myself."

"Amanda, please stay." His hand grabbed my

wrist and I didn't try to shake him off.

"You can't seriously expect me to stay here with you. You're lying to my face and you aren't even subtle about it."

"I'm not lying," William insisted. "I'm deliberately not talking about it because I don't want to lie to you."

"Why not just tell me?" He still had hold of my wrist. The electricity from his skin on mine made me weak at the knees. I had to get out of here soon, before my heart could take over from my brain.

"I can't tell you, Amanda. You don't want to be involved in this. I'm keeping it from you for your own protection."

"Don't give me that bullshit. I'm a journalist. I'm not going to stay out of a story because you say it's for my own protection."

"I need you to trust me."

"You don't trust me enough to tell me what you're doing. Why on Earth should I trust you?"

William sighed and let go of my wrist. I immediately felt less whole, as if he had taken part of me with him as he let go.

"Do you trust Carter Murphy?" William asked.

I frowned at the mention of his name. *Please, God, don't tell me Carter is involved in all this somehow? No, he couldn't be. Could he?*

"Yes, I trust Carter. Why?"

"Speak to Carter. Tell him that I'm keeping a secret from you and ask him if you can trust me."

"Carter knows what you're doing?"

"He knows some of it. And he supports me. Will you speak to Carter?"

I nodded. "I'll get in touch with him. I'm not sure if he's even in the country, though."

117

"He's not. He's in England, but I'm sure you can still find a time to talk. Do you promise you'll talk to him?"

I nodded. "I don't owe you anything, William, but I want to find out what the hell is going on. I'm not going to give this up, you know."

"Yeah, you're far too stubborn for that, it seems." He smiled at me and, against my better judgment, I let him kiss me on the cheek before I left.

I felt a little concerned that Carter knew what was going on here. He was the one who had put me in touch with William in the first place. Why would he do that if he knew William was up to something sketchy?

If Carter was in England, he would likely be asleep right now. I sent a quick email to him and Emily and headed back home. I couldn't imagine what he could say that would make me trust William again, but I wanted to hear it. I desperately wanted to trust William, but all the facts suggested I couldn't.

I didn't need protecting, even if William thought I did. If Carter and William weren't going to cooperate, then I would get the information myself, even if I had to resort to drastic measures. I would do whatever it took.

Chapter Four

Carter replied quickly for someone who likely had far more important things to do than talk to me. One day I would ask him for a favor and he would finally say no, but apparently that day was not today.

William had been right about Carter being in England, so we had to arrange a chat over Skype. I tidied the part of my bedroom that would be visible in the background and made a bit of an effort elsewhere in case I had to move my laptop. I didn't feel any particular desire to impress Carter, but I wanted to look vaguely professional.

At exactly ten in the morning—six in the evening in England—I initiated the call and waited for Carter to respond. He did so immediately, but then excused himself while he went to finish off making a cup of tea in the kitchen. He was so British sometimes.

I used the few minutes he was gone to admire his home. I'd expected it to be extravagant, but I hadn't anticipated just how spectacular it would look. The decor and structure of the living room—the part of it that I could see—were old-fashioned, but sophisticated. I felt fairly certain there would be a fireplace as well, although I couldn't see it. I'd always liked a minimalistic look best, but this had a cozy feel to it that was definitely appealing.

"Sorry about that," Carter said as he sat down in front of the screen. "I haven't had a cup of tea for a few hours."

"I don't know how you coped in America for so long," I said. "Did you have your favorite teabags imported?"

"Yep. I couldn't find anywhere in America that sold my brand. Being in prison was the tough part. Some inmates craved cigarettes; I craved tea."

"You're a walking stereotype," I joked.

"Can't help it. I blame my parents. I swear, I must have been fed that stuff out of the bottle. Anyway, enough about me. What can I do for you? Are you finally going to let me help you land a job?"

"It's about William," I said. "William Townsend."

"Ah. Yes, I figured you might want to speak to me about him at some point. Are you annoyed that I set you up with him instead of Adrian?"

I jerked my head back and caught the incredulous look on my face in the image of myself on the screen. "You knew you were setting me up with the wrong person?"

Carter smiled. "Of course. I knew you wanted to meet up with Adrian. I'm guessing you hadn't even heard of William."

"I hadn't," I admitted. "So why did you set me up for an interview with him? I went in there and completely blanked. I had no questions prepared to ask him."

"Sorry about that," Carter said, although he didn't look sorry. "I know Adrian as well, but William's a much better fit for you. Adrian is a little bit too much of a ladies' man for you, I think."

I frowned. "So you were just setting me up for a date?"

"Not just that, no. I thought you and William would be a better fit. You would never have been able to write that story by working with Adrian. He would have driven you mad."

"I'm supposed to be investigating them," I said. "I didn't want to get close to either of them."

"But you did?" Carter asked, raising his eyebrows.

I nodded reluctantly. "That's why I'm calling you. Remember how I told you I was investigating Adrian?" Carter nodded. "Well, it turns out William is involved too. We got… close before I found that out."

"And you need to know if you can trust him?"

I nodded again. "William told me you could vouch for him."

"I can," Carter said immediately. "William is one of the best men I know. You can trust him."

"But I know he's doing something illegal," I protested. "He seems to expect me to just trust him, but he won't tell me what he's doing. Can you honestly tell me that he's not up to anything illegal?"

Carter paused for so long that at one point I thought the connection had dropped and the screen had frozen.

"No," he said finally. "I can't tell you that. But I can tell you that he isn't doing anything that I wouldn't do."

"You're not going to tell me, either, are you?" I asked. I suspected Carter wanted me to figure this out for myself. He had set me up with William deliberately and he had faith in my ability to figure out what was going on. I just wished I shared Carter's confidence in me.

Carter shook his head. "It's not my story to tell you. I'm sorry, but if anyone is going to tell you, it should be William. In the meantime, you should trust him. If he's keeping things from you, then it's likely for your own good."

"That's what he said. Apparently lying to me is for my own protection."

Carter sighed and massaged his chin with his fingers. "I can't tell you, but maybe I can help convince you he's a good person. A great person, in fact."

I smiled. "That's what I wanted to hear." I realized that by saying that I was admitting that I wanted to trust William. At some point, the story had taken a back seat to my relationship with William and I hadn't even noticed it.

"His company is getting a lot of grief at the moment for using unconventional models," Carter said. He looked over his shoulder to make sure no one was around who could hear him.

"I know all about that. I was at the fashion show when they were originally unveiled."

"Have you done any research on them?"

"On the models?" I asked. "Not really. There wasn't a lot of information about them available. What should I know about them?"

"Just keep digging. I have every confidence in your ability to dig up information that people want to keep hidden."

122

I laughed at the not-so-subtle reference to how I had discovered details from Carter's past that he had been keeping secret. "Can you give me a clue, at least?"

Carter smiled, but relented. "All I can tell you is that I'm not the only mutual acquaintance that you and William have. He also knows your previous roommate."

"William knows Amy? That's interesting. Speaking of mutual acquaintances, is Emily around?" I asked.

"No, she's in another room doing the same thing I am—speaking to people in California. She's managing the business from here at the moment. She loves England, but she spends more time on video conferences than she'd like."

"Tell her I said hello and that she owes me a call. We haven't spoken much recently."

"Will do."

I desperately wanted to hang up and use the information Carter had shared to do some more research, but that felt a little rude. Instead, I grilled Carter on what he and Emily had been doing since I had last spoken to them, but he didn't give a lot away. They sounded happy, but I had the distinct feeling he was keeping some news from me. Emily would likely be more forthcoming, so I would just have to ask her the next time we spoke.

Even though Carter hadn't told me any of the important details, I felt a lot happier than I had been at the start of the call. Not only had he vouched for William—which meant a lot to me by itself—he had also suggested that whatever William was doing might not be that bad after all.

If that were the case, the story I had been working on for months would be dead, or at least would have to be drastically altered, but I might be able to keep seeing William. I didn't know if I could handle losing the story, but if Carter was right, then maybe there was no story to tell anyway. First I had to be sure that Carter was right. What was so special about those models?

Chapter Five

If I picked up the phone and called Amy, she would probably tell me right away what the hell was going on. That was certainly tempting, but I was determined to figure it out by myself. Carter had confidence in me and asking Amy felt like cheating.

William had already left me messages asking if I had spoken to Carter and whether I was ready to trust him again. I told him I was thinking about it. I liked Carter and I did trust him, but I wasn't about to take his word for everything, not when there was a small mystery for me to sink my teeth into.

According to Carter, the identities of the new women who were modeling for William's business should be enough for me to know what kind of man William was. That sounded simple in theory, but I'd already looked those women up online and there was little information to go on.

Each photo had some small text at the bottom giving the name of the model, but I was beginning to suspect that those names were made up. From my brief conversation with Michelle after the fashion show, I knew that they were all new models and that William had given them a job for some reason, despite the huge risk to his company.

I studied the photos again, looking for any clues, no matter how small, that might help me figure out what was so special about the women. I already knew that they were more everyday than model-like in their appearance. They were still above average in terms of looks, but they didn't look like fashion models. That was causing quite the controversy in the business world.

Another thing that caught my eye was how natural the pictures looked. The company had made no effort to Photoshop the images at all. A few models had hairs out of place and other minor "problems" that would usually be edited out before publication.

I pulled up a picture of Michelle. She was a larger lady than many, but I knew men who would love to be with someone with a body like hers. I opened up some photos of her in image editing software to take a closer look.

There were lines and stretch marks on her thighs, but nothing that most women didn't have. A photo from behind showed off her shapely rear as she turned to face the camera with a smile.

I flicked on to another photo, but then went back to the previous one. Something had caught my eye in the previous image. As Michelle turned, the top she wore had revealed some skin on her back and I could make out what looked like a tattoo.

Tattoos were typically covered up for photo shoots, but there was definitely a mark on her skin. I zoomed in a few times to get a better look. I couldn't imagine the tattoo was going to reveal anything about William, but curiosity got the better of me.

I gasped and held my hand to my mouth when I got a closer look at the "tattoo." It wasn't a tattoo at all, it was a bruise. Not a fresh one—judging by the yellowish color it would be gone in a week or so—but it was large. Easily three inches across.

I quickly downloaded images of the other models and zoomed in to see if I could see anything similar. I found three more marks on two other models that looked distinctly like bruises. All of them were fading, but there was little doubt in my mind that they had once been large and unsightly.

There might have been more, but the women were wearing too many clothes for me to see much of their skin. Only the loose-fitting or otherwise revealing clothes showed enough skin for me to make anything out. I dreaded to think how many other marks were hidden underneath.

Carter's hint about Amy came back to me. William knowing Amy had come as a bit of a shock, but it was quite possible William had no idea I was friends with her. If he did, then he would likely have enlisted her help to get me on his side.

When I had first moved in with Amy, she had been busy trying to get her business off the ground. She later confided in me that she had been raped by a former boyfriend at college and I knew she regularly attended support meetings with other victims of sexual and domestic abuse.

If Amy was somehow connected to the models then I had a good idea how those women had ended up bruised. I quickly picked up my phone and called Amy. Like Emily, she tended to be busy most of the time, but she always made time for my calls.

"Hi, Amanda," Amy said when she answered the call. "I had a feeling I might be hearing from you."

"You spoke to Carter, didn't you?" I asked, grinning from ear to ear. That man was so predictable sometimes.

"He mentioned you might be calling. I don't know why he didn't just tell you what's going on. Or William, for that matter. I swear those two just love to play games."

"It's okay, I've figured it out."

"I thought you might," Amy said.

"Most of it, anyway. I'm confused about how you know William, though."

"Remember that pitch presentation I went to when I was trying to convince people to invest in my business?"

I nodded and then realized she couldn't see me. "I remember."

"He was one of the investors. He wasn't interested in my business because he was in retail, but I guess he struck up a conversation with Matthew and I ended up meeting him again a month or so ago. I'm still a little fuzzy on how William and Matthew know Carter, mind you."

"I figure they all go to the same exclusive men's clubs and smoke cigars while they sip expensive whiskey."

Amy laughed. "You're probably right. I'm sure there are some exclusive networks I'm not allowed to be a part of. Anyway, did you have any questions? I promise I'll tell you what I know."

"I know that William has employed women you know from one of the support groups you attended. How did that come about?"

"William is amazing. Matthew and I had dinner with him one evening and somehow the topic of my background came up. I told William all about it and he asked lots of questions about how the women who are worst affected make it back into society when or if they move on. He genuinely wanted to help and said that his company employed a lot of people. It was the perfect fit. Matthew employs mainly engineers and most of these women lack the requisite skill set. William's company can take people on and train them in what they need to know."

"So William offered these women jobs and some of them ended up as models?"

"That bit surprised me as well, but yes, some of them had the confidence to get on stage and do modeling. William is entirely responsible for that. He gave them the confidence to put themselves out there again."

"And I guess changing their names was part of the process?" I asked.

"They operate under fake names at the moment. That must have made it hard for you to find out about them."

"Just a bit," I confirmed. "I think I already know the answer to this, but what do you think about William? Can I trust him? He's up to something shady and I don't know what it is."

"I haven't known him long, but what I do know about him suggests he's about as honest as they come. Amanda, if you think there is any chance he's telling you the truth, then you should just put your doubts to one side and go for it. He's worth the risk."

I sniffed and wiped a tear away from under my eye. Amy certainly had a way with words. I thanked her and hung up. With my phone still in my hand I sent a message to William asking if he wanted to go for dinner. He replied right away.

I'll pick you up at seven.

For the first time in ages, I had free time and I didn't use it to work on my story. I relaxed and watched television. I still didn't know what William was up to, but I did know the answers would be best off coming directly from him and that made all the difference.

Chapter Six

"I still can't quite believe you're here," William said as he pulled out a seat for me at the table.

"Neither can I," I replied. William was referring to me giving him a second chance, but I was thinking how surreal it was to be here in this restaurant.

The restaurant was situated on the top floor of a hotel in the middle of downtown San Francisco. You had to be a guest of the hotel to even get into the lobby and that meant having a heck of a lot of money. I'd tried to sneak in once when I desperately needed to use the bathroom, but three men had stopped me from getting anywhere near it. Now I had a table by the window of the most sought-after places to eat in the city.

"You like the view?" William asked.

"How can anyone not like that view?" I replied.

"Are you talking about the city, or the person opposite you?"

"The city," I said firmly, trying to suppress a

smile. "Although I suppose you'll do as well."

"Thank you for coming," William said after he had ordered drinks. He hadn't even needed to look at the wine list before he made his choice. We couldn't have been more different—I couldn't even tell if he had ordered red wine or white.

"I found it hard to be mad at you after speaking to Carter," I said. "He speaks very highly of you."

William nodded calmly. "I'm glad we have a mutual friend we both trust. I was worried you'd be too stubborn to listen to him."

"I was. I didn't just take his word for it. He told me something I could verify."

William frowned. "You have me a little worried now. What did he tell you?"

"We have another mutual friend," I said. "In addition to Carter, I mean."

"Emily?" William asked.

"Amy," I said. "I used to live with her. Before she met Matthew."

"Ah," William said as a look of realization crossed his face. "And you being a journalist—a particularly nosey one, at that—you probably figured it all out."

I nodded. "That's about the gist of it."

A few moments of silence descended between us. For all his bravado, William didn't take the opportunity to claim credit for what he had done. He should be proud, but he only looked annoyed that I had found out.

"I'm going to have words with Carter next time I see him," William said. The wine had arrived and we both took a few sips. For me, it was to calm my nerves, but William needed it to relax a little. "He shouldn't have told you about the models."

"I'm glad he did. You could have just told me, you know. That was a great thing you did. If I'd known about that, it would have helped me trust you."

"Trust doesn't work like that," William said. "You would still have followed your instincts and kept going with your story. In fact, I think you still want to write the story. Am I correct?"

I didn't know the answer to that question. I'd been thinking about it for hours, but I was no closer to an answer. William was a good person— any doubts I'd had about that had been evaporated by finding out what he had done for those women—but he was still doing something wrong.

However, no matter what he was doing, I knew deep down that I wouldn't write about it. That meant I had to drop the story. I just wasn't quite ready to say the words out loud yet.

"You still haven't told me what you're up to," I said. "I trust you now, but I don't think you trust me."

"I do," William said instantly. He reached out and placed his hand on mine. "This is not about how much I trust you. This is about keeping you safe."

"Safe?" My heart fluttered, so I took a few slow, deep breaths through my nose to calm myself down. The word "safe" implied "danger" and that had me as worried as I was excited. You can't be a journalist without getting at least slightly turned on by the thought of danger.

"You're a journalist, Amanda, and a damn good one at that. I know every instinct in your body is telling you to dig into this until you strike oil, but that's not a good idea. I'm asking you to leave this alone."

"What are you doing, William? If it's putting you in danger, then I have a right to know. I might be able to help."

"I can look after myself, but I can't protect you and do what I need to do at the same time."

"You make it sound like I'm just a distraction to you," I said petulantly. I knew I sounded like a child, but it was how I felt. I was done hiding my feelings from him.

"Of course you're a distraction," William replied. "Look at you. How can I not be distracted by you?"

"Flattery will get you nowhere, Mr. Townsend," I lied.

I took a long sip of my wine. It was a dry white wine with a crisp finish. I usually drank sweet wine because it tended to be cheaper, and when I drank dry wine it generally had a harsh edge. This one went down so smoothly I had to force myself to take my lips away from the cool glass.

"I was a mess before you came along," William admitted. "You're a distraction, but a good one."

I thought back to the first time I'd seen William. By his high standards, he had looked like crap. He hadn't slept and had looked troubled. I had immediately sensed something was bothering him and wanted to help him through it. Now I was wondering what I had let myself in for.

"How long has this been going on?" I asked.

William shrugged and picked up his glass. "About a year, I guess." He took a small sip of his wine and then a longer one. "But it's gotten tougher recently. At first I was stupid enough to think my money could solve the problem easily. But it can't."

"How much longer do you think it will go on for?" I asked.

"I honestly have no idea. I think the end is in sight, but then I've thought that before."

"Well, this time you're not alone."

"Amanda, I'm not getting you involved in this. You can't change my mind."

"I can and I will," I replied firmly. "You don't have to bring me in yet, but you can't stop me from spending time with you. When you need someone to talk to about this, then I'll be there for you."

William frowned and eyed me suspiciously. "Call me paranoid, but you sound more and more like a journalist every time we get together."

I held my hands up in surrender. "No story, I promise. I'm just curious now and I don't want to walk away from this."

William's frown turned into a smile. "Good. I think I could get used to having you around a bit more. But if I keep something from you, then you need to understand it's for your own good. Deal?"

"Deal."

I had assumed William was trying to keep me at a distance so that I didn't break the law, but there had been a hint of worry in his voice when he spoke about protecting me. Was that all it was? Worry about me getting in trouble with the law? Or was I detecting fear for my safety?

Either way, I wasn't about to take William's concerns lightly, but neither was I going to back off and pretend the problem didn't exist. At some point William would need my help, and I intended to be close by when he did.

Chapter Seven

I had been going through a rough patch when I'd agreed to go on a night out with Sophie and Natalie. They wanted me to let my hair down and have some fun, but all I wanted to do was spend the night with William. Still, they meant well, so I resisted the urge to feign an illness and got dressed up for a night on the town.

Just a few years ago, I had relished nights out on the town. I'd been one of the first ones in the bar and the last to leave. The hangovers always hit me hard the next day, but I would just stay under the covers and watch television all day. That was not an option anymore. I couldn't afford to spend an entire day in bed. That had to be the worst thing about being self-employed. A day in bed was a day without pay.

It was a bad attitude and I had to snap out of it. I pulled on a pair of jeans and some leather boots that by my standards were remarkably fashionable. I couldn't find a single top that I wanted to wear, so I snuck into Sophie's room to borrow one of hers. My chest was larger than hers, but I still managed to squeeze into a top without looking ridiculous.

I examined myself in the mirror and smiled. I'd never cared this much about my appearance before, but now I put effort into what I wore whenever I left the house. It might be a little vain, but the added looks from men did wonders for my confidence.

Sophie and Natalie were both heading straight to the bar after work. I left the apartment with plenty of time to spare, but the bus was late and then got stuck in rush hour traffic. By the time I arrived, Sophie and Natalie had already snagged a table and by the look of them they were on at least their second drink.

The two of them couldn't be more different from each other, but they seemed to be almost the best of friends now. At least something positive had come from my recent problems.

"Evening, ladies," I said as I removed their purses from the empty chair and sat down. "I see you started without me."

"We bought you a drink," Sophie said, sliding a half-gone margarita towards me. I examined the glass and frowned. "We might have drunk some of it," she added.

"It's your fault for being late," Natalie said. She already sounded a little tipsy, but I knew she didn't drink often.

I took a sip of my drink and realized why the girls sounded so drunk already. These things were loaded with alcohol. I'd have to take my time or I'd be way too drunk to do what I planned to do this evening.

"We had hoped to get you laid tonight,"

Sophie said in her typically less-than-discrete manner, "but since you never came home last night I'm going to assume you don't need to hook up with a guy anymore."

"Oh, I still intend to have sex tonight," I said, "but not with any strangers I meet in a bar."

"Well, that's good," Natalie said, "because we've found two men—brothers, I think—and we didn't know how to split them up between the three of us."

In all the years I had known Natalie, I had never known her to have a one night stand. We had gone to college together so that was really saying something. Sophie had brought out some added spice in Natalie that I had never been able to manage.

"Which brothers are you looking at?" I asked.

"They're at the far end of the bar," Sophie said, pointing in their general direction. "You can't see much of them from here—other than their fine asses—but I can assure you they are stunning to behold."

"I want the one on the right," Natalie said. "He looks like someone I used to have a crush on."

"I don't particularly care," Sophie said with a shrug of her shoulders. "They both look like they could do wicked things with their tongues."

"They look like they already have girlfriends," I said. "Or least like they're taken for the evening." The two men—who definitely could be brothers—were speaking to two women in short skirts and skimpy tops. The girls were thrusting their chests forward and one was twirling her hair. Subtlety was not required in this bar, apparently.

"We're going to let those girls have a shot," Sophie said, "but I'm confident they'll strike out. They're far too obvious. You need to be more discrete with men like that. They don't want women who just throw themselves at them."

I raised my eyebrows in shock. I couldn't believe I was hearing these things from Sophie. "You can do subtle?" I asked, incredulous.

"Of course," Sophie replied. "I change how I act depending on the man I'm trying to snag."

"I don't want to act differently just to impress a man," Natalie said. Her thumb moved around the rim of her glass as she stared at the man she had set her eyes on for the evening.

"When did you last have sex, dear?" Sophie asked Natalie.

Natalie opened her mouth and then closed it again. "Fair enough."

I wouldn't need alcohol to enjoy myself tonight. I could just sit back and watch these two and have a great time. Sophie convinced Natalie to play it cool with the two brothers for the time being, so we spent a few hours just drinking and talking nonsense.

Natalie kept being surprised whenever Sophie said something vaguely intelligent. I'd ceased being shocked by Sophie a while ago, but to Natalie, Sophie was a barista who hadn't been to college and was therefore not expected to keep up a conversation with someone working towards a PhD.

I'd been surprised as well at first, and one night after a few drinks I had asked Sophie why she hadn't gone to college. My memory of that night is hazy, but I know she changed the subject pretty quickly. I didn't know her well enough to pry any further, but I had a feeling she was keeping some big secrets under the pretense of being carefree and wild. Hopefully she'd tell me about them one day.

"Oh, heads up, ladies," Sophie said as she came back to the table with three fresh drinks. "The brothers have shown those other skanks the door. Now it's our turn."

"I don't know," Natalie said, eyes now fixed on her drink. Her buzz from earlier seemed to have worn off slightly. "Maybe I should just go home. I have no idea how to talk to guys in bars."

"Come with me, Natalie," Sophie said, taking Natalie by the hand. "I'm going to teach you everything you need to know. You want to come and watch too?" she asked me.

"No, I'm good, thanks. I'm going to leave now and have a little fun of my own."

I pulled out my phone and considered texting William, but decided it would be better to surprise him. Sophie and Natalie wouldn't be the only ones having a good time tonight. The brothers might be good-looking, but they had nothing on William. He'd rocked my world enough times already; now it was my turn to repay the favor.

Chapter Eight

My attempt at a surprise booty call fell somewhat flat. I didn't have a key to William's building, but I managed to follow someone else inside. That got me as far as the elevator, but at night you needed to use a keycard before choosing your floor. The security guard insisted on phoning William's apartment to confirm my visit and there went the element of surprise.

William was waiting for me in the hall with look of confusion on his face. "Have I done something wrong?" he asked. "I feel like I'm going to get in trouble for something."

"You must have a guilty mind," I replied. I walked up to him and kissed him on the cheek while I reached out and grabbed him between the legs. "I've just come here to play."

At that moment, I heard the jingle of metal on metal as someone behind me hurriedly tried to get back into their apartment while pretending they hadn't noticed me groping William. I grimaced and pushed William through the door for some privacy.

"How was your evening with Natalie and Sophie?" William asked. He smiled as he watched me try to take my boots off.

I'd deliberately not drunk that much and had insisted on buying weaker drinks after that first toxic margarita, but I was still a little tipsy and my hand-eye coordination wasn't great.

"It was fun," I remarked. "Neither of them will be going home alone tonight and I decided I wanted a little action myself."

William laughed. "Are you drunk?"

"Only a little tipsy," I replied. "I'm sober enough to know that I need you right now. My body needs you."

"And to think I was about to go to bed alone." William effortlessly swept me up off the floor and carried me into the bedroom. He threw me down onto the bed and I sank into the soft covers. William peeled off my jeans, then undressed in front of me.

Whatever happened for Sophie and Natalie tonight, I knew they wouldn't be seeing anything as spectacular as this. William had the type of stomach that I thought only existed on cover models after a lot of work in the editing department. The firm abs were always the first thing that caught my eye, but his chest was the most perfect part of him. I instinctively reached out to grab his firm pecs in the way that men usually reached longingly towards my chest.

He leaned forward and kissed me firmly on the lips while his hand rubbed the outside of my panties. "You're so wet, Amanda. Were you thinking about this the entire way here?"

"I've been thinking about this the entire night," I replied, gasping for breath between intense kisses.

"I can't wait to taste you again." William disappeared from view as he kissed my breasts, his tongue swirling slowly around my nipples as they stiffened under his touch. His lips continued moving down my body, first kissing around my belly button and then just above the line of my panties.

I knew I could just lie here and let William kiss my sex, but I wanted to show him a new side of me tonight. My fingers reached down; I grabbed his hair and pulled him back up towards me.

"Lie on your back," I commanded.

"I want to eat you," he replied. "You taste so sweet. I need to lick your beautiful pussy again."

"Not yet." I pressed my hand against his chest and he reluctantly slid off me with his cock standing at attention. I grabbed a condom from the drawer by the bed and sheathed his member before removing my soaked underwear.

Then I straddled his body and lowered my sex down onto his firm stomach. I let my wet lips slide up and down against his skin, letting him know just how much I needed this.

"Holy shit, Amanda, you're dripping down there."

"You like that?" I asked.

He nodded. "Sit on my cock," he ordered. "I need to be inside you."

I slowly moved my ass back until I felt the tip of his hard cock against my lips. I shifted so that his head was against my entrance and then pushed back, taking his cock inside me slowly, inch by inch, until he filled me.

"Oh, shit," he moaned. "I can't believe how tight you are. How do you fit all of me inside you?"

"It's easy when I'm this wet." There was some mild discomfort when his entire cock was inside me, but my body quickly adjusted to his size as the muscles in my tunnel throbbed around his huge length.

I sat up and looked him in the eyes as I rocked back and forward. His strong hands gripped my hips and he kept his length pressed against the parts of me that quickly got me panting and moaning as I felt an orgasm build inside me.

My pussy clenched around his shaft as if it didn't want to let go, but I slowly lifted my ass in the air and let his stiff cock leave my body.

"Don't tease, baby," William said. The muscles in his arms and chest strained with frustration.

"You said you wanted to taste me," I replied. I moved up his body until my channel was in front of his mouth. I leaned on the headboard and lowered my slit to his lips.

Immediately William's tongue darted into my folds as he greedily began licking the juices that were dripping from me.

I expelled the air from my lungs in a loud gasp as his tongue found my clit and started circling it in a slow, tender motion. His hands gripped my ass in response to my body squirming on his face and he buried his tongue deeper inside me.

"I'm coming," I moaned.

"Yes, baby, come on my face. I want to taste you as you come."

My fingers tightened their grip on the headboard as William took my clit into his mouth and started sucking on it, gently at first but then with more force.

I panted hard, my lungs expelling the air quicker than I could breathe it in. I felt lightheaded as the blood rushed to my sex. I came hard as he sucked my clit while flicking it lightly with his tongue.

My arms were no longer strong enough to rest against the headboard so I slipped back down his body to where his stiff length was still eagerly awaiting me. He entered my dripping pussy with ease and finished inside me while I was still shaking from the orgasm that was very visible on his face.

I fell forward, covered in a thin layer of sweat, and lay down on his chest. I breathed in the faint remains of my aroma on his face and shut my eyes.

"You should go out with Sophie and Natalie more often," William said. His own breathing was heavy but he was in better shape than I was and he recovered faster. No doubt he would be ready to go again shortly. "Being around them seems to make you a little more kinky."

"I'm always kinky," I replied. "I just needed the confidence to bring it out. There's plenty more where that came from."

"Glad to hear it." William kissed my forehead and held me tight in his arms as I let the exhaustion of a long night and a heavy orgasm send me off into a deep sleep.

Chapter Nine

"How are you feeling this morning?" William asked as I squinted, trying to adjust my eyes to the light. I could make out a smile on his face and knew he thought I was hung over.

"I'm fine, thank you." I tried to sit up but moved a little too quickly and felt lightheaded. "Okay, maybe a little tired, but that's it."

"I thought you might feel a little delicate, so I made you coffee."

I took the mug and held it in front of my face, letting the smell waft up my nose. I blew on the drink in an attempt to cool it down, but it was still far too hot to drink.

"Here, have mine," William said, taking the mug from me and passing me his. "I made this a while ago so it's a little cooler. You can finish it off."

"Thanks." I grabbed my phone from the bedside table and checked the time. No wonder I was so tired—I had only slept for about five hours. "Why are you up so early?" I asked, trying to clear my voice of the cobwebs.

William shrugged casually and took a sip of coffee from what had been my mug despite the fact that steam was still rising from the top. "I'm an early riser, I guess."

"You also go to bed late. Do you just not need sleep?" I'd done my share of late nights and could function for a few days on little sleep, but I always looked like crap when I did so. William looked fresh and wide awake.

"I don't need as much as most people, it seems. I also like working early and late, because there are fewer distractions. Well, there are *usually* fewer distractions. Last night being the exception."

I raised my eyebrows. "I hope that's not a complaint?" I joked.

"No, no, certainly not. You took me by surprise, that's all. A very pleasant surprise indeed."

"Today is Saturday, right?" I asked. Not having a Monday-to-Friday job made it a lot harder to keep track of the weekends, but I vaguely remembered Natalie talking about how she was looking forward to the weekend last night. Sophie had been complaining because she had to work Saturdays, but she'd admitted she needed the hours.

"Certainly is. However, I'll need to work for a little while. I need to finish off what I was working on last night."

"Do you have a spare computer?" I asked. "I didn't bring my laptop with me because I came straight from the bar. I feel kind of naked without a computer and internet connection in front of me."

"You *are* naked," William said, nodding down

towards my exposed chest. "And I'm not going to argue if you want to keep it that way."

I quickly pulled the cover up over my chest in a belated attempt at modesty and started digging around for my clothes.

"There's a computer in the second bedroom," William said. "The one with all the books. It's more of an office now, I suppose. The computer's not great, but I never got around to buying a new one because I always work on my laptop. It should do for a few hours, though."

William's idea of a 'not great' computer was still a heck of a lot faster than my old laptop. The computer was maybe a few years old, but he'd hardly ever used it so there was nothing hogging up all the memory.

I opened up my email and found a few leads for new stories. My article on William had proven popular with the online magazine publisher I'd sold it to and the editor there wanted me to write more articles on CEOs from a personal angle. He had even lined up a few interviews for me.

My article about William had been a touch cruel, so I was surprised that other CEOs wanted me to interview them. I checked a few of them out and they were all young men who were running tech companies in the area. Their online profiles didn't make them look at all appealing and usually I wouldn't bother interviewing them, but it would be nice to get the dirt on them.

I began to type out a reply to the email, but decided to put it to one side for the time being. Interviewing CEOs that I didn't respect sounded a bit like what Sophie had proposed to me not so long ago—writing about the seedy personal lives of the rich and fabulous. These CEOs might not be movie stars, but in Silicon Valley they were placed on an even higher level than that.

Instead of accepting the interviews, I decided to dig around for my own story and hope I could sell it to the same place. For a while now, I'd wanted to write a piece on the employees who worked at one of the big technology companies and find out what it was like for them when the money ran out and the company went bust.

The computer had none of the software on it that I liked to use, so I started downloading a few of my favorites and explored the office while I waited. I'd already had a good look at the books William kept on the shelves and there wasn't much else in the room.

Near the desk were a few shelves with random DVDs and assorted files and pieces of paper. William probably bought movies digitally now and probably kept his filing electronic, so that explained why this all looked old and untouched.

My eyes lingered on something that looked out of place. Between old bills was a photo frame that looked like it had been shoved there without much thought. William had given me permission to explore, so I picked up the frame and looked at the photo inside.

I laughed quietly when I saw the picture of William as a teenager with his brother and, presumably, his sister. I'd assumed he'd always been strikingly handsome, but he looked skinny and awkward in this picture. Adrian was wearing a massive grin that made it clear he had always been a little cocky and arrogant.

I'd never met their sister, but she looked familiar. She must have been about twelve or thirteen in this picture and she was wearing braces, but there was no mistaking that face. Standing right there in front of her two big brothers was Olivia, the girl I had overheard being mentioned by Professor Winston in his conversation with Adrian. Olivia was William's sister.

"You weren't supposed to see that."

I jumped and spun around in my chair to see William standing in the doorway. He did not look pleased.

Chapter Ten

"What are you doing with that?" William asked. His eyes were transfixed by the photo in my hand.

"I found it," I replied. "It was out in the open. It's not like I went through your drawers or anything."

"You should put it back."

I placed the photo down on the desk, but left it face up. "I'm not about to pretend I didn't see this. Your sister—her name's Olivia, isn't it?"

"I never told you her name. How do you know that?"

"I overheard it one day when I was spy... following your brother. He met with some law professor and the man mentioned her name."

"So you included her as part of your investigation?" he asked. I nodded. "And that's why you had a picture of her up on your laptop when I saw you in the coffee shop?"

I sighed and then nodded again as I realized how stupid I had been. When William saw Adrian and Olivia on my screen in the coffee shop, he had said something like, "Why are you investigating my family?" Not "brother"; he'd said "family." Adrian *and* Olivia.

"You already knew I was investigating her, didn't you?" I said. "It was on my laptop that day."

William nodded firmly. He still looked annoyed, but perhaps a touch less angry. "I thought you were spying on her as well, but from the way you reacted it was clear you had no idea she was my sister. I was hoping to keep it that way."

"Why?" I asked. "This actually makes a lot of sense. I wish you'd told me. Olivia disappeared from her legal career a few years ago and you did say your sister was going through some difficulties. That makes sense. You could have told me."

"It's... complicated. Are you still investigating her?"

"No," I said, quickly shaking my head. "I told you, I stopped that story."

"I know you stopped looking into Adrian, but I thought maybe you were still... Never mind."

I frowned and stared at William. He looked sullen and uncomfortable, almost like he had the first time I met him in his office. Why had he asked about me investigating Olivia?

"Is there something I should know about her?" I asked. "You've told me the truth about her, haven't you?"

William nodded. "Everything I've told you about her has been true."

I laughed. I couldn't help it. I hadn't been a journalist that long, but answers like that made it clear I didn't know the whole story.

"You've told me the truth," I said calmly, "but

there's a lot you haven't told me. Would that be accurate?"

"I've only ever kept things from you for your own good, Amanda. You need to trust me on that."

I struggled to think what could be so bad about Olivia that he wouldn't want to tell me. He had told me about her problems. There could be drink or drugs involved, but he wouldn't need to keep that from me.

William went to get a chair from the other room and I took the opportunity to run a quick search. I pulled up the website for the California Bar Association and looked up Olivia Young.

"She's been disbarred," I said as William walked back into the room.

"You just can't help but spy on people," William remarked.

"It's who I am," I replied.

William stared at me and then smiled. "Yeah, I suppose it is. She's no longer a member of the California Bar, but I don't think she was formally disbarred. She just stopped paying her dues, so they cancelled her membership."

"Why?"

"Like I said, she has problems in her personal life and they took over for a few years. She was in no shape to do much of anything, let alone practice law."

"I'm sorry."

"It's not your fault. Just don't go digging up information on her, please."

"She's part of this whole thing, isn't she?" I asked. "Olivia is somehow involved in whatever it is you and your brother are doing behind closed doors?"

I didn't need to hear William's confirmation; it

was clear from the look in his eyes.

"She's not doing anything illegal, or even morally dubious."

"But you are?"

"I'm not doing anything I'm ashamed of, Amanda, but yes, some of it is likely illegal. That's why I don't want you to be a part of it. If something goes wrong, I don't want you anywhere near this thing. I'm trying to protect you."

"I don't need protecting, William. I'm a big girl. I can look after myself. Look, I promised to let this story die, and I will, but I want you to know I'm here if you need me. You never know, I might be able to help."

William laughed and pulled me up from the chair. "I have no doubt about that at all. But that doesn't change anything."

"I'm not your sister. I don't need protecting."

William took hold of my hands and pulled me in towards him. "You can't blame me for wanting to protect you. I'm used to getting and having whatever I want—that's the main perk of being rich—but when I saw my sister's life get torn apart, I felt completely and utterly helpless. That's not a feeling I like, and I will do whatever it takes to make sure no one I care about has to go through anything like that again."

I couldn't see William's face, but I knew what he was going through from the mix of emotions in his voice. There was anger over what had happened to his sister, guilt that he couldn't stop it, and sadness for what she'd gone through.

"As much as I would love to be with you all the time," I said slowly, "you are going to have to let me out of your sight occasionally."

William laughed and let go of me. "Don't

154

worry, I'm not quite the crazy, obsessive type. Not yet, anyway. In fact, I'm going to have to let you out of my sight for a few days next week."

"Oh? Why?" Now I sounded like the obsessed one. I was already dreading the nights when I would have to sleep in my bed alone. The whole concept sounded so boring. For the first time, I primarily thought of beds as a place for sex, not somewhere I reluctantly retired to at the end of a long day of work.

William took a deep breath and looked nervous. Clearly, I wasn't going to like what he told me. "I'm going to Washington, D.C. for a few days. I have some business to take care of and I need to do it alone."

William's idea of 'business' in D.C. was probably similar to his brother's. There was no way I would be staying in San Francisco while he went to illicit meetings with U.S. senators. One way or another, I would be going with him.

Chapter Eleven

My first thought had been to make my own way to D.C. and try to follow William around like I had done with Adrian, but that wouldn't work this time. Adrian hadn't known who I was, so I'd managed to get close to him. William would spot me a mile off. Also, I didn't have the money for the flight and hotels in D.C. didn't come cheap either.

"I'm coming with you," I said. I had to convince William to take me along or I'd be stuck at home while he put himself at risk in the corruption capital of the country.

"No, you're not," William replied defiantly. "It's not a good idea for us to be in the same city when I do this. If something goes wrong and the authorities look into my travels, how will it look when they see you coming with me?"

"We'll pretend I'm doing a story on you. It's not that far-fetched," I said before William could argue that point. "I did publish an article on you, and you really did want a chance to set the record straight. I'll even write up some notes so that it looks like I'm doing an article."

William considered that for a few moments, but ended up shaking his head. "It's still not a good idea. Why do you want to come, anyway? D.C. isn't that exciting, and I'll be in meetings most of the time. Does that really interest you?"

"Actually, yes, it does. I want a better idea of how these things work."

"Lobbying is a lot like making sausages. You don't want to see what goes on. If you do, you'll never look at our laws the same way again."

"I'm not completely clueless," I said. "I have an idea of how things work, but I want to see people doing it. I'll leave you alone the entire trip and focus on trying to catch politicians in the act."

"Sounds dangerous," William said. "Where has your passion for this come from all of a sudden? Is this the sort of journalism you want to do?"

"It's not sudden. I was following a lead on a corruption story when I met you, remember? I don't know what kind of journalist I want to be yet, but these stories are important. People should know what their elected officials are doing."

"Most of it's completely legal and above board. I know lobbying is horrible, but you aren't going to get any attention talking about it. No one seems to care."

"They should," I replied. William flinched in surprise as I raised my voice. "Lobbying might be legal, but it goes too far sometimes. People can die." My voice shook with the final word, but I kept the tears at bay. I could let my anger be the emotion dictating this conversation, but not sadness.

"Die? What are you talking about, Amanda? I

don't think people die because of lobbying."

"My father did."

William frowned and stared into my eyes. I had told him my father had died in a car crash, which wasn't a million miles from the truth, but he was probably fairly confused right now. It would be a minor miracle if I made it through this conversation without crying, but for once my stubbornness might come in handy.

"Lobbying caused your father's car crash?" William asked. "I don't understand."

"That's because I didn't tell you the whole story," I replied. "And don't even think about giving me some lecture on how I should always tell you everything."

"I wasn't going to. But if you want me to understand this, then you'll have to tell me more."

Whenever I talked about my dad, I did so as a daughter who mourned the loss of her father. I often imagined writing a story about my father and how he had died, but in that case I would do so as a journalist—stick to the facts and leave emotion out of it. That's what I did now.

"My father was in the Army. He never described himself as a soldier, though. He drove trucks in Afghanistan, so he liked to say he was a regular truck driver. 'The only difference between someone driving across America and me is that the roads in Afghanistan aren't quite as good.'"

"That's very modest of him. He probably said those things so you wouldn't worry."

I nodded. "He was like that. We knew he understated the danger he was in, but the lie had good intentions behind it and it did help me sleep at night. The only thing he complained about was the quality of the vehicles he was driving and the

158

replacement parts he got sent."

"I hear that a lot of the equipment our soldiers use is out of date," William said. "Everyone acknowledges it, but no one wants to write the check to buy new stuff."

"It's not just the money, it's the whole supply chain. My father died while making a routine drive taking food to some of the cities surrounding the capital. The truck broke down. He tried to fix it, but the parts didn't fit properly and were incompatible with the vehicle. They waited for help to arrive, but it never did."

"You don't have to tell me these details if you don't want to."

If I stopped to think about it, then I would never be able to finish. I ignored him and went on. "Some Afghan rebels found them and opened fire on the truck. My father was killed in the gunfire, but not before he saved someone's life. I don't know the details, but he won a medal for his bravery. I don't like to look at it."

"I don't blame you."

William waited patiently for me to continue talking. I knew he wanted to ask me what the hell all this had to do with lobbying, but he didn't say anything.

"I hadn't even decided I wanted to be a journalist at that point, but we raised the issue of faulty equipment with the officer who commiserated us about his death. I was young, but I still recognized that we were being given the brush-off. I looked into the issue while I was in college. It turned out that the company supplying the parts for the vehicles had only gotten the contract after some intense and expensive lobbying."

159

"They bought the contract, in other words?"

I nodded. "You spend enough money taking the right people to dinner and it's no great surprise when you win the contract bid. The company was vastly under-qualified for such a big contract and it had an appalling reputation for safety. It should never have been allowed near that contract."

"That does explain why you don't like the lobbying process. Did the story ever go anywhere?"

"No," I replied. "The guilty parties had already retired and refused all my attempts to interview them. Even the CEO at the company had left. No doubt he's enjoying his money on some tropical island somewhere."

"I don't want to sound harsh, but do you really think you can accomplish anything in D.C. in just five days? This stuff is all done behind closed doors."

"Actually, some of the conversations are outside. Ironically, that's often considered to be more private. They can keep the conversation off the books that way, I suppose. I don't have high expectations, but since you're already going, I may as well tag along, right?"

William closed his eyes and sighed. He had the look of a man who was about to say something he would later regret.

"I suppose it'll be nice to have you around," he said at last. "Just promise me you'll stay out of my way when I'm working. I meant what I said earlier. I don't want you involved in any of that."

"Deal." I was going back to D.C. and this time I would come back with a complete story, hopefully not one involving the man I was sleeping with.

Chapter Twelve

William took charge of all the arrangements; I just had to show up with enough clothes to get me through five days. I didn't care too much about what I would wear during the day, but William would want to eat out in the evening and I didn't have enough formal wear for five nights.

Sophie worked on Saturdays, often with a hangover, but Natalie was available to spend a few hours shopping with me. Natalie was nowhere near as fashionable as Sophie, but she was still in another league from me. I would end up with clothes that looked modern, at least, which was a step up from most of my current wardrobe.

I met Natalie at the mall and laughed when I saw her wearing sunglasses indoors.

"Feeling a little worse for wear from last night, are you?" I asked.

"The light hurts my eyes and I'm exhausted," she replied. She took the sunglasses off slowly, as if she was scared of what she might see.

"You look fine," I lied. She did look tired, but

she had done a decent enough job covering up the bags under her eyes. "Can I assume that you enjoyed the rest of your evening? You obviously didn't get much sleep."

Natalie smiled, but then quickly stopped herself. "I can't believe what I did last night. I'm not normally like that. I can't even remember his name. You won't tell anyone, will you?"

"There's nothing wrong with hooking up with a guy on a night out. You shouldn't feel bad for having some fun. Sophie does it all the time, and I would have as well if I weren't with William. So… what was he like?"

The smile reappeared on Natalie's face and this time it stayed there. "He was… energetic. But I'm not going to see him again. It was just a one-off."

"Sometimes that's the best way. You're too busy for a relationship right now."

"I thought the same thing about you not so long ago, but you're managing to juggle work and play quite successfully at the moment."

"I don't know about that," I said. "I've agreed to hold off on my story about Adrian at William's insistence."

"That doesn't sound like you at all. Are you sure you're okay with that?"

I nodded and smiled. "Yes, that's the strange thing. William has told me some of the story, but not all of it. I know I shouldn't trust him as much as I do, but I have a few friends who can vouch for him. If what he says is true, then I'm not going to want to write that story anyway."

Natalie didn't have the trust in William that I did, but I couldn't expect her to. I took it for granted that he was trustworthy, but until I had spoken to Carter and Amy, I hadn't trusted him either. Now I trusted him completely.

Natalie took me into a few of the shops that I knew by name, but usually walked right past. Any store that had people greeting you as you walked in kind of freaked me out a little, although I had no idea why. I knew my taste in clothes was awful, so I didn't want to be judged on my way in and out of the store. It didn't make a lot of sense, but that was what went through my mind.

Shopping with Natalie was a lot easier than it had been with Sophie, although slightly less fun as well. Natalie pointed out tops, skirts, and jeans and for the most part she didn't make me try any of it on.

"I need some shorts and light dresses," I said to Natalie after we had picked out some jeans. "D.C. is still hot at this time of year and it's humid too. If I walk around in pants, they'll end up stuck to me and that isn't a pleasant experience in denim."

"Oh, okay," Natalie said, quickly putting down a top that would be far too heavy for the D.C. heat. "I've never been there, but I always assumed the weather was similar to San Francisco. The city was built on a swamp, though, so I should have guessed it would be humid."

"That's why Congress takes time off in the summer."

"I assumed our politicians just liked to take long vacations," Natalie remarked.

"That's too," I admitted. "But the weather there can be brutal. Over a hundred degrees, and with that humidity..." I shuddered. My only demand to William was that the hotel have good air conditioning and be near a subway station so that I wouldn't have to walk around in the sun if I didn't want to."

"What about the flight out there?" Natalie asked. "Do you think you'll travel first class? Or does he have a private jet?"

"I don't think he has a jet. First class or business class, I suppose. I can't imagine him squeezing into the economy seats."

"Exciting stuff," Natalie admitted. "I can definitely see why he was able to sweep you off your feet so quickly."

"That's not why I'm with him, Natalie. Other than going to a nice restaurant, we haven't done anything that a normal couple couldn't do. Well, the sheets on his bed are nicer than most, but other than that he's just like any other guy."

"Would you have dropped the story so quickly for any other guy?" Natalie asked.

Natalie had clearly wanted to ask me these questions for some time and was only just now getting around to it. She might not realize it, but she was calling me a gold-digger. If I didn't know her so well, I would have walked away, but I knew she didn't mean to be malicious.

"I have my reasons for dropping the story," I said. "And I intend to find a better one while we're in DC. Don't worry, I'm not a pushover with him, and he hasn't bought his way into my affection."

"Glad to hear it. Just don't forget me when you're hanging out with the rich and famous."

"I'll wave to you from my first class seat while I'm drinking my champagne," I joked. Travelling first class would be very different from my last trip to D.C., when I had been squeezed between two overweight gentlemen and could barely move the entire time.

The flights would be a lot different, but what I did in D.C. would be similar. There wouldn't be much time for visits to the White House and the Washington Monument. There was nothing I could do about the people who had indirectly killed my father, but I could catch the next batch of sleazy politicians. There were plenty of them out there, and D.C. was the place to find them.

Chapter Thirteen

"Where are we going?" I asked. William had hired a driver take us to the airport, and we were headed south out of the city. I had assumed we were going to San Francisco International Airport, but the driver went right past it.

"My plane is kept on a private airfield. It's only about twenty minutes away."

"Oh my God, you mean we *are* taking a private plane to D.C.? Natalie said you might have a plane, but I didn't believe it."

Judging by William's casual shrug, he didn't seem to think owning a private jet was anything out of the ordinary. "I don't like airports. Even when I travel first class, there are still too many people around, and security annoys me. I often need to fly on short notice, so having a plane is important."

"I bet it helps impress people, as well," I remarked. In my head, I liked to think of William as a normal guy. When I thought about him as a rich, handsome man, my brain ended up flooded with images of him as a playboy. I pictured him coming off a plane with a woman on each arm and a champagne glass in his hand.

"I've used it to bring people around to my way of thinking," William admitted.

"I don't think I want to know."

"Employees," William added.

"That doesn't make me feel any better."

"I offer the use of my jet as a fringe benefit when I'm trying to headhunt an important employee. It's amazing how many people have been perfectly happy in their jobs until the use of a private jet is on the table."

I couldn't help but laugh. The only fringe benefit my friends and I ever cared about was health insurance. It had never even occurred to me that planes would be used to tempt an employee to join a company.

The car drove up to a set of security gates which promptly opened when William rolled down the window to show his face. Then we drove straight up to a hanger and stopped outside. A small cart pulled the airplane out right in front of us.

Every time I went to an airport I was paranoid about breaking one of the many rules and ending up under the watchful eye of the Transportation Security Administration. Being able to walk around on the tarmac felt inherently wrong and I half expected to see security guards running towards us with guns at any minute.

"Amanda?" William yelled over the sound of another airplane taking off not far from us. "Come on, the plane's ready to go."

A man was already carrying my luggage, so I strolled towards the plane with nothing in my hands. *This feels so wrong.*

The plane looked narrow and thin from the outside, but once I'd climbed the stairs and stepped inside, I saw something I had never seen before on a plane—empty spaces. There were seats and tables at the sides of the plane and what looked like a bar in the middle, but even with all that there were still gaps large enough to do yoga in. Nothing about this felt normal.

"What do you think?" William asked. "The flight is so smooth you'll forget you're flying. There are plenty of tables if you want to work, and the jet has WiFi."

I always tried—and usually failed—to sleep on flights, so I was tempted to crash on one of the beds and wake up in D.C., but that seemed like a waste of such an awe-inspiring experience.

"Is it too early for a drink?" I asked, nodding towards the bar.

"Not if we're on D.C. time, it's not," William said with a grin. The man who had brought our bags on board scurried over to the bar to make us some drinks.

We sat down opposite each other and flattened the table so that I could put my feet up on William's lap for a foot rub. His strong hands pressed firmly into my tired feet as I leaned back sipping a vodka tonic.

The staff left us to prepare for takeoff, leaving William and me alone for the first time. "Is it wrong that all I can think about right now is joining the mile high club?" I asked. I didn't know whether it was the drink talking or the excellent foot rub, but either way I could think of nothing else right now.

"Nothing wrong with that," William said, his fingers squeezing the sole of my foot. "I wish you hadn't said anything, though."

"Why?"

"Because now all I can think of is fucking you, but we're still on the ground." William pressed a button and spoke to the captain through a speaker, making it very clear that he would like to take off as soon as possible.

Just minutes later, the engines started up and the seat began to vibrate underneath me. The power of the engines was too much for me to handle. I pulled my feet off William's lap and got down on my knees in front of him.

"How long before we're a mile up?" I asked, unzipping his fly.

"About ten minutes."

"Think you can last that long?"

I pulled out his cock and took one long, slow lick from the base of the shaft up to the tip. My lips parted and I took his head inside my mouth. I sucked hard on the sensitive head while flicking my tongue against it like William had done with my clit.

"Oh, shit," he moaned. "I'm not going to make it to a mile up if you keep going like that."

I took my mouth off his cock and looked up at him. "You want me to stop?" I ran my tongue slowly around my lips as my hand gently stroked his shaft.

"Fuck, no," he said. He grabbed the back of my head and pushed me back down on his cock. I felt the plane leave the ground as I sucked hard on his thick meat.

"Let me know as soon as we're a mile up in the air," William said to the pilot over the speaker. "As fast as possible, please."

"Yes, sir," the pilot replied. I could hear the

smile in the pilot's voice as he imagined what was going to happen once we were a mile up. I didn't care. I had the plane throbbing under my knees and William's cock throbbing in my mouth.

This never happened when I travelled economy class.

Chapter Fourteen

The jet landed far outside Washington, D.C.—no one was allowed to fly over the capital—and we had an hour's drive from the airfield to the city. By the time we got into the city it was late in the evening, local time so we just grabbed room service and chilled in front of the television.

Any hopes of this being a romantic trip were shattered when I woke up the next morning to find that William had already left to do whatever "work" he was here to do.

William had picked out a hotel near the White House, although the view from our room was of the National Mall and the Washington Monument. The hotel boasted a rooftop terrace that provided a view over the White House and William said I could go and work up there if I wanted. Call me paranoid, but I didn't want to be investigating politicians while in full view of the snipers who paraded the roof of the White House.

I settled for spending a few hours in the hotel before going out and exploring the city. I had seen all the sights before and it was too hot to be wandering around the National Mall. The hotel had a decent—albeit expensive—WiFi connection, which was likely more than you could say about the local coffee shops, so I set myself up at a desk and got to work.

Washington, D.C. was home to hundreds of politicians, and I couldn't hope to spy on even a small percentage of them in my time here. Even if I did, I would be incredibly fortunate to catch one of them in the act.

I needed to be smart about how I spent my time, but the number of politicians here was an advantage in some ways. As long as I knew where to look and who to look for, I had a good chance of seeing one of them acting inappropriately. If I had to, I could even try setting some bait myself, but that was a last resort.

There were probably hundreds of ways politicians could break the rules, but I wanted to focus on the issue that had caused my father's death—the seedy business of selling goods and services to the U.S. government.

Before the government spent any money, it had to enter into a tedious bidding process where companies would offer their goods and compete on price. The government had to be careful with taxpayer dollars, so it would usually choose the cheapest option.

There were a number of ways this process could be manipulated and abused. The bidding was supposed to be anonymous, so if someone leaked the bids then another company could come in and lowball. More obviously, the person making the final decision could be bribed to choose one of the more expensive bids.

I narrowed down the people I would be focusing on by targeting those who helped make the decisions and the rules surrounding the process. They sat on a committee together and the members came from both of the major parties. I now had a list of ten people—much more manageable.

Once I had committed the names and faces to memory, I had to figure out where to catch them in action. They wouldn't be stupid enough to meet in their offices. Every visitor to the office was logged in, which created a paper trail. If they were doing something unethical or illegal it would be out in the open and to the general public it would look like a normal, boring conversation between two people in suits.

A few places sprang to mind as possible destinations, but with only five days I had to be more certain. They would probably meet near the Capitol so that the politician didn't have to walk far. Having a car with a security team drive you to a meeting point was not exactly subtle.

I did what I always did when I need answers—I looked online. Plenty of websites reported on suspicious-looking meetings, but once the location of those meetings had been "outed" it would stop being used. The pattern was repeated constantly; a politician would be spotted a few times over the course of a month and would then pop up a month later somewhere else. Presumably once word got out, the politician in question would be spooked and would suggest a new meeting place. None of the people I was following had been spotted anywhere recently, so I would have to think of something else.

I started going through the social media sites

on my phone and soon found my first real lead. When searching for the names of politicians, I occasionally found a photo where someone had proudly snapped their local politician in D.C. I found Congressman Phillips in the background of a photo holding a taco with a comment stating that "I travelled all the way to D.C. and ended up buying food at the same place as my local congressman. #congressmanphillips."

The congressman might have been holding a taco, but he couldn't have looked less interested in it. He was standing under a tree and talking to another man near the food truck. Even though they were both holding food, the meeting was clearly not an opportunity to sample some of the local delights. The man meeting with the politician was looking directly at the camera, as if he was suspicious of the tourists and likely everyone else around him. Not subtle at all.

The lunch crowd wouldn't gather for another hour or so, but the subway system here could take a while and I wanted to find a good spot to camp out. I threw my laptop in a backpack and left the luxury of my air-conditioned hotel room to go and sit in the sun.

The wall of humidity hit me as soon as I left the hotel. I wanted to turn around and walk straight back inside, but instead I made it to the subway, which was a touch cooler.

I felt surprisingly nervous on my way to the collection of food trucks near the Capitol. My last experience in D.C. didn't help calm my nerves at all—if anything, I was more nervous now than I had been before. Maybe last time I'd been running on adrenaline? Or maybe all of Natalie's warnings about how dangerous this was were having some effect on me?

I found a bench under a tree which offered some relief from the sun, but not the humidity. I pulled out a book and pretended to read while looking around for Congressman Phillips or any of my other targets.

None of them appeared. I stayed there throughout the entire lunch hour and didn't see a single person. It had been a long shot and I still had four more days, but if this happened again tomorrow I'd need to consider other options.

As I walked back to the subway station, I received a text from William inviting me to meet him at a law firm on H Street. H Street was famous for being full of lawyers, lobbyists, and lobbyists disguised as lawyers.

I didn't know why William had changed his mind about letting me be a part of whatever he was doing, but I wasn't going to hang around and ask questions. I headed straight over to H Street and waited for him in the lobby.

I was about to see how the sausage was made and to my surprise the nerves had been replaced with excitement. Even if I didn't like what I saw, William was letting me in to another part of his life that had previously been private. No matter what happened with my new investigation, something positive would come from this trip to D.C., and that brought a smile to my face as William walked through the door.

Chapter Fifteen

"What are you looking so pleased about?" William asked as we headed to the elevator for our meeting. "Should I be worried?"

"I'm just pleased that you're letting me be a part of this after insisting that I couldn't come along to any of your meetings."

William frowned and then realized what I meant. "Oh. Well, actually, this meeting isn't part of… my other project."

"What's it for, then?" I asked.

"I'm meeting with a new legal team," William replied. "I'm going to give these guys a project to work on for my company."

"Don't you already have lawyers? Why would you want some who are based in D.C.?" I considered the possibility that William was just trying to throw me off the scent, but that didn't make much sense. He could have had this meeting without me and I would never have noticed.

"I do, but I'm just going to send a few billable

hours their way. I'm doing a favor for a friend."

"Sounds almost as unethical as whatever else it is you're doing. Why did you invite me along?"

William shrugged and looked offended that I wasn't happy to be here. "I thought you might like to see me work. We're not going to be able to spend much time together on this trip, and I miss you."

"Damn, that's a good answer," I replied. "Alright, come on, then. I guess it'll be fun to watch you work."

William and I approached a secretary when we left the elevator and she showed us to a large conference room with a selection of drinks already laid out.

"I can get you tea or coffee if you like," the secretary said. "Or you can just help yourself to one of the cold drinks on the table."

I needed caffeine, but after a few hours of sitting outside in the sun I couldn't handle a hot drink. I had only just stopped sweating and my shirt was still clinging to my back, so I declined the coffee and grabbed a Diet Coke.

A parade of high-priced lawyers walked into the conference room and introduced themselves to William, who in turn introduced me as his assistant. I made a mental note to chastise him for that later.

There were five lawyers in total. One older man was definitely a partner and would likely be the one selling the law firm's expertise. One man and two women looked to be in their thirties and were presumably senior associates. The final girl, who introduced herself as Rachel in a timid, nervous voice, had to be an intern of some kind.

That assumption was confirmed when all the other lawyers acted as if she weren't even there.

After some painful small talk, one of the partners asked William how they could help. William explained that his company had recently started working with victims of domestic violence and that they needed a firm with a dedicated background of pro bono work in that area.

"So you want us to do pro bono work for your company?" the partner asked. "We do have a pro bono program, but I'm not sure your firm would qualify for those benefits."

"That's not quite it," William replied. "These women—they're mainly women—need someone to help with things like restraining orders and in some cases need new identities. I want you to do that work through your pro bono program. In exchange, you can be in charge of all my company's employment law matters. As you know, we have thousands of employees, so it's a big job. Regular, billable work. Not too challenging, so you can put an associate on it."

"We would love to do that work," the partner said excitedly. The man might be near retirement, but his eyes lit up at the thought of bringing in easy work that an associate could complete while he collected the money. "Anton, here"—he pointed to one of the senior associates—"is an expert in most employment law matters."

"Excellent," William replied. "I'm sure we can work together for some time."

"If you don't mind me saying, though," the partner added, "I don't think we're the best people to work on these pro bono matters. You'd be better off with a firm local to San Francisco because restraining orders need someone to go to court for you."

"You have an office in the Bay Area," William said. "While most of the women brought in through the program so far have been from in and around San Francisco, it's a program that I hope to expand nationally."

"Still," the partner continued, "I would feel more comfortable if you had a local contact in the area." The partner obviously loved the idea of low-level work bringing in big money, but he didn't seem so keen on the thought of pro bono work consuming an associate's working hours.

"Let me make something clear," William said, leaning forward onto his elbows. "You are only getting the billable work because I'm convinced that this is the best firm to handle the pro bono work. If the pro bono work goes, then so does the billable work."

"Understood. Do we have anyone who can do that work?" the partner asked the associate nearest him.

"You do," William interrupted before the associate could reply. William nodded towards Rachel, who was sitting at the end of the table diligently taking notes.

The associate whispered Rachel's name in the ear of the partner to save him from embarrassment. "Rachel? Do you have experience in this area?" the partner asked.

"Yes sir," Rachel replied. "Sort of. I'm a member of my law school's society that helps domestic violence victims in the community."

"You're being modest, Rachel," William added. "You're not a member of the society. You're the founder. And you wrote an excellent paper on the recent failure of Congress to pass laws protecting victims. Not many law students get published while they're still in law school. Congratulations."

"Thank you," Rachel murmured quietly.

"I suggest you do your best to hang on to this one," William said to the partner. "She's the entire reason I'm here today." His words were clear—*lose her and lose the work.*

William went into more detail about the work he would need done over the next few months. Shortly afterward a paralegal brought in an engagement letter which William signed immediately.

The lawyers got up and started to file out of the room.

"Rachel," William called out. "Would you mind staying behind for a few minutes? You took a lot of notes, but as you can see, my assistant didn't do the same." I pursed my lips and dug my fingers into the palm of my hand. As soon as we were somewhere private, he was going to get an earful. "Do you mind if we take down some of the important dates that were discussed?"

"Of course." Rachel came back into the room so that it was just the three of us.

"They're going to do everything in their power to keep you at the firm now," William said, ignoring her notes.

"Thank you," Rachel said quietly. "I didn't think anyone would ever read that paper I wrote."

"I meant what I said. It was a great paper."

"How did you find it?" Rachel asked. "It was only just published."

"Let's just say we have a mutual friend," William replied. "I owed him a favor and this was the only way I could think of to help. I know he cares a lot about your success."

Rachel nodded, and I had a feeling she knew exactly who the mutual friend was.

"I know you may not stay here after you finish law school either way, but if you want to stay on, they'll find a role for you."

"Thank you," Rachel said again.

William didn't offer any explanation of what I had just seen and I decided not to ask. He had just done something nice for a stranger; he seemed to do that a lot. And really, I didn't need to know why he did those things. It was enough for me that he did them.

Chapter Sixteen

The next day turned out to be a complete waste of time. I went to the same place at lunchtime and hung around a few more potential hot spots in the afternoon. I kept telling myself that the chances were always slim, but that didn't make me feel better when I came up empty-handed. I desperately wanted to discover something on this trip. What kind of journalist would I be if I couldn't find a politician doing something wrong in D.C.?

On the third day, I decided to give the same locations one more try and then I would move on. I didn't know where else I would look, but I couldn't keep showing up at the same places every day without any results.

Late in the afternoon, I took up a position on the same bench under the tree and pulled out my laptop. Clouds filled the sky today and the lack of sunlight made it a lot easier to use my computer. If anything, the weather was even more humid than it had been and my clothes were stuck to me by the time I sat down. At least everyone was in the same position; the uncomfortable heat should hide my nerves on the off chance I actually saw something today.

I refreshed my memory on what the politicians looked like by pulling the pictures up on my laptop and then started streaming some music. I didn't really need the music, but having earbuds in my ears was a surefire way to stop strangers from attempting to strike up any conversation.

Watching people was surprisingly tiring. My eyes flicked to every new person who walked into my field of view until I knew they weren't up to anything more than just getting some food. The tourists stood out easily and I ignored them, but most of the visitors were from the nearby buildings and dressed in full suit-and-tie. The men in particular looked nondescript and I had to carefully look at each one before ruling them out.

After a few hours, my mind could do most of it on autopilot and I started ignoring people without even thinking about it. One man caught my eye when he stood with his back to me on the grass twenty feet away. I had no idea what he looked like, but he wasn't standing in line for food, nor was he even close enough to read the menu items on the board. Also, unlike everyone who stopped and waited for a friend, he wasn't using his phone. He just stood there, arms straight by his sides, clearly waiting for someone.

He couldn't see me, so I quickly threw my things into my bag and ran up to the food truck with the shortest line. I bought a bottle of water and walked back to my bench, making sure to take a good, long look at the man on the way.

He was one of them. I couldn't remember his name, but I recognized that face. I opened the pictures up on my phone and found him. Congressman Hutchins. He had dyed his hair since the photo was taken, because there wasn't a gray hair on his head anymore, whereas previously there had been a few streaks of it at his temples.

I opened up the recording app on my phone and started recording the sound and video. The crowds were dying down, so there was a chance I might be able to get a recording of what I heard, although I would need to get closer.

I moved again and sat down on the grass underneath a tree while Hutchins still had his back to me. So long as he didn't move I should be able to stay put and hear everything.

Hutchins started looking at his watch and shuffling his feet as he got impatient over the delay. Finally, after five more minutes had gone by, a tall man arrived on the scene and approached Hutchins. The man didn't look familiar, but then I hadn't expected him to. He passed a salad in a plastic container to Hutchins and kept one for himself. Neither of the two looked in the mood to eat and I couldn't see any forks in their hands, but they did look a little less conspicuous now.

The tall man didn't look directly at me, but he would be able to see me in his peripheral vision, so I couldn't just sit there and blatantly video the conversation. I put my phone down in a position that hopefully would capture some of the events and went back to using my laptop.

The two of them started off with some basic pleasantries, but quickly got down to business. "I spoke to my team, but they can't improve on the bid," the tall man said.

"Can't?" Hutchins asked. "Or don't want to, Zach?"

"Does it matter? I want to get this done, and I don't want to change the bid. The profit will provide a nice return for shareholders, but it's not excessive."

"And no doubt you'll get a decent bonus out of it?"

Zach sighed. "Let's not go through this again. Are you going to help me out with this or not? Let me know if I should start looking for people who are more receptive to my employer's contributions."

"I have an idea," Hutchins said quickly. "You'll need to admit another member onto your board."

"Who?"

"Doesn't matter. Just make sure they're a minority. There's a bill going through that will allow me to give precedence to businesses that are run by minority groups."

"There are already loads of bills like that," Zach replied. "Our company's too big to qualify for the benefits and having one board member who's a minority won't help with that."

"This is a new, one-off bill. It's been badly drafted and has loopholes a mile wide."

"Then it'll never pass."

"It's passed the House," Hutchins said. "But you're right, it won't pass the Senate. It doesn't need to. I can make my decision based on pending legislation if I have a reasonable belief it will pass. No one's going to call me out on giving a grant to a minority-owned business just because the legislation didn't go through. It would be political suicide."

Zach said something that I couldn't hear, but he looked happy and I caught a nod of the head. There might be some technical details to iron out, but I had a feeling Zach's company would end up winning the contract.

There were many schemes in place to promote minority-owned businesses in the U.S., as there were for women-owned and veteran-owned businesses, and they worked towards a noble goal. The federal government was one of the biggest individual spenders in the entire world. If even a small percentage of its spending went towards those types of businesses it could make a huge difference in correcting inequality.

Good intentions, however, were open to abuse. The rules had to be finely crafted to ensure that only those who were supposed to benefit actually did so. It sounded easy in theory, but was a nightmare in practice. If legislation had been passed in a hurry then there was a good chance it could be taken advantage of, and that's exactly what these two intended.

I let them walk away and spent the rest of the afternoon visiting museums before returning to the hotel around six. I didn't even care what William had been up to. I had found something much better and it would lead to a huge story that might set up my entire career.

Chapter Seventeen

"You look rather pleased with yourself," William said when I walked into the hotel room. "Should I be worried?"

"Not at all," I replied. "Let's just say I had a productive afternoon."

"That doesn't make me feel better."

I kissed him on the cheek and proceeded to peel off the sweaty clothes that were completely pasted to me after spending so much time outside in the humid, muggy air.

"Don't worry, we haven't entered the comfort zone yet," I said when I noticed the surprised look on William's face. He hadn't been expecting the sudden strip tease, but he seemed okay with it. "I'm too hot to keep these clothes on, but we have a few more weeks before I start shaving my legs in front of you."

"I'm just annoyed with myself now, that's all."

"Why?"

"Because I made a reservation for dinner at seven, but all I want to do now is throw you down on the bed and have my way with you."

I just about had time to shower and get ready, but only just. There certainly wasn't enough time for William to join me, which was what I had initially planned. "Then it'll just have to wait for tonight," I replied, talking to myself as much as William. "Where are we going?"

"The restaurant on the rooftop. I popped up there earlier and the view is every bit as good as you would imagine. We have a table in the corner with the best view of the White House."

"That place is expensive even by your standards. I don't have any outfits that would be appropriate."

I'd seen visitors entering the hotel and getting in the exclusive elevator that served the restaurant. Not one of them had been wearing an outfit that cost less than a thousand dollars. Even with my limited knowledge, I could recognize extravagant expense when I saw it and there would be plenty on show in that restaurant.

"It just so happens I brought a dress with me that you can wear," William said as he pulled a small box out of his suitcase.

I opened the box and saw the blue dress that I had tried on after the big fashion show. I held it up against my body and looked at myself in the mirror. I already knew how it looked on me, but I felt as excited as I had the first time I'd tried it on.

"You left in kind of a rush that day and left it behind," William said. "I want to see you in it again. And this time I want to take it off."

I almost wished we were going to a restaurant further away, so I could soak up all the looks that strangers were giving me. Even in this restaurant, people looked at William and me as if we were a fairy tale couple, a princess with her Prince Charming. It sounded cheesy, but as we were escorted to our seats I heard more than one person make a similar comment and I couldn't help but smile.

"You don't need me to tell you this," William said as he looked into my eyes, "but you look stunning tonight."

"It's this dress," I replied. "It's hard not to look good in a dress this exquisite."

"The dress only looks that good when you wear it," William insisted. "I've seen that dress on models and it didn't look anywhere near as special. The woman makes the dress, not the other way around."

"Careful, you're starting to sound like a fashion designer. You were right about the view," I added, not-so-subtly changing the subject.

The sun wouldn't set for another hour or so, but the humidity had dropped and a refreshing breeze was blowing in from the east. We had to keep our napkins weighed down on the table, but at least I wouldn't spend the evening sweating.

"The President isn't at home today," William remarked. "Neither is the First Lady."

"How can you tell?" I asked.

"There's more security when one of them is home. There are no snipers on the roof today, and fewer guards on the grounds."

"You sound like you're casing the joint," I joked. "Or do you have plans to live there one day?"

"God, no, not a chance. I like a degree of privacy in my life. I already have more of a public profile than I'd like, but that's nothing compared to what politicians face."

"The reporters here would have a field day investigating your private life."

"My life isn't quite as tawdry as you seem to believe," William replied. "Although there certainly are a few ex-girlfriends that I don't want coming out of the woodwork." He smiled, but the grin disappeared quickly.

Much to my own surprise, I didn't feel particularly jealous towards what I was sure was a long list of ex-girlfriends, but the way his smile had vanished so quickly when he was talking about his past was a touch disconcerting. Still, we hadn't been dating long; I had plenty of time to remove the last memories of former lovers from his mind. I intended to get started on that right after dinner.

The food came served in tiny portions, but there were enough of them that I had to pass on dessert. We could always order room service later, but for now I just wanted to get William back downstairs and I could tell he wanted much the same thing.

The door to our hotel room hadn't shut before William pressed his lips against mine in a hard, passionate embrace. I stumbled back against the wall before lifting my leg and hooking my thigh around him for support.

The dress parted at the side as William's hand ran up the bare skin of my leg. I pressed myself against him and felt his erection trying to burst through his pants. My hands fumbled at his belt as his fingers worked their way between my legs.

"I've wanted to do this all night," William whispered in my ear. "Every man on the roof mentally undressed you, and now I get to do it for real."

He took my hand and led me over to the bed. He stood behind me like he had done that day at the fashion show, but this time he pulled down the zipper at the back of the dress and let if fall to the floor.

I heard him step back and knew he was looking at my naked body. "You're not wearing any panties." The words came out as a growl and I knew he would take me soon.

"There didn't seem like much point," I replied softly.

William's clothes dropped to the floor and he pressed his naked body against mine. His lips brushed my neck lightly as he reached around and softly squeezed my breasts. His breath on my skin sent shivers down my spine and my nipples hardened to his touch.

William grabbed me by the waist and pushed me forward onto the bed. I fell onto my stomach and parted my legs wide enough for him to land between them. He kept kissing my neck as his cock parted my wet folds and brought the evening to a passionate finish.

Chapter Eighteen

Now that I had a name and a face, I could spend my time in D.C. much more productively. None of the information I found online about Congressman Hutchins made him sound especially corrupt, but if that information were public he wouldn't be a politician in the first place.

Crucially, I now knew where he worked, so if he went to any additional lunch meetings I would be able to follow him and listen in. First thing in the morning I went to the Capitol Hill area of D.C. and hung out by his building. In the morning there were enough people around that no one noticed me, but once the commuters had all arrived at work I had to take a seat on a bench and pretend to use my laptop.

The building had multiple entrances and exits, but only one had a specific lane for cars to pull over and pick up their employer. Hutchins might walk to his destination, but my instincts told me he would still use the same exit out of habit.

Even keeping an eye on the exit, I could

easily have missed him. Every man walking into that building wore a similar-looking suit and tie combo and Hutchins didn't have any distinctive characteristics. The odds were not in my favor, but I got lucky.

A man with a slender frame walked out the door accompanied by two larger men, presumably security. It was him. I hadn't noticed any security with him yesterday, but I kept my gaze down to keep them from recognizing me.

The lack of other people in the streets meant I had to keep my distance, but conversely I had an uninterrupted view of Hutchins and could easily follow him from over a block away.

He didn't go far. He made the short walk to the Ulysses S. Grant Memorial and any hope I had of catching him in the act again disappeared when I saw who awaited him there.

Hutchins approached a group of kids on a field trip and gave them a speech on the great work done by the American government in the Capitol building. My stomach felt uneasy watching someone I knew to be corrupt talking to a bunch of impressionable children, but I couldn't do anything about it.

I stood near the water and wandered up and down pretending to talk on my phone to look less suspicious. Hutchins spoke to the children for nearly thirty minutes explaining how Congress worked—or how it should work, at least—and then answered questions. I had to give it to him, he took his time and only left when he had been there for an hour and had to go vote on a matter before the House. As excuses went, that wasn't a bad one.

Hutchins walked into the Capitol building, so I

couldn't follow him. A quick look on my phone confirmed that the House did have a vote going on and Hutchins was expected to participate.

I didn't have anything else to do, so I decided to wait for Hutchins to leave the building. Tourists were gathering around the monument in the center, so I took a seat on the ground just outside one of the lesser-visited memorials to the side.

Other than tourists asking me to take a photo of them, no one bothered me while I sat and flicked through the social apps on my phone. I had a bunch of messages from Sophie that I'd ignored. None of them were particularly important, but I felt bad for ignoring her.

Apparently Adrian had come into the restaurant where she worked, which meant she'd seen him two times in the flesh now. I still didn't know how I felt about Adrian, but I hoped she had restrained herself around him. William thought those two were made for each other, but I thought the two of them might be a little too similar. Something would have to give, and I worried that Sophie would end up getting hurt.

The statue behind me got little attention, but after I had been there an hour some tourists walked behind me and stood near it. I looked up in front of me and noticed a man in a suit and dark sunglasses, with a distinctive coil hanging from his ear. He was obviously part of a security detail, which meant someone important must be nearby.

I looked to my left and saw two more men. There was another to my right and all of them were looking directly at me.

My heart froze. I wanted to stand up and run, but that would look suspicious. Besides, my legs had turned to jelly beneath me so I wouldn't be running anywhere.

I angled my head down to my laptop and then tried to look at the security guards in my peripheral vision. The guards were looking in my direction, but they were all wearing sunglasses so it was hard to tell if they were staring at me.

I breathed a sigh of relief when I realized that they were looking just above me and not at me. They were protecting whomever was behind me looking at the statue. Given the location, I assumed the person behind me was a congressman.

The congressman—from the sound of his shoes as he walked I was fairly sure it was a man—paced slowly around the statue until another man joined him.

I considered leaving, but I didn't want to draw attention to myself. Besides, I had been here first; I wasn't about to be chased out of a public space.

"Let's make this quick," a deep voice said. The speaker was standing just feet behind me, but he was on the other side of a stone wall and wouldn't be able to see me sitting on the ground. "There's not much I can do. I'm sorry, William. I don't think I can help you."

William? Surely it couldn't be my William? I forced myself to remain in position, although I desperately wanted to turn my head and look over the barrier to see if it was him.

"Not *much* you can do," William said.

My William. That was definitely him. I had stumbled on one of his meetings. He'd be pissed if he saw me here and would probably assume I had followed him.

"So you can do something?" William continued.

The other man sighed. "It's not going to be easy, but yes, there is something I can do. You're risking a hell of a lot."

"I'd risk everything for her," William replied.

"You really care about her, don't you?" the man asked.

"I love her with all my heart," William said. Was he talking about me? He couldn't be. Why would he talk about me to a politician? "I haven't seen Kaylee in months, and it breaks my heart."

He wasn't talking about me. I couldn't breathe. He loved someone he hadn't seen for months. Who was Kaylee? She must be an ex-girlfriend.

"My life isn't complete without her, Robert. I'm going to do whatever it takes to get her back. Just tell me what it is I need to do."

I had at least four security agents looking in my direction. I couldn't react. I couldn't move as I heard my boyfriend talk about the love of his life. Someone he hadn't seen for months. Someone who wasn't me.

Part Three

Chapter One

The message came through quicker than I had expected.

We need to speak as soon as possible. Are you free?

For a few seconds my heart stopped in my chest as I imagined the email had come from William. He might well have sent me a message like that, but I had blocked all his messages, emails, and calls so I would never know about them.

This email had not come from William; it had come from the editor at a large national news organization. I knew exactly why she needed to talk to me. Yesterday I had sent her a copy of my story revealing that Congressman Hutchins had been taking bribes in exchange for lucrative government contracts.

I'd never written a story so fast. All the facts and evidence I needed had seemingly fallen into my lap and I had a complete article within two weeks. The story was good enough to be published in a national paper, but that didn't mean any of them would bite. I had no contacts, so my email would have gone straight to the bottom of the pile. Of course I held out hope that it would get picked up at some point, but I never expected that to happen within twenty-four hours.

The editor, Lauren, gave me her direct line number and told me to call as soon as possible. I picked up my phone and dialed her number. She answered after the second ring. "Lauren Turner."

"Ms. Turner? This is Amanda Gibson. I wrote the article about—"

"Amanda, hello. Please call me Lauren. I'm so glad you called me. Listen, as you've no doubt guessed, we want to run your story as soon as possible. It's going to be huge."

"I'm glad you liked it," I replied calmly, trying to keep the excitement out of my voice. I wanted Lauren to think I was a professional who did stories like this all the time. We would have to negotiate a payment soon and I wanted to be on a strong footing.

"Listen, I'm sure you appreciate that the subject matter is a little controversial. The article is being run through our legal team right now to make sure we aren't going to get sued for printing this thing."

"You won't get sued," I said confidently. "It's all true and I have the evidence to prove it."

"I know. I reviewed the evidence you sent me. I just need to know how you got it all. The legal team is going to want to know, so I figured I might as well ask you now. That way we can save time and get this story published even quicker."

I lied and told Lauren that I had gone to D.C.

specifically to spy on Congressman Hutchins. I didn't mention William for fear that she'd ask questions about him that I couldn't answer.

"I followed a hunch and made a recording of the congressman while I was in D.C.," I continued. "You have a copy. With that evidence I knew I was on the right track."

"And what about the other conversations and the copies of incriminating emails? How on earth did you get those? If hacking was involved, then we may not be able to use them. That's a pretty sensitive topic these days."

"No, I didn't hack anything. Nothing like that. Once I got back to California, I found out who the congressman had met with and arranged a meeting with him."

The meeting had been easy to arrange. After interviewing William, I had a minor reputation for interviewing CEOs and I used that to my advantage. Fortunately, the CEO, Zach Creston, had an office in San Francisco. He assumed the interview was about his life as a successful CEO, but instead I confronted him with the evidence from D.C. He crumbled before my eyes.

He didn't seem to feel any guilt for what he'd done, and he couldn't wait to spill the beans on his relationship with the congressman. I was taken aback by how easy it was, but on further investigation it turned out that he was having an affair with a woman in D.C. and didn't want his wife to even know he'd been there. Once I agreed to keep his name out of the story, he spilled the beans. Unfortunately I must have accidentally stopped the recording at that point. Oops.

"Are you going to get any comment from the congressman before you go to print?" I asked. I had called the congressman's office to see if he had anything to say for himself, but had never heard back from him. This newspaper had a solid reputation, so if Lauren called she would be much more likely to get a response.

"I don't have anything official yet," Lauren replied. "But I have a source in his office who told me the congressman is going to retire early. He probably won't pull the trigger until we go live with our story, but it's going to happen. You've caught one of them, Amanda. That's an incredible accomplishment, especially for a young journalist with no contacts in politics."

"Thank you," I replied. I didn't feel deserving of her praise. The entire thing still felt like a fluke. I would never get that fortunate again, I was sure, so I intended to milk this story for all it was worth. This would be the story to make my career—if I made the most of it.

"I hope you're prepared for the changes this is going to bring to your life," Lauren said.

"Changes?"

"I have to be honest, you're not suddenly going to become famous from this story. Most of the country only pays passing attention to politics, but in certain circles you'll be a big name for a few months at least. If you play this right, you could end up being a point of contact for political stories. Have you considered moving to D.C.?"

Lauren's paper was headquartered in D.C., but they had offices all over the country. I hoped to do more work for them, but had no intention of moving to Washington, D.C.

"The weather's a little hot for me," I replied. The weather was one of the reasons, but not the only one. I didn't like the vibe there. Compared to northern California, D.C. was far too stuffy and dull for my liking.

"Well, I'd love for you to write another story, and you don't need to be based in D.C. to write it. In fact, you're already in the perfect location to follow through with this lead."

"I'd love to do more work for you," I said honestly. Lauren's paper paid far more than any other website or organization I had sold stories to, and it was far more prestigious to boot. I also needed the distraction. Working on the story had been the only thing that kept me from thinking of William twenty-four hours a day. Keeping busy meant I only thought of him about twenty hours a day. It was an improvement. "What lead do you have for me?" I asked.

"It's your own lead, really," Lauren said. "I can't take credit for it."

"My lead? I don't have any other leads at the moment."

"You may not have realized you had it," Lauren explained. "You remember that recording you made of the congressman? The one outside the Capitol building?"

I nodded. I had recorded the congressman even though he hadn't met with anyone on that occasion. All my recordings had come out surprisingly well even though there were a lot of crowds around.

"You must have left the recording going once he left. About an hour later the recording picked up two men talking behind you."

William. My phone had picked up the conversation between William and a man I didn't know. I shivered. Even thinking about that conversation made me feel ill.

"The conversation probably sounded innocuous enough at first," Lauren continued. "You wouldn't have given it a second thought. I listened to it a few times and I think they're up to something."

"Who's they?" I asked. I still didn't want to admit I knew William, and I genuinely had no idea who the other man had been.

"Those voices belonged to Senator Robert Larson and William Townsend. Townsend is the hotshot CEO of a fashion company. I think you have another story on your hands here. You interested?"

Chapter Two

I felt like I was going around in circles. No matter what path I took, the story always found a way back to William. Months ago I had been researching Adrian Townsend and had ended up in William's office thanks to an intervention from my friend Carter. Lauren obviously hadn't read my resume or she would have noticed I knew who William was from my prior interview.

Then, when I went back to investigating Adrian, I discovered that William was behind the entire thing. I dropped the story and went to D.C. to follow through on other leads, but managed to overhear a conversation between William and a senator. If I believed in fate—and at this point I was starting to—I would think that William and I were destined to be a part of each other's lives, albeit not in the way I had hoped.

When I overheard that conversation in D.C. between William and another man, my brain had focused on one sentence.

I love her with all my heart.

He loved another woman. Once those words

hit my ears, everything that came after them was irrelevant. I think the conversation lasted for a few more minutes before the two of them went their separate ways, but it could have been hours for all I could tell.

I had sat there not moving until they left and all the security guards cleared the area. I didn't cry until I was back in the hotel room. Somehow being surrounded by people helped keep my emotions hidden deep inside, but once the door shut and I was alone in my room, the tears had poured out.

If it hadn't been for my desperate need to get out of the hotel before William returned, I likely would have stayed in bed until I cried myself to sleep. Instead, I packed my bags as quickly as possible and headed to the door.

Just before leaving I decided to go back to the hotel and leave William a handwritten note to tell him that I was going home to San Francisco and that he shouldn't contact me. I didn't leave the note for his benefit. I didn't owe him anything, however I didn't want him thinking I had gone missing and call the police. The last thing I needed was the police tracing my whereabouts over the last few days.

The last minute plane seats I booked were far less comfortable than the ones I arrived in, but they sufficed to get me far away from William. Now my editor was asking me to write a story about him. There was no way I could do that.

"I had no idea I recorded Senator Larson and William Townsend. Are you sure it was William? I did an interview with him not that long ago and I think I would recognize the voice."

"Oh, yes, I forgot you had done that. Wow, what are the odds, eh? Yes, it's definitely him. We have software to check voices and it was a strong match."

"I've heard of Senator Larson," I said, trying to take the conversation away from William. "Who is he?"

"He's one of the senators from California," Lauren said. "He hasn't been up for election for about five years, though, and you may have not been eligible to vote then."

I had voted five years ago, but at that age my interest in politics had been nominal. I just voted for the Democratic candidates without giving it too much thought. I'd probably voted for this Larson guy, and now he was involved with William. If I weren't so distraught I would have marveled at the coincidence.

"What do you think the story is?" I asked. "I don't remember hearing anything particularly interesting."

"I don't know exactly," Lauren admitted. "But it sounds like Townsend needed a favor and the senator agreed to help him out."

"It's probably nothing," I replied casually. "If no money changed hands, then it could just be one friend helping out another."

"I think you're right in that respect," Lauren said. "This did sound like one friend doing a favor for another, but there's something more to it than that. For one thing, they went to great lengths to have a conversation in private. I don't know how they missed you, but they thought they were alone."

"I was behind a fence," I explained. "I was sitting there waiting for Congressman Hutchins to leave the Capitol. I'd like to pretend it was a work of genius on my part, but it was just a coincidence."

"You make your own luck in this game. It was good work, Amanda. Townsend asked the senator about a woman named Kaylee."

The air got stuck in my lungs at the mention of her name and I had to remind my body to resume breathing. This was only the second time I'd heard that name spoken aloud and it had a chilling impact on me.

"I think she might be in jail or something," Lauren continued. "Townsend spoke about getting her out and the senator said he could help but that it was risky. I admit that's not a lot to go on, but there's definitely a story here. Do you want it? I appreciate that you might be exhausted after the last one, but I wanted to offer it to you first."

"Thanks," I replied. I most certainly did *not* want the story, but if I didn't take it then Lauren would just offer it to someone else. "Do you think there's a conflict for me here? What with the previous article I wrote on Mr. Townsend?"

"Not at all," Lauren replied. "That makes you perfect for this. You already know him. Maybe you can use that to get an interview."

"I don't have the time to fly back to D.C. right now," I explained. "Maybe I can pick it up in a month or two?"

"That's the best part," Lauren said excitedly. "Senator Larson is back in California now, and so is Townsend. I'm getting the impression you aren't interested, though. You can pass if you like. I'm going to make sure you're well paid for this piece, so you won't need money for a few months."

I took the phone away from my mouth and breathed a sigh of relief. Spending so much time with William had distracted me from my own personal finances, which weren't looking so hot right now. Hearing that Lauren would pay me a decent amount for the story was music to my ears.

"It's not that I don't want to do it," I lied. "I just want to make sure I'm the best person for the job. I'll take the project on. Give me a few weeks to do some initial research and I'll get back to you."

"Excellent. Let me know if you need any advances for expenses. I might be able to help with connections as well, but you should start with Townsend and work from there."

"Thanks, Lauren."

I had bought myself a few weeks, but at some point I would have to give Lauren some information on William and Senator Larson. That meant either making something up or finding out the truth. I hated the thought of lying; it could destroy my career just as it was getting started. However, I couldn't bear to find out more about Kaylee. Just knowing William loved another woman was enough.

I decided to give myself twenty-four hours to think it through. One whole day for my subconscious to make up its mind. I opened up Netflix and put on a show that didn't require much thought. I had earned a day of rest at least. Tomorrow I might have to start this whole thing all over again. I'd come full circle and once again ended up back at William.

Chapter Three

I came to a decision, but I didn't like it. According to my subconscious, the best thing for me to do right now was to speak to William and ask him about Kaylee. It was a stupid decision. It only took me seconds to think of ten reasons why it was an awful idea. Unfortunately, nothing else made sense.

If I ignored the problem, then some other reporter would pick up the story and William's relationship with Kaylee would be in the papers and online. I didn't want that to happen, so in some ways talking to William was perhaps sensible.

Of course, it would utterly destroy me and ruin everything I had done to keep him out of my life since our trip to D.C. That should have been enough of a reason to go nowhere near him, but my brain wouldn't let me forget about him. One way or another, I had to know about Kaylee. That meant speaking to William.

There was no way in hell I was going to call him or go round to his apartment. That would look like I was apologizing. I had to bump into William naturally.

William had come round to my apartment a few times since he finished up in D.C. Much to my disappointment, he had not ended his trip early when I came home. He had stayed there and finished up whatever he had to do involving Kaylee. I shouldn't be surprised given that I knew he loved her, but it still hurt.

Sophie had made excuses for me every time he came round to my apartment, but there hadn't been much I could do to stop him seeing me when I left the apartment. He hadn't given up easily. William knew which coffee shops I preferred to work in and Natalie had reported seeing him turn up on a regular basis and leave after looking around and not seeing me there. Now I could use that to my advantage.

I grabbed my laptop and headed to the coffee shop. If I hung out there long enough, William was bound to show up looking for me. I hoped.

All the tables in the café were taken, so I started looking around for spare seats by the wall or on the edge of someone else's table. The atmosphere wasn't exactly friendly, but everyone was working and usually didn't care if people sat at their table.

"Amanda," a voice called out. A male voice, but not William.

I looked around. The shout had come from behind me, but I couldn't place the voice. Then I saw a man stand up and wave at me.

"John?"

"Hi, Amanda," John replied as he made space at the table and removed his bag from the spare chair. "I didn't know you came here too. Do you work nearby?"

"Sort of," I replied as I sat down. "I live nearby, but I work from home, so I suppose that's the same thing."

I hadn't seen John since the incident with Emily and Carter and the lawsuit I had helped them with. We had hit if off, though, and John was incredibly friendly. He was one of those guys it was tough not to like.

"How are things?" John asked. "Did you manage to get a job with a newspaper? I know Carter talked about setting you up with something last time I spoke to him."

"I decided to go it alone," I said. "I like the freedom of doing my own thing. I wouldn't mind a regular paycheck, mind you, but I'm not complaining."

"I couldn't imagine working a regular job," John said. "My boyfriend's a waiter and he works so hard, but doesn't get paid a lot. I landed on my feet starting a business with Emily."

"She says the same about you," I said. "You two were a team and you both made that company into a success."

"Maybe," John said with a smile.

"Haven't you made a load of money from the company already?" I asked. "What are you doing slumming it with us normal people?"

"Most of the value is in company stock and I don't intend to sell. I have a nice little safety net, but I don't feel the need to spend money recklessly. Besides, I don't want to rub Michael's nose in it."

"Fair enough. Is Emily still in England? I wish she'd come home more often."

"Yes, and I wish she'd come back too. She loves it there, though, so I only see her via webcam or on one of those fleeting visits of hers. Can't say I blame her, though. Have you seen the house she lives in with Carter? Holy crap, that place is nice."

"I saw part of it when I had a video call with Carter. It looks like an old building. Must have cost a fortune."

"Every time I talk to Emily, she's calling from a different room. I don't know how many they have, but there must be at least twenty. They have a staff just to keep the place clean."

"Okay, *now* I'm jealous. No one has picked up my dirty clothes since I moved away from home. I could get used to that."

John went to say something, but seemed to change his mind and took a sip of his coffee instead.

"What is it?" I asked.

"I almost said something I'm not supposed to know," John said.

"Let me guess, Emily or Carter told you I was in a relationship with William Townsend?"

"Maybe," he replied with a cheeky grin. "I'm gay. You can't expect me to stay away from gossip."

"Has anyone ever told you that you only play the gay card when it suits you?"

"No," John replied thoughtfully. "Although I'm surprised you're first. You'd think someone would have picked up on it by now. Anyway, don't blame Emily. She just can't keep secrets from me. We're business partners, so there has to be complete honesty."

"It doesn't really matter," I replied calmly. "We

were seeing each other, but it didn't last long."

"You mean the two of you have split up already?" I nodded. "What happened?"

"It's complicated."

"That's a shame. That is one good-looking man, and Emily spoke very highly of him. So you're definitely not seeing him anymore?"

"Definitely."

"You're sure?"

I frowned. "Yes, John, I'm sure. I think I would know if I were still seeing someone."

"Huh. Because a man who looks a lot like William has just walked in and he's coming straight towards us."

I closed my eyes and took a couple of deep breaths to compose myself. My plan had worked. William had come to the café and found me. That was the easy part. Now I just had to speak to him.

I turned around and looked straight up at William as he approached the table. He didn't say anything—just looked down at me, staring into my eyes.

"We need to talk," I said. "Let's go somewhere private."

Chapter Four

"We're not going to your apartment," I whispered to William as we walked out of the café. I didn't trust myself to be alone with him in private.

"Let's go to the park," William said. "There'll be plenty of people around at this time of day."

We found a bench in the sun and sat down. I did get a touch of déjà vu sitting on a park bench in the sun again, but the cool San Francisco breeze and lack of humidity reminded me I was back in California and not D.C.

William looked strangely calm. I had expected him to either be pleading for forgiveness or angry with me for abandoning him. He seemed neither. Did that mean he didn't care about me anymore? Perhaps he had accepted that Kaylee was the only woman for him? If he had her back in his life, then he wouldn't need me anymore.

"You took some drastic measures to avoid having to see me again," William said. He kept his eyes facing directly forward as he spoke, not turning to look at me. "I can only think of one reason why you would have done that. You know, don't you?"

"You've tried this on me before," I replied, remembering one of William's previous "confessions" where he'd tried to get me to tell him what he had done wrong. He had been more playful that day. Now he looked deadly serious. He wasn't messing around.

"You know about Kaylee," he said slowly, still not looking at me.

I nodded, but he couldn't see me. "Yes. I know about her." I still couldn't say her name out loud.

"How?"

"I overheard a conversation between you and Senator Larson by the Capitol. I'd rather not go into the details about what I heard you say, but it was enough to know I needed to cease all contact with you."

"But now you've changed your mind?"

"No, not exactly. It's complicated. I need to know what you talked to the senator about, but not for my own benefit."

"I'm not sure I understand, but I don't care. I've been desperate to tell you ever since I saw your note in the hotel room."

"Not desperate enough to leave D.C. and come back to San Francisco immediately," I said bitterly. I wouldn't have agreed to see him anyway, but it would have been reassuring to know he would cancel part of his trip for me.

"I couldn't," William replied. "I wanted to—more than you can imagine—but I had to stay in D.C. until I had sorted a few things out."

What did that mean? Did he have Kaylee back in his life now? That would explain why he wouldn't even look at me now.

We stopped speaking while a young mom walked past with her two children, one in her arms and the other running ahead kicking a ball around despite his mom's orders not to run off.

"Do you have her back now?" I asked.

"No," William said, shaking his head. "I don't. Not yet."

"I'm sorry," I lied. "I hope you get her back soon. It sounds like you care a lot about her."

"I do. She's very important to me."

"You said you love her," I reminded him. "I heard you. You said you love her more than anyone else."

"I shouldn't have said that," William said. "I mean, I do love her, but I didn't mean for you to hear that."

"I wish I hadn't, I can assure you."

A young girl rode by us on a bike with the training wheels still on and a cute little basket on the front. William smiled as she waved at us and left her mother far behind.

"There's no need to be jealous," William said. He turned to look at me and I immediately got lost in those deep, dark eyes.

"Who said I was jealous? I'm angry. Disappointed. I guess I was jealous, but I'm not anymore." There was some truth to that. I found it hard to be jealous of someone I didn't know. I didn't even have a picture of her that I could direct my hatred towards. I knew nothing about her.

William stayed silent for a few more moments and then laughed.

"Is something funny?" I asked.

"Not really," he said, but he was still grinning. "None of this is funny, but, well, maybe we can laugh about this one day. God, I hope so."

I couldn't imagine what set of events would have to happen for me to ever laugh about this. I would hopefully put it behind me one day, but I wouldn't forget William in a hurry, or the way he broke my heart.

William dug his hand into his pocket and pulled out his wallet. He didn't carry a lot of cash, so there wasn't much in there apart from a few bank cards. His fingers reached behind one of the cards and pulled out a picture.

"I know it's a little old-fashioned to have hard copies of pictures these days," William said as he passed it to me, "but I like it."

I took the picture carefully in my hand. It had frayed around the edges from being kept in his wallet, but the image still exuded vibrant color, so it couldn't be that old. The photo was of a young girl about five years old. She beamed the kind of happy smile that only a child can.

"If you're jealous," William said, "there's no need to be. That's Kaylee. She's six years old now. I love her with all my heart."

I smiled. I couldn't help it. Kaylee was a child? I had been jealous of a child all this time? My happiness didn't last long as I thought about what this might mean. I didn't mind that William had a child, although keeping it from me had been dishonest.

The more troubling issue was picturing Kaylee in the context of the conversation I had overheard in D.C. Lauren had thought that Kaylee might be in jail, but clearly that couldn't be the case if Kaylee was a child. So why did William need the help of Senator Larson? Perhaps Lauren was right—this could be a big story after all.

"Why didn't you tell me?" I asked. I couldn't

217

take my eyes away from the photo. The girl didn't look at all like William, but the shape of her face did remind me of someone.

"I should have," William admitted. "I can trust you with anything. I know that now, but this is a secret I've kept for years. It feels odd to talk about her."

"I don't care that you have a child," I said truthfully. "I just wish you hadn't lied about it. You swore you were telling me the truth."

"No, I swore I wasn't lying to you. I admitted that I had secrets."

"This is a pretty big secret, William."

William looked away again. "She's not my child."

I frowned. "Then whose—" Kaylee did look familiar, and now I knew where from. She looked like William's sister. "Kaylee is Olivia's child, isn't she?"

William nodded. "I'm her uncle, but sometimes I feel more like her father. She's been taken from us, and I'm going to get her back."

Chapter Five

"Can we go back to my apartment?" William asked. "I know you wanted to be in public, but I'd rather not have this conversation where people can overhear all the details."

We made small talk as we walked back to his place, but William found it difficult to relax, and I wasn't entirely sure how I should feel towards him. My overriding instincts were telling me that he needed my help and support, but a nagging voice at the back of my head kept reminding me that he had been dishonest and had kept things from me.

As I walked through the door, my first thought was that we had walked into the wrong apartment. The suitcases William had taken to D.C. were still on the floor and largely unpacked, plates and bowls littered the living room, and empty pots and pans were scattered all over the kitchen.

"Did your housekeeper call in sick or something?" I asked as I stepped over one of the suitcases.

"I had to tell her not to come for a few weeks," William replied. "I can't risk her finding anything out, so it's best she not be here."

"And this is what happens when you don't have a housekeeper to clean up after you?"

William cringed and had the decency to look a touch embarrassed. "I'm not all that domesticated. I've lived by myself for so long I've never needed to give it much thought."

"You're lucky you're rich," I said. I tried to resist the urge to clean up after him, but had to move some clothes just to find a seat on the sofa.

"I'll clean it up later today, I promise. I hadn't realized it had gotten so bad. You stay there. Give me ten minutes to clean up the worst of it."

As soon as William left the room, I pulled out my laptop and sent an email to Lauren. My editor had been right about there being a story here, but I also knew I didn't want to write it.

Whatever the exact details ended up being, this was clearly a story centering around a child, and I didn't want her dragged into the middle of a political issue that had nothing to do with her.

My email to Lauren explained that Senator Larson and William knew each other from previous fundraising events and that they had a mutual acquaintance. In my version of events, Kaylee was a former flame of William's with whom he had been more infatuated than he liked to admit. The senator knew the woman from law school and had promised to help repair the barriers after William cheated on her.

Lauren would be disappointed to read the story, but not exactly surprised either. It would fit with the stereotype of a billionaire who throws his toys out of the stroller when he can't get what he wants. If Lauren ever caught me in the lie, my career would sink as quickly as it had risen, but that was a risk I had to take.

William had gone to a lot of effort to keep this whole thing secret and if it weren't for me, Lauren would never have found out in the first place. The least I could do was cover it up.

"There we go," William said, and he fell down onto the sofa in mock exhaustion after ten minutes' work. "Good as new."

I raised my eyebrows as I looked around the room. He had moved some of the mess and shoved it out of sight, but that was about the extent of it. "You tidy up like a man, you know that?"

"I'll get the housekeeper back in," William conceded. "The risk is worth it. You don't want to know what I saw growing in the sink."

"You're right, I don't. So then, are you going to tell me what's going on with Kaylee and your sister?"

William nodded. "I've told you about Olivia already. There isn't much else left to say other than that she had a kid with some jerk who promptly left her. I have no idea how a guy like him could father someone as beautiful and charismatic as Kaylee."

"She must get it from her mother."

"That's what I like to think," William said. "Olivia used to be like that once, but now… She's in a bad way. Has been for some time."

"I'm guessing you started looking after Kaylee when Olivia was unable to?" Olivia likely had drink or drug problems, but William didn't like to go into details and I didn't particularly need to know anyway.

"Yes. Adrian and I spent a lot of time with Kaylee, but Adrian had less time to spend with her as his business took off."

"You have a business to run too," I pointed out. "You shouldn't have had to raise her by yourself."

"I wanted to. At first, I pretended that looking after her was a chore, but I must have enjoyed it, otherwise I would have just paid for a babysitter."

"She looks like a lot of fun." I still had the photo in my hand and kept looking down at it every few seconds. Kaylee was undeniably cute, but there was also a hint of mischief in her eyes. I imagined she could be a handful when she wanted to be, although that was likely true of all kids.

"She is."

"So, where is she now?" I asked. "I'd love to meet her. I don't have a lot of experience around kids, but if you can manage it, then it can't be that hard."

"Thanks," William said. He pretended to sound offended, but I saw him smile.

"You're welcome."

"A year ago, Child Protective Services took Kaylee from her mother."

"Oh my God, I'm so sorry. But can't you fight that? You're her uncle. You can ask to be her guardian. Or adopt her."

William's head sunk forward. "I tried. It didn't work. There was a hearing. The court rejected my claim and ordered her back into protective services. They haven't been able to place her with a family, so she's been there ever since."

"That's crazy. Why on earth would they do that when she could have been placed with her uncle?"

"It's my fault," William said slowly. "I blew it."

"It's not your fault," I insisted. "Can you

222

appeal? Do you know why you weren't awarded custody?"

"The judge didn't approve of Adrian and me. She thought we were playboys and didn't want to put a child into that kind of lifestyle. That's not why this is my fault. Adrian and I, we were the ones who called CPS in the first place. We're the reason Kaylee was taken from my sister. We're the reason she's now without parents. I have to do something, Amanda. I have to get Kaylee out of there."

Chapter Six

I had no doubt in my mind that Kaylee would have been better with William than in the system. She would have a loving, doting parent who had the means to provide her with whatever she wanted.

I needed a moment to clear my head so I went to the kitchen and made some coffee. I hadn't ordered any while we were in the café because I had been distracted by John, and now my body craved caffeinated refreshment.

I tried to piece together what was going on, but there were still too many gaps in my knowledge. How would a senator be able to help get a child away from CPS? He would have a lot of influence, but ultimately the case had gone to court and a politician couldn't just overrule that.

Then there was the briefcase that Adrian had collected from Professor Winston. Something in that briefcase would help get Kaylee back, but I had no idea what it could be. How would an old law professor working in international law be able to help get a child out of protective services?

I made both coffees strong, but added some

milk to mine. William preferred black coffee, but I needed something to take the edge off the bitter taste. I couldn't tell whether my brain worked quicker with coffee or if it just refused to work without it, but either way I felt better as soon as the aroma reached my nose. Now I could think. If William needed ideas, I might actually be able to help.

"Here you go," I said, passing William the coffee, which he immediately started drinking even though the water was barely below boiling temperature. "You're going to burn your tongue one day doing that."

"My tongue is just fine, thank you. I'm sure you can attest to that."

I grinned and sat down next to him. I realized I'd already forgiven him. It hadn't taken long, but everything he said made so much sense I couldn't help but accept what he'd told me. I pulled out my phone and fiddled with the settings to unblock William. I had never deleted his number from my contacts. That was a clear sign I hadn't been ready to forget him.

"What are we going to do?" I asked. "I don't know much about how this works. Can you apply to adopt her again?"

"No," William said, shaking his head. "I can apply, but my lawyer advised me that it'll take a long time. Years. While the appeal is ongoing, she won't be eligible for adoption elsewhere. Obviously it would kill me to see her adopted by another family, but I would prefer that to the current situation. If I'm going to act, I need to do it quickly."

"What happened with your sister? Can she clean herself up and ask to take Kaylee back into her care?"

William shook his head. "We can't get her into shape. We've tried. We paid for the best treatment money can buy, but it's no good. Adrian even moved in with her for a while to see if that would help."

"Does she have a drug problem?"

"Not any more," William said. "But she did. The problems are now mental. We don't even know what caused them, although I'm fairly certain her ex-boyfriend, Kaylee's father, had something to do with it. If we could get her back to normal, she could apply for custody of Kaylee, but that will take longer than my appeal."

"You've obviously been working on something. What are you planning? Maybe I can help. I don't know if you've noticed, but I'm pretty good at uncovering secrets people want to keep hidden."

William laughed. "Yes, Sophie told me you'd sold a big story on Congressman Hutchins. Quite impressive."

"You've been talking to Sophie?" I asked.

"She shared some updates on what you were working on as an excuse for why you were too busy to come to the door. Plus, she's still hoping I'll set her up with Adrian. Apparently she keeps bumping into him. She's convinced herself the two of them are fated to be together."

"Oh, God, that girl is kind of crazy sometimes."

"She's interesting. She pretends to be a little ditzy, but I think that's all an act."

"You're not actually thinking of setting her up with Adrian, are you?"

"Why not?" William asked. "They might be a good match. I'm not going to do anything just yet—Adrian's too distracted at the moment—but maybe in the future."

I still had an irrational dislike of Adrian, but that wasn't fair. At first, I had assumed he was corrupt, but everything he had been doing was for Kaylee. Adrian was only as guilty as William, so I should cut him some slack. It would be nice to see Sophie settle down, and if she spent time with Adrian I would have fewer strange men in my apartment.

"Let's wait until all this is sorted out first. I assume you have a plan in place to get Kaylee back. What are we going to do? And before you say anything, it *is* a 'we.' I'm working with you on this."

"I'm not going to argue with that. There's still a part of me that wants to keep you out of this in case it goes wrong, but I need your help. I had hoped to do this by myself, but Kaylee is more important than my ego."

"How is the senator involved in all this?" I asked.

"He's an old friend. His dad was friends with my dad. We saw a lot of each other as kids but then lost contact until we started seeing each other at fundraising events. I didn't want to ask him for help, but I had no choice."

"What can a senator do, though? Does he have any power in all this?"

"He has some influence, but he's taking a huge risk for me. Robert's putting pressure on people within the system to have the case reopened without going through all the usual channels. He thinks he's found a procedural problem with the case that might be enough to justify a rehearing. I usually hate it when

227

technicalities force retrials, but in this case I can live with it."

"If anyone finds out he got personally involved in a case, he'll never get re-elected," I pointed out. I tended to picture all politicians as selfish, but maybe there were some good ones out there after all.

"Like I said, he's taking a huge risk. Robert's a good man. I wish there were more like him in D.C., but he's one of a few. I know he's frustrated with politics, so he's doing this because it means he can help someone."

"So the plan is to get the case reopened. Who's to say that the same judge won't hear the case and refuse to grant you custody again?"

"It's a possibility," William admitted. "I have a backup plan in that case, but I'd rather not go through with it."

The briefcase. "I saw Adrian pick up a briefcase after meeting with Professor Winston in a restaurant. That's your backup plan, isn't it?"

William nodded, but wouldn't say anything.

"What's in the briefcase?" I asked.

"Something I hope never sees the light of day. I'll tell you if I have to, but for now I'd rather pretend it doesn't exist."

"Okay, I can live with that. For now, let's just focus on getting this case reopened. We'll have Kaylee back in no time."

Chapter Seven

I tried doing some research on family law matters, but I didn't have anywhere near enough time to wrap my head around such a complex subject. Besides, I wasn't a lawyer and didn't think like one. Even finding which laws were relevant was harder than I anticipated. I prided myself on finding the information I wanted online, but when it came to legal research I was well and truly out of my depth.

"I'm getting hungry," William said, looking at the time on his phone. "It's nearly seven o'clock. Do you want to eat?"

"It's seven o'clock already?" I exclaimed. "I've been looking at this stuff for three hours now."

"I know. I didn't want to disturb you. You're cute when you're concentrating on something complicated."

The second I stopped working I realized how hungry I was. My stomach growled loudly enough for William to hear.

"I guess that's a 'yes' to dinner, then?" William asked with a smile. "You want to get takeout?"

"No, let's eat out tonight. If we stay here then we'll have to tidy up first so we have somewhere to sit at the table."

"Fair point. Come on, then, let's get a move on. I have a place in mind, but the chef is infuriatingly slow."

My stomach growled again. This time I suspected the growl was in protest of the small portions we would inevitably get at one of William's preferred restaurants. The food was no doubt of top quality, but right now I was craving something fried.

"Can I choose the restaurant this time?" I asked. "I need a big portion of something disgustingly unhealthy and I don't want to wait two hours for it to be cooked."

William shrugged and grabbed his keys from the table. "Fine by me. At least that way I won't have to make small talk with all the boring regulars. The choice is all yours."

"This is your choice?" William asked as we stood outside a popular southern-style diner in downtown San Francisco, looking at the menu. "I'm not sure what half of the items on here are."

"Now you know how I feel when you take me to restaurants where half of the menu is in French. Besides, you grew up poor. Don't tell me you've never had this kind of food before."

"My mom would never have let me eat this stuff as a kid. How about you choose for me? I always do that for you when we go to one of my restaurants, so it's only fair."

I laughed and grabbed William by the hand to

drag him inside. The restaurant was a little rough around the edges, but the food was genuinely excellent and they made fresh fruit smoothies that were so good I preferred drinking them to cocktails.

Even though I'd been here many times before, I didn't have a lot of experience with the menu. On my first visit I'd ordered chicken with waffles and it was so good that I hadn't been able to order anything else since. I'd seen friends order the pork belly over grits and that looked good, but it might be a little too unfamiliar for William.

"Let's both get the chicken and waffles," I said to William. "No starters or side dishes, though. They do great beignets that I want for dessert."

"Do chicken and waffles go together?" William asked. "Sounds like an unusual combination to me."

"It works, trust me." I ordered the food, but let William choose his own drink. We both ended up going with an apple and mango smoothie, though. The waitress either thought we were cute or boring for getting the same food; I couldn't quite tell which.

"So," William began, leaning forward and staring into my eyes, "tell me about this story you were working on while you were blocking all my calls and messages."

"Oh, yeah, sorry about that. I suppose I should apologize. I got that completely wrong."

William shook his head. "No apology required. You jumped to the most logical conclusion. Besides, it's my fault for not letting you in on everything. At least the trip to D.C. ended up being productive for you after all."

"I can't believe how well it all came together," I admitted. "Managing to catch a corrupt congressman talking about accepting bribes for contracts was lucky enough, but I figured it would take me months of digging from there to get a story."

"What happened?" William asked. "Did he just confess to everything?"

"No, but it sounds like he will. The other man did confess, though. He'd been having an affair and didn't want anyone to find out. It was all pretty easy after that."

"You only managed to get the story so easily because you have great instincts. Honestly, if I had brought you in on all this from the start, I'd probably have Kaylee back already."

Just mentioning her name seemed to drain the energy out of him. I wanted to take his mind off her and nearly suggested going for a drink after our meal, but I was far too exhausted myself. The story had kept me awake for an unhealthy amount of time and right now I needed some sleep.

When the food arrived, William looked like he didn't know where to start. The portion was huge and I suddenly felt like I'd been a little too ambitious. Despite a cautious start, I soon noticed William devouring the food and there was nothing left on his plate by the time he put down his knife and fork.

"Are you going to admit to enjoying that?"

"Nope," William replied. "Because then I'll never hear the end of it. You still want dessert?"

I shook my head. "I'm stuffed, and I'm also kind of tired. Can we just head home?"

"Of course. Your eyes do look a little heavy. I think an early night's in order."

I raised my eyebrows and tried to give him a flirty smile, but I knew I wouldn't have the energy to do anything more than sleep in bed tonight. Sure enough, the last thing I remember from that evening was collapsing down on the soft sheets and telling William I'd just rest my eyes for ten minutes. I didn't open them again until morning.

Chapter Eight

"Good morning."

I felt William's strong arms hugging me in close to his chest. I was still fully clothed, but he had gotten undressed and his chest warmed my face.

"Morning," I replied, clearing my throat as I did so. The light streaming in through the blinds meant it must be at least eight in the morning. I'd slept for over ten hours.

"Feeling a little better?" William asked. "You slept like a log the entire night. You didn't even stir when I got into bed."

"I guess I was tired. Were you tempted to wake me up when you came to bed? I wouldn't have minded."

The long sleep had done me a world of good. Instead of taking half an hour to feel awake, my mind was already buzzing and raring to go. My eyes were wide open and I could have jumped out of bed if I wanted to. My desire to stay in William's arms had nothing to do with wanting to go back to sleep.

"I wanted to undress you when I came to bed," William said. "But I thought it might be a little weird if you woke up naked."

"For future reference, you should definitely feel free to undress me. In fact, I'm feeling kind of trapped in all these clothes. Feel like helping me out of them?"

"I think I can manage that."

William rolled me onto my back and pulled my top off over my head. I cringed when I saw the old bra that I had shoved on yesterday. I'd had no intention of sleeping with William when I got dressed, but fortunately he discarded the bra with a hunger I had missed in my weeks apart from him.

"God, I've missed these," he said as his left hand squeezed my breast. He placed his lips over my nipple and sucked hard as I squirmed under his touch.

I reached under the covers to explore William's naked body. My fingers ran down over his firm abs until I found his hard shaft waiting for me.

"I'm about ready to blow," William said. "As soon as I get inside you. These last few weeks have been painful without your tight pussy to help me relieve the stress."

William moved his hands down to the waistband of my pants and pulled them down my legs, taking my panties with them. I felt free. Being naked in bed with William was liberating. It wasn't just what he could do with his cock; it was much more than that. As our naked bodies mingled together I felt complete in a way that I never did without him.

William's head moved down my body,

heading towards my sex. I grabbed his hair and pulled him back up until his lips locked with mine, our tongues clashing in my mouth.

"Just fuck me," I whispered in his ear. "I can't wait any longer to feel you inside me. I want to feel the flesh of your cock as you explode inside me."

"Are you sure?" William asked.

I nodded, using my leg to pull his body on top of mine. My pussy was already dripping wet and he entered me with ease.

"That feels so good, Amanda," he moaned in my ear. "I love feeling your wetness on my cock as I fuck your tight little pussy."

My fingers dug into the firm skin of his back as he ground his hips on top of mine. I needed this so much. I hadn't even masturbated since the last time we'd fucked in D.C. and I felt ready to blow. I came within minutes, digging my nails into his back as his muscles tensed up and his cock exploded, leaving a sticky goodness inside me.

William reluctantly rolled off and lay next to me as we both recovered. Sticky sweat covered my body and the insides of my thighs were wet with my excitement.

"I'm so glad you came to find me in the coffee shop," I said once my breath was slow enough for me to speak. "I needed that."

"Me too," William replied. He turned to lie on his side and face me. His fingers danced lightly over my stomach, occasionally moving up and teasing my erect nipples. "I just wish you didn't have to go through all that pain and doubt over these last few weeks. It must have been awful for you to hear what you did and not know who I was talking about."

"It was," I replied, "but it wasn't your fault.

You didn't know I was listening and I jumped to the wrong conclusion. I just tried to not think about it. That's why I threw myself into that other story."

"I wish I'd never said it."

"Don't say that," I said. "You do love her, and I can hardly blame you for that. It's sweet that you feel so strongly for her."

"I could have phrased it differently. I don't love her more than anyone else in the world. I love her, but there's room for me to love more than one person."

William stared into my eyes with a serious look on his face. I felt scared and my heart raced in my chest. A big moment was coming and I was entirely unprepared for it.

"I love you," William said. "Kaylee was the only girl in my heart, but now there's two and I love you both."

My mouth suddenly felt dry and nerves clenched hold of my stomach. I didn't know what to do. This was how I'd always felt before exams, knowing that whatever happened next might change my life entirely.

I suddenly felt sick, but I didn't take my eyes off of William. His eyes held a hopeful expectation, but the longer I went without saying anything the more his eyes began to lose hope.

"I… I've never said that before," I muttered.

"It's okay," William said. "You don't have to say anything." I could tell he would be heartbroken if I didn't.

"No one has ever said those words to me. Except for family." My voice was weak and timid; I didn't know if I would have the strength to say it with the conviction I wanted.

"Let's just get up and get dressed," William

said, finally turning his eyes away from me. "I shouldn't have said it. That was too soon."

"Wait," I said. I reached out and grabbed his arm. He paused for a moment before turning to look at me again. The nerves were still there, but that didn't mean I was uncertain. I knew what I wanted to say, I just had to say it. "I love you too."

Chapter Nine

I spent the rest of the week walking around with a huge grin on my face. Sophie knew something was up immediately, so I told her what William and I had said to each other. It still seemed somewhat surreal. Sophie asked if things were moving too fast, but I didn't feel that way at all.

To Sophie, I probably looked like a living cliché, but I really did feel like I was walking on air. I knew William and I had a tough time ahead of us, but we were working together now so the problems didn't feel insurmountable.

John got in touch and invited me out for drinks. I had assumed he was just being polite after our last meeting got interrupted, but he genuinely did want to get together one day after work. William was busy catching up on all the business issues he'd been postponing, so I jumped at the chance to socialize. Now that I was officially in love, I found I wanted to spend as much time out and about as possible. Being indoors seemed like a waste of my good mood.

John selected a bar downtown that I had

never heard of before, but they had music and cheap drinks so it ticked all the boxes as far as I was concerned. I arrived a little early so I ordered a gin and tonic and took a seat at a table in the corner. I'd brought a book along with me, but the music was too loud for me to concentrate on reading. Plus, it felt a little odd to be reading a book in a dark bar.

I settled for doing what everyone else was doing and stared at my phone instead. Ever since I'd found out about Kaylee and what had happened to her, my mind had started running through theories and ways I might be able to help. Instinctively, I knew it was useless—William had high-priced lawyers who hadn't been able to help, so what good would I do? However, while I waited for John to arrive it seemed like the only thing worth occupying my mind with.

The woman who had caused all the problems for William was Judge Madelyn Roscoe. The judge had refused to send Kaylee to live with William because—according to her, at least—William lived a playboy lifestyle and couldn't be trusted to bring up a child. You only had to look into William's eyes when he talked about Kaylee to know that he would make a great parent for her.

I assumed Madelyn Roscoe would be an elderly, conservative judge who was out of touch with the way the world worked in the 21st century, but that wasn't the case. She looked about fifty— which wasn't old for a judge—and her election campaigns were based on a liberal agenda. She made no secret of being pro gay marriage and her support for equal rights was plastered all over her website.

Judge Roscoe sat in family court, so the

cases she heard were mainly divorce and child custody cases. I didn't have access to most of her case decisions, but a few were published and generally she gave decisions in line with the values she'd talked about when she was trying to get elected. So why had she taken such a dislike to William?

"Who's that?" John asked as he sat down next to me.

"Oh, hi, John. You want me to get you a drink? I have a tab open."

"I just ordered one. They'll bring it over in a minute. Do I know her?" He nodded again to my phone. I had a picture on my screen of the judge from her website biography.

"Oh, no, I doubt it. She's a judge. Does she look familiar?" I passed John the phone and he took a close look at the picture as a waiter dropped off something blue and toxic looking.

"She does look familiar," John said. "I don't know any judges, though. I can't place where I know her from. Damn, that's going to annoy me now."

"Try not to think about it. It'll come to you eventually. If you do figure out where you know her from, let me know."

John frowned. "Are you working on another story? Oh, do I get to be a part of a scandal? That sounds exciting."

"I am, but I have to keep my cards close to my chest, I'm afraid."

"I suppose I can let you off that one. I know Emily already owes you one because of your discretion. So, what's the plan for tonight?"

Plan? I had assumed we'd just meet for a few drinks and then go our separate ways. It sounded like John had a full night planned.

"You want to go somewhere else after this?" I asked. I tried to sound eager, but despite my vastly improved mood since William had told me he loved me, I still felt a way off from a night of dancing.

"I haven't been out in ages," John said. "Michael has to work nights all the time, so I need a good dance and I don't like to do it alone."

I sighed and gulped my drink. "All right, but you have to pretend to be straight and stop other men from grabbing at me."

"I'll do my best, darling," John said in an exaggeratedly campy tone with his pinky extended into the air. "Come on, let's go to the first bar we hear playing a Taylor Swift song."

Water. I need water. My mouth was so dry. I felt like I had woken up in the middle of the desert. My cellphone vibrated on a hard surface nearby. There probably wasn't cellphone reception in the desert.

I was in my bedroom. In bed. Well, *on* the bed fully clothed. *Never again. I'm never going drinking with John again.*

My head hurt like hell, but I forced my eyes open and picked up my phone from the table. A message from William.

It's on. We're going to meet with Rob Larson. Come to my place ASAP.

Chapter Ten

I had heard people describe shocking events as being "sobering," as if merely hearing surprising news could shake off all the cobwebs, wake up your brain, and rehydrate your body. William's message had definitely shocked me, but my body refused to sober up.

I got out of bed gingerly and threw on some clothes. I should have showered and washed my hair, but then I'd have to wait for it to dry and I had the distinct impression I didn't have time for such luxuries.

I didn't hold politicians in especially high regard, but even so, meeting a senator was a big deal and usually I would make an effort. I felt like I should wear a dress at the very least, but the only dresses I owned—and that were clean—were better suited to a night out rather than meeting an elected official.

I couldn't stomach cereal, so I prepared a couple of slices of dry toast and, for a few blissful minutes after eating it, I felt like my hangover was going to disappear and let me get on with my day.

I hadn't even made it out of my building before that proved to be nothing but wishful thinking.

There was a light breeze in the air, but to me it felt like a gale force wind battering against my head. No matter which direction I faced the wind seemed to blow directly into me, making my headache worse with each step.

I stopped at a convenience store on the way to William's to pick up an energy drink and that did make me feel less queasy, but it did nothing for the headache. At least the wind gave me a decent excuse for showing up with bed hair. The mirror in the elevator gave me a chance to smooth down my hair and tidy up my clothes, but it would still be immediately obvious that I had just rolled out of bed.

Two deep voices came from inside William's apartment. Both voices were familiar. A feeling of déjà vu came over me briefly as once again I found myself listening to a conversation between William and Senator Larson while hidden out of sight. My stomach contracted until my mind reminded my body that this time there would be no feeling of heartbreak at what I overheard.

William's door was usually unlocked while he was at home, but I knocked anyway. I couldn't be sure what William had told the senator about our relationship and if I just strolled right in, it would be obvious we were an item.

"Come in," William called.

I took a deep breath and tried to ignore my body telling me to crawl back into bed and go back to sleep. William walked up and kissed me as soon as I walked inside, letting me know there was no need to keep our relationship a secret.

"Rob, this is Amanda," William said,

introducing me to the senator.

"William has told me all about you," Senator Larson said as he shook my hand. "You sound like quite the remarkable woman."

"Thank you, Senator," I replied.

"Please, call me Rob or Robert. I hate the formal title and it doesn't seem appropriate today, given what we're here to discuss."

Robert's official photos all made him look like he was about forty, but he had to be in his early thirties. His staff must have made him look older in the pictures to give him an air of authority, but they needn't have bothered. Even dressed in a polo shirt and chinos, he exuded a sense of power and confidence that was almost on a par with William's. Robert didn't have the same financial influence, but he clearly exerted a lot of power.

"Okay, Robert it is," I replied. "I hope you don't mind me saying, but you're young for a senator."

William groaned and looked up at the ceiling and back down again. "Don't tell him that. He has enough of an ego as it is."

Robert laughed. "Ignore him. He's just jealous that I've met the president. I only got elected because the previous candidate had to pull out at the last minute. I took his place as the Democratic candidate and reaped the rewards of all his hard work."

"Well, I'm still impressed," I said. "And I'm also impressed by men who can make billions of dollars before their thirtieth birthday," I said to William before giving him a kiss on the cheek and letting him wrap his strong arm around my shoulders.

"I can see why you like her," Robert said.

"She's not intimidated by you. You always needed someone who would stand up to you."

"She certainly does that," William said. "Okay, let's get down to business, shall we?"

The smile quickly disappeared from Robert's face as we all sat down around the table. I moved gingerly so as not trigger any desire to throw up, but if anyone noticed my trepidation they didn't say anything.

"Sorry for insisting on this meeting at such short notice," Robert said. "I'm only in the area for a few days and it's nigh on impossible to get my security team to leave me alone for five minutes. Fortunately this building has more security than the White House, so I got permission to come up here alone."

"It's no problem," William said. "I'm just glad you're here. Does your presence mean you have good news?"

"Yes," Robert said, although he didn't sound enthusiastic. "Some good news, some bad news."

"Let's start with the good news first," William said.

"The good news is that Kaylee's case has been reopened."

"That's great news," I exclaimed. "How did you manage that?" I regretted my question as soon as I asked it, because there was a good chance I didn't want to hear exactly how he'd arranged it.

"I asked nicely," Robert replied. "It's amazing how people are prepared to forget protocol when they're faced with a request from a U.S. senator."

"When?" William asked eagerly. "When will her case be heard?"

"Soon," Robert said. "But that brings me to

246

the bad news. I'm sorry, William. There was nothing I could do about the next step. You don't get to pick and choose the judge."

"Shit," William said tersely.

"The judge is Roscoe?" I asked. It seemed the most likely explanation, but I wanted to be sure I was on the right wavelength.

Robert nodded. "We already know she isn't your friend, but maybe she'll change her mind. There is another option, but I don't think you'll like it."

"What is it?" William asked. "I don't want Kaylee to have to go through all this only to be knocked back into the system by that bitch. What's the other option?"

"Wait until after the next election," Robert replied.

"That's a good idea," I said. "She may not get re-elected, and then you can try again."

"No, she'll get re-elected," Robert said. "She won the last one by a landslide."

"So why wait until after the elections?" I asked.

"Because *I* may not stand for re-election. When I'm no longer a senator I can get more involved in the case. I'll still have influence, but won't have to worry about abusing my position to interfere in state matters. I will even get a job with CPS if I have to."

"Robert's a lawyer as well as a senator," William said when he saw how confused I looked. "I bet you're thinking you picked the wrong guy now, aren't you," he joked.

"I know, I know," I replied. "But sometimes a girl just has to settle for a handsome billionaire."

I looked back to Robert and saw him smiling

at us. "You two are cute."

A few moments of silence passed until William spoke up. "I can't wait that long. I know these things take time, but I've waited long enough. I'm not a patient man. Not where Kaylee is concerned."

"What are you going to do?" Robert asked.

"I'm not going to tell you." Robert went to speak, but William spoke over him. "I appreciate everything you've done so far, but you should stay clear of what happens next."

Robert nodded and stood up to leave. "Good luck, William."

"Thanks," William replied, shaking Robert's hand. "I can't live without her any longer. I'm going to get Kaylee back, whatever it takes."

Chapter Eleven

"We shouldn't be doing this," I warned William. I knew nothing about legal practice or how to deal with court hearings, but I knew that it was a really bad idea to confront a judge before the hearing.

"I need to give her a chance," William replied. "I want to give her a chance to do the right thing before I completely fuck up her life."

"Couldn't you be held in contempt of court?" I asked. "There are bound to be rules against talking to judges who are sitting on cases you have an interest in."

"Probably," William replied. "But what's the worst that can happen? If she reports me for it, that means she wasn't going to decide in my favor anyway. I'd rather not resort to blackmailing her if I can help it."

"You're too nice," I replied. "Going by what I know about the last hearing, it sounds like she deserves to be punished."

There was no public transcript of the original hearing available because a minor was involved, but William had told me that the judge had made the reasoning for her decision clear. She didn't like William and Adrian and felt they didn't deserve to have custody of a child.

The whole thing still sounded a little odd to me. In public, the judge insisted she was as liberal as anyone, so why would she care if someone like William took custody of Kaylee? I suspected William had played the field a bit in the past, but that was no reason to deny him the chance to look after Kaylee. With William, Kaylee could grow up having whatever she wanted. As a child waiting to be placed with a foster family, she wouldn't get much of anything beyond three meals a day and some secondhand clothes.

We waited outside the court for the judge to arrive. She didn't have a case until ten o'clock so we arrived thirty minutes early to lie in wait. The courtroom was small, but even so there were remarkably few people going inside. The lawyers were easy to spot. Most of them were carrying briefcases and were dressed in suits and ties, but they looked rushed and stressed as they jogged up the steps to the entrance.

I didn't see any young children being taken into the courtroom, but that was probably for the best. I certainly didn't want Kaylee to be in the courtroom when such a big decision was made about her future, especially if the decision was one William didn't like. I dreaded to think what his reaction would be if he lost this case and had to look at Kaylee as she was being taken away.

"There she is," William said. He was already halfway to the judge before I even spotted her getting out of her car.

I jogged to catch up with him, but he didn't slow down. The plan was to catch up with Judge

Roscoe as far from the courtroom as possible. The courthouse had security and if any of them saw a judge being harassed we'd find ourselves in trouble pretty quickly.

William was on her before she had even locked her car. He slowed as he approached to seem less threatening. He'd made it clear that this wasn't about scaring the judge or threatening her. He wanted to give her a chance to explain her previous actions and do the right thing.

"Judge Roscoe," William said as he approached. "I'm William Townsend."

"I know who you are, Mr. Townsend. And I know that you shouldn't be here. I suggest you walk away very quickly."

The judge had recognized William right away. With the amount of cases she heard, there was no way she should be able to recognize one person that easily. William had been right: the judge had it in for him and likely his brother as well.

If she did have some personal reason to dislike William, she should never have heard the case in the first place. Any judge can step aside if they have a conflict of interest; that was what she should have done the first time and it was what she should do this time.

"I want to know why you decided not to let Kaylee live with me. You must have had a reason. You owe me an explanation."

"I owe you nothing," the judge spat back. "You heard my explanation and I included it in my written report."

"That wasn't the real reason," William insisted. He was doing a remarkably good job of remaining calm. "I know there's more to it than that."

"Step aside, Mr. Townsend. I can easily call security from here."

"I've appealed the decision," William said. "You've been assigned to the case again."

"Yes, I saw that," the judge said. If she was feeling under any pressure from this meeting, she wasn't showing it. "I'm going to make my decision in accordance with the law, as I always do. I see nothing in you or your brother that has changed recently, so I'm sure my decision will be an easy one."

"I implore you to make an impartial decision," William said. "Whatever it is you don't like about me and my brother, please put it to one side for the sake of this little girl. Her life will be so much better with me. Either step aside or make the right decision."

"Oh, I do *not* like where this is going, Mr. Townsend," the judge said, a slight smile appearing on her face. "Is this the part where you attempt to bribe a judge? Please tell me it is. I do love seeing billionaires end up in prison because they don't get their own way on something."

"No blackmail," William said. "Not yet, anyway. If, and this is just an if, I had anything I could use to blackmail a judge, I might just release it to the general public and let them be the judge and jury."

This must have something to do with the briefcase, I thought. What did William have in there that he could use to scare the judge? Judge Roscoe and William stared at each other for a few seconds, until the judge finally looked away.

"Goodbye, Mr. Townsend. If I see you within fifty feet of me or this courthouse again, I will have you held in contempt."

I caught the look of worry on her face as she walked away. Unfortunately, while she might have skeletons in the closet, she didn't look like she was about to give in to William's requests.

"What now?" I asked.

William sighed. "I think it's time you finally met my brother."

Chapter Twelve

"Why are we going to see your brother?" I asked. "And where are we going?"

William led the way from the courthouse and called a car to take us to the other end of the city. We weren't going to Adrian's place of work. Judging by all the large apartment buildings around us, we were probably going to his house.

"Adrian will be at home right now," William said. "Alone, hopefully."

"Are we going to get the briefcase?" I asked.

William didn't respond for a few seconds. "He has it with him. I'd rather not take it, but it looks like that's the only option."

"What's so bad about the briefcase?" I asked. "I think it's time you told me. We're about to go talk to your brother about it. I can hardly contribute to the conversation if I don't know what we're talking about."

"I'll tell you if I end up taking it."

"William, I'm going to look stupid in there if I have to sit still and keep my mouth shut. Is that really what you want your brother to think of me?"

William took a deep breath and let out a long, slow sigh. His fingers gripped the door handle; I didn't know if he was mad at me for pressuring him or just angry about what was in the briefcase.

"It's information," William said. "Photos, emails, and even a few handwritten letters."

I had a strong feeling I knew what was in the briefcase. "She had an affair," I said. "With the professor who gave Adrian the briefcase."

William nodded. "I wish it was just that. She has a family□; a husband and three kids. She's had a string of affairs ever since she was married and going by these emails, she doesn't think any of her children were fathered by her husband."

"Oh, Jesus. That's awful for the kids."

"Exactly. One of them is about seventeen, but the others are younger. This would tear the family apart."

"She has it coming to her," I said. "The kids will move on from this. You shouldn't feel bad about using this against her. I don't know how she has the nerve to criticize your lifestyle."

"She's a hypocrite," William said. "But she's mastered her public persona. She wins each judicial election in a landslide, but behind closed doors she's a vile human being."

"Vile? There's something else, isn't there? What else is in the briefcase?"

The car stopped outside a large apartment building and the driver opened the door. William got out first and helped me out of the car, but he still hadn't answered my question.

"I'll tell you upstairs," William said. "I don't want to talk about it outside."

A few months ago, being in an apartment like

this would have been awe-inspiring, but having been in William's apartment I was now getting used to it. Going back to my own place would be painful.

Adrian opened the door to his apartment and immediately gave William a hug, as if they hadn't seen each other in a while.

"You must be Amanda," Adrian said as he gave me a kiss on the cheek. "Nice to meet you."

Adrian's apartment was roughly the same size as William's but it couldn't have looked more different. William kept things minimalistic, whereas Adrian had flashy devices and gadgets everywhere the eye could see. I didn't even know what all the toys did. One device looked like a speaker, but then it spoke with a woman's voice to remind Adrian of an appointment he had in thirty minutes.

"Pleased to meet you at last," I replied. I initially felt uncomfortable being so close to the man I had been spying on not so long ago, but it was hard to be mad at a man with such a cheerful smile.

"Amanda's met you before," William said. "Sort of. She spied on you while you were meeting with Professor Winston."

"Oh yes, I forgot about that. I guess if William's invited you here, that means you're no longer investigating me."

"Not actively," I replied with a smile. "If you want to give me a story, though, I'm all ears."

"I like this one," Adrian said. "She has a little more bite than the ones you usually pick."

"Speaking of who you like," I said quickly, sensing an opportunity, "I have a friend who has kind of a crush on you. You've bumped into her a few times already, actually. Her name's Sophie Klein."

The color drained from Adrian's face at the mention of Sophie's name and for the first time since we had arrived he looked speechless.

"You alright?" William said, looking somewhat bemused. "You don't usually get spooked at the thought of meeting a woman."

"Huh? Oh, yeah, I'm fine," Adrian replied, then turned and walked over to a dining table. "Let's get started, shall we?"

William looked at me and shrugged. We sat down at the table and Adrian dropped the briefcase on top.

"Do you know what's in here?" Adrian asked me.

I nodded. "Mostly."

"I haven't told her about the articles yet," William said.

"Now would be a good time," I said.

"Judge Roscoe was very active when she was in law school," Adrian explained. "She wrote a lot of articles and impressed all her professors with the quality of her writing. Unfortunately the content of what she wrote wasn't so well-received."

William grabbed the briefcase and opened it. "She presents herself as some uber-liberal judge, because that's what it takes to get elected here, but her actual beliefs are a world away." He handed me some of the articles.

The titles of the articles were ambiguous, but I only had to flick through the introductory comments of each to notice how inflammatory her opinions were. When she was in law school, the judge had held strong views about homosexuality and what should happen to those who practiced it.

Her legal argument was weakly supported by random quotes taken out of context, but the rest was her opinion.

Adrian had been right about her writing. She could structure her thoughts well, it was just that in this case her thoughts were abhorrent.

"How has this never gotten out?" I asked. "Surely one of her opponents would have found this stuff and used it against her."

"She had them destroyed and removed from her academic record. Or at least she thought she did. I'm still not sure how, but she was in law school in the days before everything was done online, so that helps."

"This would destroy her," I remarked. "Why are you hesitating about bringing this out into the open?"

"*I'm* not hesitating," Adrian said. "I think we should do it immediately."

"I didn't want this to come out if it didn't have to," William said. "Just think how many court cases will get delayed after she's forced to resign. Her cases affect children's lives, and they'll be left in limbo until someone replaces her. Also, I looked into it and most of her decisions have been sensible. She's screwed us over, but otherwise she's decided cases pretty consistently. I didn't want to do this just to get revenge on her."

"But we're going to do this now, right?" Adrian asked. "I'm assuming that's why you're here?"

William nodded. "I think we have to. I don't see any other way. If it looks like she's going to decide against us again, then I'll show her this and see if she wants to reconsider."

"This is risky," I said. "She has already

threatened to have you held in contempt of court if you talk to her again."

"Let someone else do it," Adrian said. "I know a lot of people who'd spend a few months in jail in return for a few hundred thousand dollars. There's no need to put yourself through this."

William shook his head aggressively. "I can't. I can't let anyone else be responsible for this. I need to get Kaylee back, and I'm not about to put her future in someone else's hands."

Adrian went to argue, but then closed his mouth and nodded. "Okay, let's figure out how we're going to do this."

Chapter Thirteen

We had a week until the trial and no matter how much I racked my brain there didn't seem to be anything productive to do while we waited. I just had to be patient. Every journalist needs a degree of patience, but it wasn't a skill I had developed yet. Hopefully it would come with time, although I hoped to pick it up sooner rather than later.

My brain couldn't even begin to focus on a new story. I still had some money in the bank from my report on the corrupt congressman, but when you're freelancing, it's best not to rest on your laurels.

I decided to take some of Sophie's advice and focus on a few celebrity pieces just to keep my writing skills active. These days it was easy enough to write a few thousand words on a popular topic, add some appropriate celebrity photos and sell it to a website for a few hundred bucks. That sort of money wouldn't pay the rent, but it would cover my bills. I used a pen name to ensure I kept my reputation for hard-hitting journalism intact.

The website published the story remarkably quickly—they obviously didn't do a lot of fact-checking on stories like this one—so within a few days I had a story online that I could share with friends. I shared the story on my social website without telling anyone I had written it and it received more engagement than any of my more serious work ever had. I'm not sure quite what that says about my friends, but at least they enjoyed my writing.

William had been frustratingly busy and I had barely seen him all week. I stayed at his place one night but, like a drug, that wasn't enough and I needed more. I picked up my phone to ask if he was free, but received a message from him before I could finish typing.

I have tickets for the 49ers game tonight. Are you free?

I checked the time. The Thursday night games usually kicked off at seven o'clock and it was already five o'clock. We might just about make it down to Santa Clara in time for kickoff, but only if we left soon. The traffic at this time of day was a nightmare.

I quickly deleted the half-finished message I had been typing and sent a reply. *I'd love to go, but we'd have to leave soon.*

I'm outside your building now. Come on down.

William hadn't struck me at first as being the overly spontaneous type, but he certainly could be when he felt like it. I grabbed an old Niners sweater I kept in the closet and ran out of my apartment and into the waiting car.

I couldn't keep my hands off William the entire ride to the stadium, but he had some work to finish up and couldn't go thirty seconds without his phone vibrating for a new email.

This was my first time visiting the new 49ers stadium and the traffic around it was just as bad as I had been told. Fortunately William's driver took us straight to an exclusive parking lot where we could avoid the worst of it.

"Is it safe to assume you bought the most outrageously expensive seats you could get your hands on?" I asked. We were walking against the flow of the crowd toward a door with security guards standing outside it.

"You wouldn't be too far off," William replied. "We have an executive suite on the fifty yard line. It's not technically the most expensive one. The one next to us is slightly bigger, but one of the players bought that for friends and they get priority."

"So we have to slum it in the second-best suite, do we? Well, I guess I can live with that."

Once we'd gotten past security, a host escorted us up to the suite, which was big enough to hold fifteen people at least. There was a bar stocked with local craft beers and a full shelf of liquor. Two members of staff stood nearby to see to our every desire.

One of the waiters handed me a menu, so we ordered some appetizers and drinks.

"There are no prices on the menu," I said to William. The last time I'd gone to a football game, I'd paid $6 for a hot dog and $10 for a bad beer. I dreaded to think how much all this cost.

"It's all included in the price of the suite," William replied. "And no, I'm not telling you how much it costs."

"That's probably for the best. I imagine this

one night here could have paid for my entire college education. Is anyone else joining us?" I asked, looking around at all the empty seats.

"Nope, it's just us. If I invited anyone, it would have turned into a networking event or a business thing and I hate those. I can never understand why people go to football games and then do nothing but talk business."

"What about Adrian?" I asked. "Sophie's going to kill me when she finds out. This could have been a double date opportunity, you know."

"It's difficult around Adrian at the moment," William replied. "This whole thing with Kaylee has led to some tension between us. We didn't always agree on the best approach. We're still close, though, and once this is over things will be back to normal."

Watching football in such comfort felt utterly surreal. We had a soft leather sofa which made it like watching a game from home, the drinks service of a bar, and the atmosphere of being at the game. It was the best of all worlds.

By half time, I had a good idea why the conversation often turned towards business. Sometimes the games were just dull. Or depressing. In this case, the game was both. The 49ers hadn't found their rhythm at all and went into the second half down by ten. That soon turned into a thirteen-point deficit after the restart and things didn't look like they'd be getting better any time soon.

Just outside the suite was a row of seats that we could go out and sit on if we wanted to and the regular fans were right in front of that. I walked over and stood by the window to try to take it all in.

"I'm surprised people don't try to peek

through the window and see who's in here," I said. "I know if I were sitting right in front of an expensive suite I'd want to know who was inside in case they were famous."

"It's one-way glass, so they can't see in," William said. "Actually, the glass can switch from regular two-way glass to one-way glass at the press of a button. I have it set to one-way at the moment."

"Why?" I asked.

William didn't answer and instead turned to look back at the two waiters who were standing by the door in case we needed more drinks or food.

"We don't need anything else for the time being," William said to them. "I'll press the button if we need any further assistance." The two waiters nodded and left the room. "The glass is one-way in case I want to do something to you that's not suitable for viewing by the general public."

William moved behind me. One hand went to my stomach and the other went down my top and cupped my breast. I let him press his body against mine, his cock throbbing urgently against my ass.

"I can't be around you and not want to fuck you, Amanda," he said before fiercely kissing my neck. His hand moved slowly down from my stomach to between my legs. "I can feel how wet you are even through your pants. Take them off."

I hesitated at getting undressed so close to strangers, but they couldn't see me. I pulled down my pants and left my bottom half completely exposed and naked. William removed my top and bra to reveal my firm nipples.

Just ten feet in front of me was a group of men who—if it weren't for the one-way glass—would be able to turn around and see my complete nakedness. I felt terrified and excited. I didn't know how much I could trust the one-way glass, but I didn't care. The priority was getting William's cock inside me.

I heard his pants fall to the floor and felt his shaft rub against my flesh. The tip of his cock was already wet with his excitement. I leaned forward and pressed my hands against the cold glass to present my wet entrance to him.

"I love fucking you from behind," William said. "I get to see my hard cock sliding in and out of that beautiful wet pussy."

"Take me," I moaned. "Please, hurry. I need you inside me so fucking much right now."

William grabbed my hair and pulled my head back to give me another kiss on the neck. The other hand grabbed my breast as he thrust himself forward into my eager folds.

I let out a low, guttural groan as he entered me. I felt certain the people in front of me could hear, but if they did, none of them reacted to it. William pushed himself all the way inside me and moved his hands down to my hips. I steadied myself firmly against the glass as William pulled out, then slammed himself back inside me.

My moaning got louder each time his cock filled me. If the football fans couldn't hear me, then the waiters outside almost certainly could. I didn't care.

"I'm close," I moaned. "God, I'm so close."

William reached around and his fingers started rubbing my clit. Slowly at first, but then faster, always keeping it in pace with his thrusting.

"You're so beautiful," William said as he fucked me. "I love watching you come."

His words released the pressure that had built inside and I came hard the next time his cock entered me. My legs spasmed under me as I lost all the strength in my body. William supported me until he released his orgasm inside me moments later, then carried me back to the sofa to recover.

I wanted to lie down and get my breath back, but the game wasn't far from over and the wait staff would be back in soon. I got dressed although the sweat dripping down my back meant that I no longer needed the sweater.

William called the staff back into the room, but I couldn't look in their direction. My face would give me away instantly.

"Two glasses of wine, please," William said to the staff. "And I suddenly have quite an appetite. Please bring in another tray of those nachos." The staff disappeared and William turned to face me. "I've never been quite so happy after seeing my team lose by so much. We should watch games together more often."

"You read my mind."

This time on the way home William turned his phone off and didn't respond to emails. The trip back to San Francisco didn't take as long at night, but I enjoyed every minute of it.

Chapter Fourteen

Friday was the day of the hearing. I kept referring to it as the 'day of the trial' in my head, because it sure as hell felt like William was on trial. As the individual requesting custody of Kaylee, the proceedings would center around him. To me, it seemed like the easiest way to resolve the issue would be to ask Kaylee what she wanted to do, but apparently that wasn't how it worked, at least not with a child this young.

Our hearing time was three in the afternoon, which made us the last ones for the day. That didn't sound like anywhere near enough time to decide something so important, but the judge's calendar was split into one-hour blocks and no one was allocated more than two hours.

William and I went to the courthouse together, but he was soon whisked away by his lawyers, who wanted to go over his answers in more detail and make sure he was going to say the right thing. He'd been avoiding speaking to his legal counsel as much as possible. He felt that if he answered from the heart, that would be enough. I tended to agree with his lawyers—he should focus on saying the right things at the right time, even if that felt a little orchestrated.

Ten minutes before the hearing's start time, the doors to the courtroom opened and I stepped inside to take a seat in the public gallery. I chose a seat close to the front so that William could see me if he needed any support.

The courtroom was smaller than I had imagined, although it was no less intimidating for it. Even though the setting looked familiar from television, the high seat for the judge immediately gave off a sense of power over the lawyers who had to speak from a much lower and more modest table opposite the judge.

William would be talking from a witness box which was also raised from the floor, but still left him sitting much lower than the judge. If William were being grilled by lawyers, then the height would give him a slight advantage; however, in this case the judge would be grilling him and her sense of power would be exaggerated.

Fortunately, William didn't fear the judge and I didn't think her title or appearance in the courtroom would bother him. Even in the business world he didn't seem to put a lot of stock in titles and didn't care who he should look up to. I'd seen him treat baristas with the same respect he would treat the CEO of a Fortune 500 company, maybe more.

Judge Roscoe appeared in the courtroom and slumped down in her seat, motioning to her clerks to get the proceedings underway. If she had seen William, she didn't react to him at all. She couldn't have looked less interested, as if she had already mentally clocked out for the weekend.

William took his position in the witness box. To my surprise, he did look visibly nervous. I thought back to the day I had first met him in his office and how stressed he had looked. I hadn't known it at the time, but he was worried about Kaylee even then. He'd been thinking about this moment ever since the last hearing and now the moment was here. He wasn't nervous about facing the judge; he was nervous about losing Kaylee. William knew if it went wrong this time, he might not get another shot.

The judge started off by going through the procedural history of the previous hearing, during which she referred to Kaylee as the "subject" of the hearing. She also made it clear that this new hearing was the result of "unusual procedural issues." This wasn't a good start.

Finally, she turned to William and asked him a few basic questions about who he was and his relationship to Kaylee. William answered calmly and slowly, but it wasn't long before the judge revealed her true colors.

"Why did you try to take the subject away from your sister?" the judge asked. "That's quite a drastic step to take, Mr. Townsend."

"It was drastic," William replied, "but I didn't have any choice. My sister had changed a lot in the last couple of years. She had issues with the father of the child and that led to her drinking too much. In the end she turned to drugs."

"I agree, that doesn't sound like a safe environment for a child," the judge said. To anyone else in the courtroom she probably sounded sympathetic, but I knew it was an act.

"How long was it from when she started taking drugs to when you finally decided to call the authorities?"

"I don't know exactly when she started, but I noticed about a year before I put in the call."

"A *year*?" the judge asked incredulously. "You thought it was acceptable to leave the child with a drug addict for a year?"

"I didn't leave Kaylee with my sister," William replied. His words were calm and collected, but I could hear frustration slipping into his voice. *Stay calm, William.* "I looked after her most of the time. We tried to get my sister help. When it became clear that she wasn't improving, that was when I decided to call Child Protective Services for Kaylee."

"Did your sister, the mother of the child, consent to you taking the child, Mr. Townsend?"

At this point, one of William's lawyers stood up and asked permission to speak. I had expected him to yell "objection," but apparently that wasn't the procedure in this court.

"My client is not on trial here," the lawyer said. "There is no evidence to suggest he kidnapped the child at any stage and such allegations are far out of this court's jurisdiction."

"I'm just trying to establish the facts," the judge replied defensively. William started to answer the original question, but the judge took the lawyer's comments to heart and changed the conversation. "When potential parents are being considered for adoption, they must meet very strict criteria before they can welcome a new child into their home. They typically must be able to provide a stable home life for the child. Tell me, are you married, Mr. Townsend?"

"No," William replied through gritted teeth.

"I see. Are you in a stable relationship?"

William looked at me and I nodded. We hadn't been going out that long, but I loved him and we were as stable as any other couple I knew.

"Yes," William replied. "I am."

The judge raised her eyebrows and did a poor job of hiding her surprise at such news. She hadn't been expecting that. She had seen me with William, but she must have assumed I was his assistant or just a friend.

"That's good," the judge replied. "I'm impressed, Mr. Townsend, because from what I see in the official court records from the last hearing, you admitted to having a string of short-term dalliances with members of the opposite sex. From what I can tell, these women considered themselves lucky if they were able to stick around for breakfast."

There were a few murmurs of laughter from journalists gathered at the back of the courtroom and even the judge's clerks smiled. I didn't find it so amusing, but kept my face composed and smiled at William to show my support. It didn't change how I felt about him; the past was the past as far as I was concerned. So long as the judge didn't insist on going through the gory details, I should be able to make it through without needing to stick my fingers in my ears.

"Whatever I've done in the past isn't important," William replied. "Even then, I always put Kaylee first and I will continue to do so. I'm her uncle, and if she were here now she'd tell you that she wants to live with me."

"I'm sure she would," the judge replied. "What young child wouldn't want to live with a rich

271

uncle who can buy her whatever she wants without a moment's hesitation? Children are easily influenced, and while I'm happy to take her opinion into consideration, I'm more concerned with the long-term safety and well-being of the child."

"Kaylee should be with me," William insisted again. "She's been through enough already. Why take her away from the family that loves her?"

"Because, Mr. Townsend, her family consists of a drug addict and two brothers who seem to have a running competition for who can sleep with the most women."

The judge continued to grill William on every part of his lifestyle. After finally moving on from his past relationships, she asked about his job and how he would look after the child as a single parent while running a billion-dollar business. William had answers for everything, but the judge never looked convinced.

I hoped William would mention the work he had done for victims of domestic violence. The judge would probably not care, but it would look good on the official record. However, William still felt obliged to keep the details of that to himself so as not to put the spotlight on the women.

By the time the judge was done it was nearly five o'clock. William had done a phenomenal job of answering all her questions while remaining calm, but I sensed it wouldn't be enough. The judge had made up her mind even before the hearing had begun.

"There's no time left for my deliberation," the judge said as she stood up. "I will deliver my decision first thing Monday morning."

William sighed and rolled his eyes. This weekend was going to be torture. The judge had likely dragged the whole thing out just so that she could make him wait over the weekend.

I met up with William and Adrian—who had been sitting behind me the entire time—and we went for coffee. The mood was predictably despondent.

"That didn't go well," Adrian said. "I think we need to consider plan B."

Chapter Fifteen

William wouldn't even let Adrian consider 'plan B,' and he shut down all of Adrian's attempts to talk about it. A silence descended between the two brothers and I occupied an awkward space alongside them.

"Let's do something tonight," I said. "Go to a play, watch baseball, anything to take our minds off this." It had only been twenty-four hours since the football game, but that had helped William relax, and with any luck it would do the same tonight.

"The Giants aren't playing at home tonight," Adrian said instantly. He must be a fan. I didn't follow baseball too closely, but I went to games with friends when the chance came up. "I guess we could fly out to New York and catch the game tomorrow night?"

I still couldn't get used to flying around the country at such short notice, as if getting on a plane were as simple as riding the bus. I had to book plane trips months in advance to try to get the cheapest tickets and I had to start saving for the tickets months before that.

"I'm not leaving the city this weekend," William said firmly. "I need to be close to Kaylee, even if I can't see her."

Adrian nodded in agreement and pulled out his phone to look for events going on nearby. "There aren't any plays I want to see," he said. "And the selection of movies is terrible."

"What about a concert?" I suggested. I had a particular concert in mind, but I wanted to warm them up to the idea first. My favorite singer was performing tonight and tomorrow night, but tickets were impossible to get without paying hundreds of dollars.

Adrian kept scrolling through lists on his phone, but he didn't seem impressed with what was available. "I haven't even heard of half of these people," he said. "Here." He passed the phone to William. "You have a look."

"I would have thought you'd be up to date with the latest music," I said to Adrian as William looked at the phone. "Don't you spend a lot of time in bars and clubs?"

Adrian gave a hearty laugh. "True, but my attention is usually not on the music, if you get my drift."

I rolled my eyes and smiled. He really would be perfect for Sophie.

"Oh, God," William groaned. "We've been played," he said to his brother.

"What do you mean?" Adrian asked.

"I think Amanda knew exactly what she wanted to do tonight and which concert she wanted to go to."

I gave a big, cheesy grin to William. "Please," I pleaded, trying to give him my best puppy dog eyes. "You know you'll enjoy it."

"I didn't see anything on that list William would enjoy," Adrian said. "What did you have in mind?" William handed the phone back to Adrian so Adrian could see what he'd found. "Oh. Well, I suppose it'll be fun in an ironic kind of way."

"And the best thing is, I know Sophie is a fan too," I added. "I can invite her. I think she's supposed to work tonight, but I'm sure she could find someone to cover for her. She wouldn't want to miss this."

Adrian turned white and took a sip from his glass of water. Every time I mentioned Sophie he would act strangely. He acted like a guy who was intimidated by women, not one who had a reputation as a playboy.

"On second thought," Adrian said, "I don't think I could handle two or three hours of that music. But it's a good idea, and I'm sure you'll have a lot of fun, William."

William sighed as if he were uncomfortable. "I don't know. This is a big ask."

"Oh, come on," I pleaded. "It'll be fun, and with Sophie there you can zone out occasionally. I'll even let you send work emails during the breaks."

"You're too kind," William replied.

"Is that a yes?" I asked.

"I can't believe I'm doing this," William said as he started purchasing the tickets on his phone. "I'm getting us a box, though. I don't think I can handle being surrounded by thousands of screaming girls."

"That's fine with me. The boxes are actually near the front." William sighed again and cursed under his breath, but he bought the tickets while I got right on the phone to Sophie. "Hey, Sophie, can you get tonight off work?"

"Sure," she replied. "I cover for people all the time. They owe me some favors. Why? What have you got planned?"

"We have box seats for a concert tonight. We're going to spend the evening singing along with Taylor Swift."

Chapter Sixteen

"Here goes nothing," William said as the judge's car pulled up in the parking lot on Monday morning.

For a few hours on Friday night, I had been able to forget about this hearing and relax, but once the concert was over William and I had spent the weekend together, barely able to think about anything else. Now the moment of truth was here.

Last time we had approached the judge it had been to give her a warning, to let her know that we didn't intend to go down without a fight. I had hoped she would listen to us. Now I found myself about to blackmail a judge. How had it come to this? Not so long ago, I'd been the one vigorously opposed to all forms of corruption. Now I was doing it myself.

Of course, I firmly believed that the judge was the corrupt one here. I was merely fighting fire with fire. Deep down, I didn't feel any guilt for what I was about to do and that meant I must be doing the right thing. If I weren't, my gut would tell me about it. Right now I was nervous, but that was it.

William and I approached the judge. This time she saw us coming and waited for us with a grin on her face.

"Please tell me you're about to do something stupid," Judge Roscoe said. "I'd love to have you spend a few months in prison."

"You haven't filed the decision yet," William said. "It's not too late to do the right thing."

"I believe I *am* doing the right thing," the judge replied. "Is this where you throw money at me and hope I'll take the bait?"

"I don't need money to convince you to change your mind."

The judge frowned. She was curious. She should have just walked away, but she was arrogant and didn't think anyone could stop her. "And what might that be, Mr. Townsend?"

"I want you to know that I'm not enjoying this," William said, taking a thick envelope out of his bag. "I don't take pleasure in other people's pain."

"You think you can cause me pain?" the judge asked. The power had gone to her head. She thought she was invincible.

"Not you, no. But it'll be bad for your family." William handed the judge copies of emails that made her transgressions crystal clear. "There are more like that. These emails will find their way out into the open and your family will be torn apart. Do you really want your husband to go through that?"

The judge took her time going through the emails and the color drained from her face each time she turned a page. The emails didn't just make it clear she had slept with Professor Winston. They also listed her personal preferences in bed, some of which were unusual, to say the least. I didn't care about that part of it, but she would lose all respect as a judge—particularly in family court—if those emails came out.

"This will definitely cause me embarrassment, Mr. Townsend. You're right there."

"Just let me take care of my niece and these will all go away."

"But my husband loves me," the judge continued. "And I think he knows about the affairs anyway. He's never said anything, but he isn't stupid. Sorry, Mr. Townsend, but I'm a woman of principle and I'm not about to give in to someone blackmailing me."

William cursed and took a thick pile of papers out of the envelope. "We also have these. You thought they were destroyed, but we have copies. How would this go down with the electorate, do you think? You run as a liberal, but these views…well, they're somewhat ultra-conservative, don't you think?"

The judge flicked through the papers, but didn't spend much time reading them. She knew what the papers were and likely remembered exactly what was in them.

"How did you get these?" she asked.

"That doesn't matter. The important thing is that I have them and I will make them public. You're a strong writer, Judge Roscoe, but I don't think the electorate will appreciate your viewpoints on issues such as gay rights and race relations."

The judge didn't speak for a long time and William became impatient. "You wouldn't be making the wrong decision," he said. "Giving me custody of Kaylee is the right thing to do. You know that. I love that girl and there isn't a thing I wouldn't do for her."

"Do you know why I pretended to be a liberal all these years?" the judge asked.

"Because you're in a district that always votes for liberal judges," I replied. The judge looked at me as if noticing my presence for the first time. "You don't have a lot of competition in the family law field, so long as you get the support of a few big donors, you're practically guaranteed election as a judge."

"That's true," the judge admitted, "but that's not the reason. I could have just moved to a more conservative district if I'd wanted to. No, the reason I act like a liberal in public is because liberals are just so damn forgiving."

"You think the voters will forgive you for all this?" William asked.

"Not at first," the judge admitted. "But I'm not up for election for a few more years, anyway. The old stuff I wrote in law school looks bad, but I can pretend my viewpoints 'evolved' over the years. And the affairs aren't important. A president got sucked off in the Oval Office, for Christ's sake. They aren't going to care what a judge does when she's not wearing her robes."

"You're bluffing," William said. "But I'm not. I will release this information."

"I'm not bluffing. Go ahead and release it. You won't get custody of that child."

William didn't speak. He looked on the edge of exploding, but I couldn't let him lose his cool in public.

"Why?" I asked. "Why is it that you don't want William to get custody of Kaylee? There must be more to it than just you disapproving of how he used to sleep around."

"Used to? Don't kid yourself, dear. He'll go back to doing that soon enough. And when he does, he'll leave a trail of broken hearts behind him just like his brother did."

"Adrian?" I asked. "What do you mean? Who did Adrian hurt?"

"Who didn't he hurt?" the judge said angrily. "My daughter was a fucking mess for months after he led her along. You people just screw your way around the city and don't give a second thought to those whose lives you ruin."

I heard William take a slow, deep breath next to me. "Do you mean to say," he said slowly, "that all this is because my brother slept with your daughter and didn't call her back? You're prepared to ruin a young girl's life because my brother had a one-night stand?"

"You see this kid like a daughter," the judge replied, practically spitting the words out. "Let's see how you like to watch someone's life fall apart because your brother can't keep his dick in his pants."

I couldn't believe what I was hearing and neither could William. He looked as lost for words as I was. The silence was broken by my phone ringing in my bag. I grabbed it and was about to send the call to voicemail when I saw who was calling. It was John. He had never called me before, and my instincts told me this was a call I should take.

I stepped a few steps away from the judge and answered. "Hi, John. Is this important? I'm kind of busy right now."

"Yes," John replied. "I have a feeling you're

going to want to hear this."

Chapter Seventeen

I walked far enough away that the judge and William wouldn't be able to hear my conversation, but I kept them in sight in case William lost his cool. The judge could easily have called security, but she also had the incriminating evidence in her hands. She wouldn't want to make a scene if she could avoid it.

"Okay," I said. "I have some privacy. What is it?"

"Remember when we met at the bar the other day? You had a picture of a judge up on your phone."

"I remember. I remember very well. In fact, I'm looking at her right now in the flesh."

"Is she a friend of yours?" John asked.

"No, far from it."

"Oh, thank God for that. I think I told you she looked familiar from somewhere, right?"

"Yes," I said. "You mentioned it, but you didn't know where you recognized her from. Did you remember?"

"Yep. I remember. I recognized her from one

of those camps that claim to 'cure' gay people. You know, 'pray the gay away' and that kind of thing."

"You went to one of those camps?" I asked. "It obviously doesn't work, then."

John laughed. "Yeah, I guess I needed a few more prayers. I only went undercover. A little like a journalist, I suppose. Anyway, I applied for a job there so that I could talk to all the kids who were finding the going a little tough. I had to tone down my personality a bit."

"You managed to convince people you were straight? I don't know about a journalist, but you might make a good actor."

"I still don't know how I managed it. I didn't stay for long. Those places are dark. You can't even imagine what it feels like for these guys. Their own parents think they need fixing. It's horrible."

"Those places should be shut down," I remarked. I made a mental note to consider a future story about these groups. If John could sneak in pretending to be straight, then there was no reason I couldn't sneak in too. Anyway, that was a thought for another day. "So what does this have to do with the judge?" I asked.

"Oh, yeah. I saw the judge at the camp. She was dropping off her son. I didn't see that much of her, which is why I didn't place the face straight away, but I know it was her. I gave her the paperwork to sign and her son was assigned to my group. He even told me some stories about how she acted when she found out."

"What did she do?" I asked.

"Let's just say she got overly physical. I saw bruises."

"Holy shit," I exclaimed. "I'm sorry to hear all that, but I'm glad you told me."

"What are you going to do with the information?" John asked. "I don't really care, but I'd like to know if she's going to get what's coming to her."

"Oh, you can be sure of that. I'm going to use it to get a favor from her first, but after that we'll think of something. She's just as vile as I suspected."

"Glad to have helped," John said. "Let me know how it goes."

I quickly jogged back over to William and the judge. They were in an awkward standoff. Neither of them spoke. William wanted to wait for me and the judge knew she had to see this one out. She might not be bluffing about going through with her decision against William, but that didn't mean she wanted the information made public if there was anything else she could do about it.

"Everything okay?" William asked.

I tried to keep the grin off my face, but it was difficult. I was going to enjoy this. "How's your son?" I asked the judge. "You mentioned your daughter, but you also have a son, don't you?"

The judge's eyebrows came together as she gave me a suspicious look. "Yes, I have a son. Are you going to threaten him now as well?"

"No, not at all," I said. "I wouldn't want to step on your toes. It seems like you threaten your son enough already."

"Amanda, what's this about?" William asked. He'd been trying to keep the judge's family out of this from the beginning and probably didn't like me bringing them up.

"The judge's son is gay," I said. "He's still

gay, although she did her best to try to change that." The judge remained silent, but there was a new look of defeat in her eyes. "She tried to beat it out of him, and when that didn't work she sent him to one of those places that try to 'cure' homosexuality."

"You're kidding," William said incredulously. "That's insane."

"It is," I said. "But it's true. I have proof. The electorate might forgive marital indiscretion and mistakes you made decades ago, but they aren't like to forgive this. Not in a progressive place like San Francisco."

William and I both stared at the judge and waited for her to speak. She knew she had lost, but desperate people sometimes do stupid things. There was still a chance she would try to call security on us.

"Leave my son out of this," the judge said. "He's going through a tough time. I don't want this to be public. It would destroy him."

"It sounds to me like you've already done your best to destroy him," I said.

"We'll leave him out of it," William said. "But I think you know what you need to do."

The judge nodded and handed back the pile of incriminating papers. "Let's get this over and done with."

After everything we had been through, I'd expected a big audience for such a momentous moment, but there were few people in attendance. A couple of journalists had returned, but the courtroom was almost empty.

The judge kept to her word and ordered that

Kaylee be delivered to the custody of William at the earliest possible opportunity. The lack of surprise in the courtroom spoke to how little attention the journalists had been paying to the proceedings.

William had been holding my hand tightly, but he relaxed his grip and sighed loudly when the judge announced her decision. He hadn't believed it would actually happen until the words came out of her mouth.

The clerk of the court eventually provided us with a written court order and we went straight to the center where Kaylee was being held to demand her release into William's care.

The whole thing took a frustratingly long time to go through. Child Protective Services insisted on verifying the order with the court and had to get three different people to sign off on the release. Neither of us complained—something so important should not be done lightly—but it was undeniably frustrating nonetheless.

Finally, a door opened at the far end of the waiting room and a man walked out with a scared young girl holding his hand. She looked confused, but she had been well looked after and the staff stood behind her with tears in their eyes as they said their goodbyes.

I nudged William, who had his eyes down, looking at his feet. I pointed over to Kaylee just as she spotted William.

"Uncle William!" she yelled, letting go of the man's hand and running towards us.

William stood up and lifted her up into the air for a big hug. He didn't let her go until Kaylee spotted me.

"Uncle William, who's this lady?"

Epilogue

I lived just minutes from Golden Gate Park, but I had never been there for a picnic. That soon changed, once we had Kaylee in our lives. She liked nothing better than cycling around the park on her new bike.

"We'll be able to take the training wheels off soon," I said to William. He was lying back on the grass with his bare chest glistening in the sun. I'd long since given up glaring at the women who stared at William as they walked past as if I weren't there.

"She's a fast learner, isn't she?" William replied.

"Uncle William, come and play!" Kaylee yelled as she cycled toward us, only just stopping in time.

William sighed as if he didn't want to move, but he quickly got up and let Kaylee chase him around the park. Her little legs pedaled furiously as she tried to catch up with William and she never seemed to get tired.

As soon as Kaylee came to live with William,

he had started looking for a new place to live. His apartment wasn't well suited to a young child, so he picked out a four-bedroom house near the park. He also invited me to come and live with him. It took me all of three seconds to say yes, and not much longer to pack up my things and move.

William paid a year's worth of rent on my old apartment so Sophie wouldn't feel the need to get a new roommate, although she was the social type and would likely have someone else move in soon.

We initially told Kaylee I was a friend of William's, but children are far smarter than adults usually give them credit for. She soon started referring to me as Auntie Amanda and told her friends I was William's girlfriend. I didn't bother to correct her.

"I nearly caught you," Kaylee yelled as she reached out and just about missed grabbing William's shorts.

I didn't explain my living arrangements to my mom and sister until they started talking about coming to visit me. My mom couldn't believe that I was now looking after a child.

"You landed on your feet with William, though," she said during a video chat with her and my sister.

"I expect she spends more time on her back than her feet," my sister joked.

My mom scolded my sister, but I caught her smiling. "Are you ready to be a mom to this kid?" she asked. "She sounds lovely, but you've taken on a lot of responsibility here."

When I convinced my mom I was ready, I convinced myself at the same time. It helped that

William cut back on work, and we had plenty of paid help. I couldn't deny it would be a lot harder without that, but Kaylee brought so much joy into our lives she was completely worth it.

I reached down and spread some cheese over the crackers that William had included in the picnic. A glass of wine would have rounded the afternoon off, but we didn't drink in front of Kaylee. Kaylee asked about her mom sometimes and William told her she was sick and being looked after. Kaylee didn't remember that her mom drank and took drugs, but even so, it seemed reckless to drink in front of her.

My phone vibrated, but I couldn't see anything on the screen because the sun was shining so brightly. I adjusted the display and read the message. It was from Sophie.

You would not believe who I'm seeing tonight.

Attached was a screen shot of her phone. A new contact had been added. The name displayed was "Adrian Townsend."

Sophie had dreamt about hooking up with Adrian, but whenever I mentioned her name to him, he had never looked interested. Something must have changed.

I was about to reply when I heard the sound of Kaylee cycling towards me.

"Auntie Amanda, will you play with me? Uncle William's too tired."

William didn't look tired, but he enjoyed watching me play with Kaylee as much as I liked watching him.

"Okay, Kaylee," I said, then stood up and brushed off the loose grass. "But I warn you, I'm much harder to catch than Uncle William. Ready, set, go."

Author's Note

Keep reading for a free preview of my Crash series.

Thank you so much for reading my book and for supporting an independent publisher. I really hope you enjoyed it—I know I loved writing it.

If I may be so bold, I would like to ask a favor of you. Most people do not leave reviews, but if you enjoyed the book (or even if you didn't and have some feedback for me) please do consider writing a review at the online store where you obtained this book. Independent publishers like myself are entirely dependent on reviews—we cannot sell books without them.

Thank you!

Now, here's a free preview of Crash

CRASH
MIRANDA DAWSON

Chapter One

I took a peak into the conference hall to look at our audience. There were hundreds or people out there. Mainly men, but with a token scattering of women in power suits. Soon they would all have their attention fixed on me. Was I ready for that? I'd never been the subject of attention like this before.

"Do you think we should do one more run through of the presentation?" I asked John. "We did slip up a little in the middle when talking about the historic financial data."

John smiled at me. "Relax, Emily. We've got this. That slip up was entirely my fault and it won't happen again. The more we stress about every little detail, the more likely we are to make a mistake."

"I can't help it," I said. "You do realize that everyone out there is going to be waiting for me to screw up?

"Not this again, Emily," John sighed. "No one in the audience even knows about your leg."

"Actually, smartass, I was referring to the fact that I am a woman. I've checked out the list of speakers for this conference, and only three women are scheduled to speak. And the other two look like they could be part-time supermodels."

John sighed again, but he didn't argue. He couldn't disagree with me on this one; Silicon Valley was still a boys club, and the vast majority of women who did make it here were attractive or had other connections. I had neither.

"The fact that you are a woman gives you an advantage, not a disadvantage," John said. "Besides, I guarantee you that most of the men in this audience would do anything to get you in the sack."

"Oh, please," I said. "I'm hardly beating men off with a stick."

"That's because you won't even let them get that close. I'll let you in on a little secret, Emily—when men think about what they like in a woman, the lower half of one leg features pretty low on the list. Now stop sulking and get ready for this presentation."

John was right. I needed to get my head in the game and stop worrying about things that were out of my control. This presentation could make or break our startup, so it had to be a good one. My paranoia about having a prosthetic leg would have to wait.

John was on fire. He spoke with a confidence I had not seen in him before as he wowed the audience of investors with the business plan for our start-up venture. LimbAnalytics had started as just an idea—something I had dabbled with in my spare time while pursuing my biology major at Stanford—but with John's help, I had made it into a business.

With the right investors, LimbAnalytics might revolutionize life for people with artificial limbs like me. To say I was excited would have been an understatement.

I scanned the room and picked out a few faces I recognized. Silicon Valley was a close-knit community, so the same people appeared at most of these events. Every face in the crowd represented cash, the lifeblood of my business.

But one face stood out from the crowd. A man stood at the back of the room whispering into a woman's ear. I saw her giggle as he handed her a business card. Based on her body language, they would be having more than a networking lunch.

I kept an eye on him as he pulled his mouth away from the woman's ear. He was captivating. I was standing on stage next to my business partner as he gave a presentation and yet all I could do was stare at this man. He wore a fitted, light gray suit that hugged his muscular arms and bulging chest. I'd never mentally undressed a man before—heck, I'd never undressed a man period—but I already had him shirtless and was unbuckling his belt in my mind.

My eyes followed him as he left the room. His tight trousers left me with a detailed view of his rear and I couldn't help but imagine sinking my teeth into it. The man was a walking Greek God— an Adonis. I ached with longing and found myself eager to get back to my hotel room and spend some time between the sheets.

"Emily?" John said next to me, sounding a little agitated.

I looked toward him and could hear the crowd murmuring and snickering at me as I stood there under the lights. I looked at our presentation and realized it was my turn to speak. Judging by the sweat glistening on John's forehead, he had been trying to get my attention for some time.

"Uh, sorry. Um..." I muttered, kicking myself for daydreaming at the worst possible time. "As John has explained the business plan, please now let me explain a little more about how LimbAnalytics works and how it will revolutionize medical treatment for people with—"

As I spoke, my fake leg hit the back of my other calf and I went flying into the podium. I tried to grab hold of it, but only succeeded in pushing it over on my way down to meet the floor. My knee took the brunt of the fall, but that wasn't my concern right now. My trouser leg had crept up and my prosthetic limb was showing to all and sundry. The gasp from the audience washed over me as John picked me up.

"At least now I have your attention," I said, rearranging my clothing. It was a bad joke, but the audience gave a polite laugh.

The rest of the presentation went surprisingly well, given that little incident. I did have to apologize to John for leaving him hanging. Apparently he had called my name at least five times with no response. I gave him some excuse about seeing an old college friend in the audience and he seemed to buy that.

It didn't matter anyway. After the presentation we were inundated with people who wanted to speak to us about our product. Intriguing people had never been a problem, though; it was getting them to invest that had caused many sleepless nights. LimbAnalytics had a great business model, but we required huge capital investment with little chance of return for five years. I had every belief we would succeed, but I couldn't blame potential investors for getting cold feet after looking at our accounts.

John and I spent the rest of the afternoon and into the early evening networking with nondescript men who all started to look alike after a while. They were all white, middle-aged, and dressed in a suit, but without the tie, which was about as formal as it got in the Valley.

The only way I could tell them apart was the way they acted with me. There was Niles, the skinny guy who kept trying to peer through the gap in my blouse. Preston kept putting his hand on my knee or on my arm whenever he made a bad joke. Richard and Wilson treated me like an idiot and assumed I wouldn't understand any of the financial aspects of investment.

None of them were ideal investors, but at least they retained my vision for the company. They were not the real problem. The problem that kept me up at night was PharmaTech, the world's largest pharmaceutical firm that had been sniffing around our company for months. They would make an offer sometime in the next few months, that much I knew. It would be an offer that would make us millionaires overnight and likely mean we would never have to work again for the rest of our lives. But they would also destroy my dream.

PharmaTech would buy the company and then immediately dismantle it because our product threatened their profits. PharmaTech made big money under the existing system and we worried them. I couldn't let them buy the company. I started LimbAnalytics to help people, not to make a rich company even richer.

"You going to call it a night, Emily?" John asked when he had finally managed to shake off the last hanger-on.

"I'm going to grab a bite to eat at the bar," I said. "I haven't eaten since breakfast and my stomach is growling. Want to join me?"

"No, better not. I promised Tom I would give him a call. He always worries that these networking trips are just orgies in disguise."

I smiled and said goodbye. John's boyfriend was a little clingy, but it was nice to see John settling down in a serious relationship. He'd spent all of college sleeping around, so a boyfriend was a big lifestyle change for him.

The hotel restaurant was small and all the tables were taken. I considered heading out into the city for food when a few people got up from the bar and vacated their seats. I grabbed a stool and skimmed the menu before settling on a large burger. It was hardly an original choice, but I needed comfort food right now.

The burger arrived quickly and I immediately set about destroying it. I didn't look entirely ladylike, but at that point I couldn't have cared less; it'd been a long day. Not a lot could have taken my attention from my dinner right then, but someone walked into my line of vision and stopped me mid-bite.

In through the hotel entrance walked the man I had seen earlier while I gave my presentation. He strolled through the door in the same gray suit, although I would never have guessed he had spent the day in it. The only change to his appearance from earlier was the rough stubble around his face. Other than that, he looked immaculate.

The man stopped to finish up a phone conversation, giving me a great opportunity to take him all in and store him in my memory for later. He held the phone in his hand; elbow bent to reveal a large bicep that seemed eager to escape his suit. His tailored shirt did not leave a lot to the imagination either, and if I had to guess, I would have imagined he had the beginning of a six-pack on his stomach.

He put the phone down and I quickly looked away to avoid getting caught, then went back to picking at my food. Just a few moments later, someone pulled out the stool next to me and took a seat.

My peripheral vision took in a gray suit. I chanced a quick look to the side as he picked up the menu. It was him. He was sitting right next to me. I could smell a faint whiff of subtle aftershave and it sent my hormones into overdrive. Suddenly I felt drunk and giddy like a schoolgirl.

The bar had emptied out somewhat while I had been eating, and there were now plenty of tables free. He did not have to sit next to me, and yet here he was. If I were to move slightly to my right, my arm would brush against his.

Why had he sat next to me? Surely he wasn't planning to hit on me? One-night stands were hardly unusual in hotels, but that sort of thing didn't happen to me. Just a few seats to my left a stunningly gorgeous woman in a red dress was drinking alone, practically screaming for a guy to buy her a drink, and yet this man, this god in human form, had chosen to sit next to me.

Maybe he had a thing for broken women? Or he could detect my innocence and wanted to teach someone "pure?" I wasn't technically a virgin, but I felt like one and I was sure I gave off that vibe.

I made an effort to eat slowly and finish my drink. Hopefully he would take note of the empty glass and decide it might need a refill.

"Hi," came a soft voice from the seat next to me. "Can I buy you a drink?"

Oh my God, it had worked. It was really happening. No one like this had ever hit on me before except at college, and that was usually as a joke.

I tried to act cool. "Sure. I'll have a vodka tonic," I said, turning my head to smile at him. But he had his back toward me. He turned and looked at me over his shoulder, staring into my eyes and looking confused. My heart sank as I saw a stick-thin, beautiful woman in a silver dress on the other side of him. It was the same woman he had been talking to during my presentation. He wasn't asking me for a drink; he was asking her. The woman snickered and made little effort to hide her amusement.

"Oh, I'm sorry," the man said, looking at me with pity. "I was asking this lady. But please, allow me to buy you a drink anyway."

I quickly rummaged around in my purse for some cash, then threw it down on the bar and ran as fast as I could with only one working leg. A few strangers cast worried looks in my direction, but I ignored them and headed straight for the elevators. Unfortunately, they were all on their way up to other floors.

I looked back over and saw them both still looking at me. The elevator took an eternity to arrive and by the time I arrived back in my room I was a hot, sweaty mess. What a fool I had been.

302

Men like that did not buy drinks for women like me.
I lay on the bed and cried myself to sleep.

Chapter Two

I couldn't face going downstairs to breakfast the next morning. It took me nearly an hour to shower and make myself look presentable, and by the time I was done, the breakfast buffet was probably just down to the dregs anyway.

My phone had a few missed calls from my mom. I'd promised to update her on how the day went and she tended to panic when I forgot to call. I contemplated just sending her a text, but I really needed to speak to a comforting voice right now.

Mom always answered the phone with a generic, "Hello?" as if she didn't know exactly who was on the other end. It usually drove me nuts, but right now I found it kind of endearing.

"Hi, Mom."

"Oh, hello, dear. How are you? How did the big day go?"

"I'm fine, mom. Sorry for not calling last night. John and I were networking into the early hours, and by the time I got back to my room I was just exhausted. I fell right to sleep." I could never outright lie to my mother, so I just kept to statements that were technically true.

"Networking?" Mom said. "I am impressed, dear."

Mom was impressed with most of what I did. I was the first in the family to go to college, so when I graduated Stanford University with a major in human biology, it was a pretty big deal. Mom didn't entirely understand my business or the amounts of money that were being bandied around, but that was probably for the best.

"It's not as exciting as it sounds, I'm afraid," I said. "Just talking to lots of rich men about money."

"Sounds exciting to me dear. I wouldn't mind spending my evenings talking to rich men who want to give me money."

"Mom!"

"What? I'm just saying that perhaps things aren't all that bad. Any chance one of these rich men wants to buy you dinner?"

"Hardly, Mother," I said. "I doubt I'm their type."

I heard my mother sigh on the other end. "Not this again, darling. You are a beautiful young woman, and when you project a little confidence, I doubt any man can resist you. No man worth having is going to care about your leg."

"I know, I know," I said, just to keep Mother happy. I didn't want to get into that discussion right now. "This is just not a good place to meet men, that's all."

"I thought it was a sausage-fest over there," Mom said. "You should be able to have your pick."

I cringed at Mom's choice of words. No one wanted to hear their mother talk about "sausage-fests." Her and Dad had started drifting apart after my brother died and Mom seemed determined to regain her lost youth. That meant talking to me like she was still twenty, and it was painful.

"I'm trying to keep it all business while I'm out here," I said. That should keep her happy. She wanted me to find a man, but she also wanted me to be successful, so work had to come first sometimes.

"Anyway, can we talk about that on your birthday? I assume you can still make it over for that weekend? I've booked a restaurant for us." It wasn't a cheap one either, but then it wasn't every year your mother turned fifty. With Dad unable to get out of work this weekend, she would only end up spending it with other couples. She hated that, so we'd arranged for her to come and spend the weekend with me in the city.

"Oh, yes," Mom said. "I'll be there. Can't wait to get out of this place, actually. The weather is getting up into the hundreds, so it's too hot to even go outside."

"All right, well, I'm going to buy your plane ticket when I get home tonight. I've got to dash now. I have one final bit of networking to do."

"Okay, dear. Do see if you can snare a man while you're at it."

"I've told you, Mom. I'm not interested in these guys."

"Not for you. For me. Have a good day."

Mothers. I checked myself in the mirror and decided to try and take Mom's words to heart. I was the founder of a popular start-up company and people were interested in me. I wasn't unattractive. When I wore trousers or a long skirt to hide my leg, I attracted a lot of glances. Bigger tits would have been nice, but the ones I had were pert and went well with my slender frame.

I pulled on a professional pair of trousers and paired it with a blouse that opened low, revealing a hint of bosom. I didn't have a lot to work with, but I was damn sure going to make the best of it. Time to go charm some investors.

Chapter Three

After two days of mingling with investors, I actually found it rather challenging to return to work. Whereas I usually leapt out of bed in the morning ready to change the world, I now found myself lingering between the sheets and reluctant to even switch on my computer.

I spent Saturday at home, but it was not exactly productive. I answered some emails and made a few minor tweaks to the code, but nothing exciting. John didn't like it when I fiddled around too much with his code, because more often than not, I broke it and he would spend days fixing it. Still, given that only a year ago I had known nothing about computer coding, the fact that I could do anything at all was an achievement.

Unfortunately I made the mistake of streaming TV shows on Netflix, and from that point, the day was over in terms of productivity.

John apparently had the same problem. "Want to work at the SF Station tomorrow?" he asked in a message. "Can't work at home with Tom around."

"Sure. See you there at 10 am."

The SF Station was our go-to coffee shop located roughly equidistant between John and me. They served excellent coffee but were criminally underrated, which meant John and I could always find a table to sit down and work.

"Usual, Emily?" Jane asked as I approached the counter.

"Yes, please, but could you drop a second shot of espresso in there today?"

"One of those days, is it?" Jane asked with a smile.

"Something like that."

John had already claimed a table in the corner that was big enough for four people. Or it was until we pulled out laptops and chargers and spread ourselves out.

"Morning," I said, sitting down adjacent to him.

"Hey," John replied. "Thanks for coming here today. I was just getting so much grief from Tom for working at the weekend. I had to get out."

"But he doesn't mind you working at the coffee shop?" I asked.

"He might," John said. "But I told him I was visiting my brother down in Palo Alto."

"Ah. Well, I would likely have come here anyway. I barely got a thing done yesterday."

"*How I Met Your Mother*?" John asked.

"*Frasier*, actually," I replied. "Haven't watched it in years, and you know what it's like once you get started."

"Only too well," John said.

We had a quick catch up on where we were with the business and then divided up a couple of important tasks. LimbAnalytics had started with us working like this in the coffee shop, so being back here with John helped me forget about the investors and really knuckle down to work.

"I'm going to need another coffee," John said after we had worked in silence for at least two hours. "You want one?"

"Oh, yes," I replied. "Soy milk latte, please."

John left the table and headed over to order the drinks. I should have asked him to grab me a snack as well. As soon as I stopped working I realized how hungry I was.

"Do you mind if I join you?" asked a man with a strong accent. Was he English?

I hated sharing a table, but the two of us could hardly justify taking up a large table if the place was busy.

Except it wasn't busy. I looked up and saw a number of empty tables in front of me. It was too late to say anything now; the stranger was taking a seat opposite me and next to John.

"Thank you," the man said.

"No problem," I muttered and took a quick look up at the man.

It was him; the guy from the bar at the conference, the man in front of whom I had completely embarrassed myself.

"Hi," he said with a grin. "Remember me?"

How could I forget him? In shock, my lungs expelled the air from my body and I saw a tiny bit of spittle escape from my mouth and land directly in front of him. He pretended not to notice. His appearance was different from the night before. The stubble had gone and a polo shirt and jeans had replaced the tailored, slim-fit suit, but his face was not one I was likely to forget in a hurry.

"Yes," I said, finally able to form a word. "I'm sorry about what happened. I hope I didn't spoil your evening."

The man looked puzzled. "Why are you sorry? That was all just a misunderstanding. These things happen."

He kept staring at me, his eyes looking deep into mine as if he were trying to read my mind. What should I say next?

The silence stretched on while he waited for me to speak. With impeccable timing, John returned to the table with my coffee.

"Oh, hello," John said to the stranger, assuming I knew him from the way we were looking at each other. "I'm John, Emily's business partner." John held out his hand to the man while I looked on, still not entirely sure what was happening.

"Hello, John. I'm Carter. Pleasure to meet you."

"Is that an English accent?" John asked, his eyes lighting up. He was a sucker for an English accent almost as much as I was. Knowing my luck, the two of them would be talking about *Doctor Who* any minute now.

"Yes," Carter replied, glancing back at me. "I'm from Winchester. It's near London," he added when John glanced at him with a confused look on his face.

"I met Carter at the conference the other night," I said, trying to take some control over the situation.

"Ah, you want to invest in LimbAnalytics?" John asked.

Carter lifted his cup to his lips, his bicep flexing under the tight shirt as he did so. God, this guy was a dream. Better, in fact. Even the men in my dreams were grounded in reality. This guy should not have been real.

Two Chinese girls at the table next to us were clearly talking about him. I didn't need to know Mandarin to recognize sexual desire when it was that obvious.

"No, no," Carter said. "I'm afraid I know nothing of technology. Not my thing at all. I just popped by to ask Emily for a favor."

It all fell into place. The other night was no doubt an illicit liaison that needed to stay secret. He had come here to ask me to keep my mouth shut. How romantic.

"How can I help you, Carter?" I asked.

Carter smiled. "You can accompany me to dinner on Friday."

Chapter Four

I saw John mouth the words, "holy crap!" He looked as excited as I should have felt.

"I, uh, I've just remembered I need to make a call outside," John said, standing up from the table so quickly he banged his knees and nearly tripped over the power cord connected to his laptop. I thought he mouthed, "go for it," as he left, but I couldn't be sure.

"You want to take me to dinner?" I asked.

"Yes, if you would be so kind." Carter leaned back in his chair and crossed one leg over the other, never losing eye contact with me.

"Look, I get that the other night was embarrassing for all concerned, but you don't need to make it up to me."

"I know," Carter said. "I'm not trying to make it up to you. I just want to buy you dinner."

"Why?" I asked. "I'm not exactly your type, am I?"

I caught a hint of confusion in Carter's face, but he did a good job of hiding his emotions.

"What is my type, exactly? I wasn't aware I had one."

"I saw the woman you were with the other night. She was stunning. Don't tell me you are interested in someone like me."

"You don't really think a lot of me, do you?" Carter asked, each word coming out soft in his English accent. "I don't have a type. I just like beautiful women, and you, Emily, are very beautiful."

He must have been lying, but what for? Did he just want to sleep with a disabled girl for a laugh? Maybe he hadn't noticed my leg? I'd assumed he'd noticed as I tripped on my way out of the restaurant, but it was possible he'd been too fixated on Miss Big Tits to notice.

"Why are you in the US?" I asked, changing the subject.

"On business," Carter replied.

"So you are only here for a week or so?"

"A couple of months, actually."

"And then you go home. I'm not looking for a short fling, I'm afraid. I suggest you stick to women who are only looking for a night of fun."

"Ouch," Carter said. He looked genuinely offended. "All I want to do is take you for dinner this Friday. Is that really so much to ask? I think I could show you a good time, and if you don't want anything else to happen, then it doesn't have to."

Carter wasn't used to people telling him no, and I must have been crazy to be doing that. I could see John staring through the window and egging me on. Was I mad to be turning him down? Carter looked genuine enough, but something didn't quite fit in this situation, and there was no way I could let myself fall for someone like him. In a few months he would head home and leave me here where no man could ever measure up.

"I don't mean to sound rude," I said. "I'm sorry. I just don't like jumping into things so quickly, and knowing that you're going home in a few months just makes this the sensible decision. Besides, I have a disability that isn't exactly conducive to having passionate flings."

Carter smiled. Was that a nice smile or a condescending one? I couldn't decide.

"You have an artificial leg, Emily. That hardly makes you incapable of going to dinner with me. Do you always do the sensible thing? Because life would be a lot more fun if you let your hair down once in a while."

"Unfortunately, yes," I replied. Every decision in my life was based on being sensible. "Anyway, it's my mom's birthday on Friday and I'm taking her for dinner."

"Okay," Carter said, standing up. "I'm not going to try and force you to do something you don't want to do. It's a shame, though, because you seem like a remarkable woman."

"Wait," I called out as Carter walked away. "How did you know I would be here?"

"Easy," Carter replied. "I saw your company name on your name badge at the convention. That company has an office nearby, according to public records. I assume it's just a PO box, or something like that?"

I nodded.

"You're a start-up. Start-ups like to work in coffee shops. I looked in a few ones nearby and bingo, here you are."

"Impressive," I said.

"Like I said, I really want to take you to dinner, and I always get what I want. Goodbye, Emily. I will see you again soon."

I gave a weak wave as he left the coffee shop. He had gone through all that effort to find me. Why would he do that for a girl who made a fool of herself in front of him?

"Are you crazy?" John yelled at me as he sat back down. "You turned him down? Are you blind?"

Everyone in the coffee shop was staring at us now.

"He just wanted a one-night stand," I said. "And yes, I know he is attractive—"

"No, he's not attractive," John said. "Brad Pitt is attractive. Carter looks like he was personally sculpted by God and then given an English accent. What were you thinking?"

"Come on, John. Doesn't this all sound a bit weird to you? He could have anyone he wants, but he decides to invite me out to dinner? He just wants to have a bit of fun with a cripple and then ditch me. Maybe he just wants to brag to his friends that he slept with a one-legged girl."

"Don't be ridiculous," John scolded. "Anyway, so what if he just does want a bit of fun? What's wrong with that? I don't mean to sound rude, Emily, but you really need to let someone in one day. And not just in your heart, if you get my meaning."

"He's not my type, John, okay? Now just leave it."

John dropped it and we got back to work, but he looked baffled and acted a little off for the rest of the day. I kept typing away, but couldn't get Carter out of my mind. Those eyes. Those arms. I just couldn't shake them.

As soon as I got home, I took some time to myself between the sheets. I shuddered to a climax imagining Carter's strong arms lifting me up and throwing me onto the bed before making me into a woman.

Every time I masturbated, I told myself that I would loosen up and get a man for real. I'd allow him to breach my sex and fill my insides with flesh in a way that my fingers just couldn't do. But then I would meet men and clam up; all the negative possibilities would take over my mind.

What if he freaked out when he saw my leg? What if I was crap in bed? Logically, I knew thinking this way was stupid, but that didn't help. I couldn't change the way I was, but didn't seem to be able to accept it either. Until I did, men like Carter would only be fucking me in my fantasies.

Chapter Five

Mom insisted on staying in a hotel even though I offered her my bed. She said she didn't want to cramp my style, but I had a horrible feeling she just didn't want me to cramp hers. My mother made no secret of her newfound lust for life, and I dreaded to think of the ways she might occupy herself with a hotel room in a big city.

On Friday night, we met at the expensive restaurant I'd picked for her meal—La Table. John and I ate here the night we first got some seed funding for the company. It was a reckless way to blow through a couple of hundred bucks, but we'd both been living on noodles for months and John convinced me that we deserved a treat.

The business was generating a bit of cash now, but this night would still represent a noticeable blow to my bank balance. Still, my mom wouldn't be turning fifty every year, and without Dad around I felt like I had to make an effort.

The restaurant was one of the few places in San Francisco that actually had a dress code, so I wore a dark blue, full-length dress with thin straps and a somewhat risky low neckline. This dress was one of the few that gave me a bit of confidence in my figure, mostly because it completely covered my leg but also because it hugged my figure, pushing my breasts up and out. The maître d' at La Table seemed to approve, judging by the lusty look he gave me.

"Good evening madam," he said, reluctantly tearing his eyes away from my chest. "Do you have a reservation?"

"Yes, table for two under the name Emily Saunders."

"Ah yes, your other guest is already at the table."

He walked me over to a little two-seater table at the back of the room. It was in the middle of an aisle and near the restroom, so we would have people squeezing past us all night. I'd been lucky to get a table at all and couldn't afford to be picky about its location.

"Happy birthday Mom," I said, wrapping my arms around her thin frame. She lost a little weight over the last few months and looked damn good. If I looked like her at fifty, I would be very happy.

"Thank you, dear. I cannot believe how fancy this place is. You really didn't need to bring me somewhere like this. Have you seen the prices?"

I smiled. Mom was used to the dirt cheap food they served in Phoenix, so the prices in San Francisco were bound to be a bit of a shock to her. "Don't worry about that, Mom. It's my treat for your birthday. Just order whatever you want."

"I'm glad you said that, because I have taken the liberty of ordering us a couple of cocktails. Ah, here they are."

Over the next hour we sampled a bit from the cocktail menu, usually ones with rude names that seemed to titillate my mother, and got through our appetizer and main course. The courses had been quite modest in size, so I contemplated squeezing in dessert.

"Mom, you getting anything?" I asked.

No reply. My mom stared into space, deep in thought. "Mom?"

"Huh? Oh, sorry, dear. Did you say something?"

"I was asking if you wanted anything for dessert?"

"What I want for dessert has just walked in through the door. Goddamn, what I wouldn't give to devour that fine specimen."

"Mom!" I exclaimed. "I don't want to hear things like that."

"Look behind you at your five o'clock and tell me you wouldn't do wicked things to that man."

I sighed, but swiveled slightly in my chair to get a better look at the object of my mom's desire. I couldn't see anyone at first, but then noticed the man with his back to me. He was pulling out the chair for his date, a stunning leggy blonde who must have come straight off the catwalk. This man certainly had a nice ass, I agreed with my mom on that point. Rich as well, judging by the location of the table which had a view out over the bay and by the fact that staff were hovering around to see to the couple's every whim and desire.

Finally the lady took her seat and the man turned round to take his own. He was stunning, all right. Stunning and familiar.

It was Carter.

About the Author

Miranda Dawson is a 25-year-old Californian who can't find the man of her dreams and so writes about him instead. She likes reading romance novels and watching scandalous television shows. Her writing is influenced by both!

You can contact me at miranda.dawson@sfpublishingllc.com or check out my Facebook page.

Printed in Great Britain
by Amazon